THE LONG WAY HOME

Fran Clark

Book Cover by Rima Salloum

ISBN: 978-0-9933381-5-1

The Long Way Home
Island Secrets Series Book 3

Also in the series:
Holding Paradise Book 1
A Prayer For Junie Book 1
When Skies Are Grey Book 4

Also by Fran Clark
Lovers

In Loving Memory of Rosemary Hester Wahby
23 October 1943 to 17 November 2023

1899

Antoine held his arms away from his body, his hands cupped, the tiny newborn child wriggling in the palms of his hands. Such a strange and beautiful creature. Skin pinkish with hues of soft sand and the gold of a setting sun. He was frozen, beguiled and falling in love again with each tangible second that passed in the heat and stillness of the room. He brought the baby a little closer to his chest when she began to wriggle and wake up. He looked at his wife, Nanette, wanting to tell her what a remarkable job she'd done, how brave of her, how courageously she'd fought to bring this gift of life into the world. Then he closed his eyes. His mind could not reconcile the thing of beauty struggling and clenching her small fists in his palms with the bed just beside him. His wife's body lay there, the sheets soaked with her blood and the tears they had both wept. She looked peaceful, now, serene. The room was in shadow with just one oil lamp lit in the corner. The black nurse had left the room for a brief moment, shaking her head and telling Antoine in French that she would give them a few moments alone. She would probably relay everything to the nuns, whom he'd heard shuffling by in the corridor, muttering and whispering and offering prayers as they'd listened to Nanette's cries.

Antoine's baby girl continued to wriggle in her father's hands. She didn't cry, but she needed warmth and security. Antoine hesitated as did the nurse who returned to the room.

She began fixing the bed, covering Nanette's body to her chest, informing Antoine that she would find something to wrap the baby in. He could sense her, looking at him from the side of her eyes, waiting patiently to see what he would do. If she could read his mind, she would know that Antoine's was thrown into confusion. *He should hand this baby to the nurse. What was he to do with a baby now?* Antoine brought the child closer to his body as if he would cuddle her, cover her delicate skin in his shirted arms, shush her, tell her there was no need to cry, that everything would be all right. In his heart, he knew this wasn't true, so instead, he placed her into the nurse's outstretched arms. The nurse bowed and laid the baby on a low wooden table while she busied herself wrapping a rough sheet around the child. Her clean white headdress was like that of the nuns who had been kind enough to take pity on the sun-drenched and exhausted couple who had arrived at the convent of St Mary and the Angels some five hours ago.

'Who will care for this child?' the nurse asked Antoine.

'I don't know,' he replied. He sat on the low stool next to the bed and stroked his wife's forehead and rested a hand on her damp cheek. 'If only we had got here sooner.'

'*Monsieur*, the consequence would have been the same. To survive what she has gone through would have been a miracle. So beautiful,' the nurse said, looking at the child.

'Yes, she is.' Antoine rested his forehead against Nanette's and took her hand, brown like the bark of cinnamon, in his, the colour of milk.

'Maybe *monsieur* has some relative somewhere?'

'Not one who will raise a child of that colour.'

'Perhaps I can suggest a solution, *monsieur*.'

Antoine's attention was still on Nanette. He looked up at the nurse, distracted.

'My godmother. She has one child already. Three years old. She would dearly love another, but the Lord has not granted her such a wish. Perhaps she…'

'Yes, whatever you suggest. I cannot look after a baby.'

'Then leave everything to me.'

'I will give you some money. I will fetch it now.'

'*Merci, monsieur.*'

'Nurse.' Antoine stood and faced her. 'Is she a good woman? Your godmother? Will she be kind?'

'Oh yes, *monsieur.* She is a Christian woman with a kind heart. Her husband works the fields, a humble man. They are a good family.'

'So. Fine. I give consent. I will return to the convent door as quickly as I can with some money—but here.' Antoine unfastened the silver locket from Nanette's neck; it caught on a sodden lock of her hair before it came away. He put it into the nurse's hand. 'This must remain with our child forever. Promise me.'

'*Oui, monsieur.*'

'And her name is Rose.'

Antoine turned, slowly, from the bed. His reasons for travelling that hot afternoon on the wagon with a heavily pregnant Nanette was to seek a place to stay in Roseau, find work and speak to the doctor he hoped would deliver the child. Now, his purpose was to make arrangements for a funeral. His footsteps were leaden as he took himself to the door, the torments of that evening heavy on his shoulders in the quiet room. Only the soft sounds from the baby could be heard. He stood before the door, not ready to leave Nanette.

'And what will *monsieur* do now?' the nurse asked.

Without turning round, he said in a low voice, 'Now I must seek the compassion of the family I deserted. I pray to God they will forgive me.'

Chapter 1

The wind that blew the trade ship in from Grenada that day was not a cool one. Quite out of character, it was warm against Rose's cheek, and she turned this way and that to look for her sister, May, who knew how to bargain with the sailors. The sailors had brought their usual wares—fabric, spices and the enormous baskets of brown chromis freshly caught by the Gouyave fishermen that very morning. Before any of these goods could reach the market traders, the settlers nearest the port would have first pick. They got a good price, but they had to be quick: the market traders would quarrel if they thought they were losing a sale, but the crafty sailors made more money selling retail.

Marceline sent her daughters to the port early. She had trained them well, but Rose found it hard to barter as well as her older sister. May was as keen as her mother.

'Do your best, Rose,' May encouraged. 'Mama wants nutmeg, cinnamon and cloves today. Remember?' Her sister nodded slowly. 'Go on.'

Rose pushed her way along the jetty and stood and watched as the large baskets and crates were unloaded from the small high-sided vessel.

'So?' A young sailor from the ship called down to her.

Rose had not realised she was being spoken to, so ignored him. She was busy inspecting more goods as they were carried off the ship.

'So, young miss.' The man called a little louder and Rose looked up. 'What I can do for you today? What is your heart's desire?'

Rose had to place her hand above her eyes to protect them from the bright sunlight. The man had a friendly voice. He wore a straw hat with a blue and red ribbon around the crown. A red rose, its stem pushed beneath the ribbon, was wilting from thirst. His shirt was a tatty white cotton with a slight rip in the breast pocket. His trousers were loose like those of the other sailors and held up by a much worn brown belt. His feet were bare. Rose could not see his face clearly, but she knew he was smiling.

'What you have in the way of spices, sir?' She looked intently at the boxes and crates just as her mother did, jerking her head upwards with raised eyebrows at everything she saw, the corners of her pursed lips turned downwards as though there was surely nothing there worth having.

'Well, I have some lovely mace, maybe some cocoa for you today?'

'Not cocoa, sir, I don't want cocoa. Ours is better here, anyway.' She crossed her arms and sighed the way her mother did, and without looking at the sailor, she asked, 'What you have in the way of nutmeg? Maybe I could use some cinnamon and cloves if they all right.'

'They more than all right.' He jumped off from the side of the ship and stood in front of her with his arms crossed, too. He was far taller than she was: broad chested. His forehead was smooth and his cheekbones high. His dark complexion contrasted with the ochre-tinged brown of Rose's skin. Her black hair was tied back by a yellow ribbon, and she worried that she would appear too juvenile to be taken seriously. At sixteen, Rose still preferred to wear her hair uncovered to town, whilst her mother and older sister wore hats or kerchiefs like most of the other women.

Rose noticed the way this man looked at her, from the simple flat shoes she wore, the calf-length dress of pale blue, the silver locket that hung from her slender neck and into her impatient light brown eyes. There, his eyes rested; he was motionless. Rose uncrossed her arms and peered into one of the large baskets.

'OK—give me a handful of this cinnamon,' she said, pointing without looking back at him. 'I will take some of those cloves—there. And a handful of the nutmeg. Tell me how much.' She turned to face him; he was still smiling.

'I can't, miss.'

'What you mean, you can't?'

'They not mine to sell, miss.'

'What you saying, sir?'

'I mean this is not my spice—look, mine over there. The cocoa and the mace. And that's all I have, miss.'

'Sir, you wasting my time.' Rose shrugged and moved over to her sister, who looked suspiciously at the tatty sailor then took her sister's hand. May made the purchases for Marceline. Holding hands the two girls walked away from the busy jetty in the direction of home. The sailor followed behind.

'I sorry. You hear?' He called after them, but they did not look back. 'I didn't mean to tease. I just wanted to help because you look so lost, miss.' Rose turned round briefly, looked the sailor up and down, scornfully, and felt herself being pulled away by May.

'Well, I see you are at the command of your big sister, I never realised you were just a little girl.'

Rose swung around and stamped her feet as she marched up to the sailor, forcing him to stop. 'I am not a little girl. I came to buy, but you don't have anything worth buying.'

'Rose, come on, we wasting time.' May carried on walking.

'So, your name is Rose.' The sailor was grinning now.

'That's not your concern. Next time you see me, *miss* will do.'

'Yes, miss.' He bowed his head in mock respect. Rose followed her sister.

'And you can call me Raphael,' he shouted, but Rose had turned onto the river path that was lined with tall reeds. She hurried to catch up with May, still stepping purposefully as if she were angry, her yellow ribbon bobbing. She paused briefly, her voice floating back to Raphael like a song from the willowy reeds: 'That's not my concern.'

She knew he was still there but that he could no longer see her, so she allowed herself to smile. First, at the cheek of the young sailor and then the nerve he had to follow her and May and call her a 'little girl'. She wasn't so little. She had left school, and she was helping her family to bring in money. She cooked and cleaned for a rich couple in town. She helped her father in his gardens to pick the produce he sold at market, and she helped her mother with most of the household chores now that May was studying to be a teacher.

'What you making that face for?' May said. She had waited for Rose at the turn-off from the river path to their house on the other side of the gravelly road.

'I'm not making a face.'

'Yes, you have a ridiculous look on your face and I don't like it.'

Rose raised her eyes to the cloudless sky and tutted. She had been thinking about Raphael. Of course she couldn't tell May because she would only berate her for wasting any thoughts on someone so poor and who couldn't afford trousers that fit or a shirt that wasn't ripped. But Rose saw past his appearance. He had a gentle voice. His eyes were kind, too, and she didn't mind the way he seemed to inspect her from head to toe. From the moment he stepped down from the ship, a sense of warmth and calm surrounded her in his presence. She wanted to believe that he'd stayed among the tall reeds of grass for quite some time, watching her catch up with May. She had felt his eyes on her back.

For three weeks, Rose thought about the sailor, waiting eagerly for when the ships from Grenada would return to the port.

The horn for the ships sounded in the distance. Rose had been up early, brushing her hair and tying it with a silk ribbon. She'd considered pinning her hair into a bun like her sister, May. She was nineteen and always wore her hair in a bun, and she looked very grown up compared to Rose. Rose smoothed the front of her dress as she went to pick up her mother's shopping basket.

'Where you going with that, young lady?' Her mother was at the front door beating out a mat and then laying it on the wooden floor just inside the door.

'To the port,' said Rose, full of enthusiasm.

'I didn't say I wanted anything today.'

Her mother, Marceline, was bustling around the main room where the family both dined and relaxed together in the evenings. A large dining table took up one-half of the room along with a large dresser of crockery, glasses and cups.

Lined on the dresser were several figurines of dancing women and of women carrying some sort of vessel. Marceline had been gifted several of these little statues since she began collecting them from market stalls in Roseau as a young woman. In the far corner of the room were two low couches that served as beds for both Rose and her sister. All their clothes were folded away in the large wardrobe in their parents' bedroom where there was a sagging double bed and a Victorian dressing table that Rose's father had been given by a white woman who left her grand home in Roseau and for whom he'd tended her gardens.

'You sure?' Rose asked. 'Not any spices, nothing?'

'No, Rose. And don't pester me because I have a busy day. I want you to clear up the front yard while I gone. I have some business today I can't miss.' Marceline was putting on her straw hat—the one that used to be for church but had now been relegated to her business bonnet. Rose had no idea what business her mother had, but she knew she had no intention of clearing up the yard that day.

Marceline left the house with a grand sweep of the front door, leaving Rose on her own. It was Friday morning, her father had left before light to tend to his crops and May was assisting at a school in Loubière as part of her teacher training. Neither would be back for hours. She waited until Marceline had shut the wooden gate to the small front yard. The rusty bolt clanked as Marceline pulled the gate to. After a few minutes, Rose wrapped a fine knitted shawl over her shoulders. Releasing her hair from the silk ribbon and letting her thick curls fall to her shoulders, Rose peeked over the gate and looked down the pathway leading to the main road. She had to make sure Marceline had gone on her way.

After closing the gate behind her, Rose folded her arms and headed to the tall grasses that led along the river to the port. She wondered if she should have carried a basket as a person shopping would, but there was no time to return home. The ship had arrived half an hour ago, and she would have to hurry.

As always, the port bustled with activity. Against the clear sky, Rose saw the sails of a ship similar to Raphael's docked alongside another. Some of the sailors were still unloading the last baskets of cargo. Market traders had already set up their stalls in the chaotic square close to the sea. Everything from the ground provisions they had grown themselves to the spices and fish the sailors had sold wholesale to the traders was on display in a random fashion. Buyers massed among the stalls, which for most traders consisted of an old blanket thrown on the ground and for others, a makeshift table. Some used the backs of their wagons. Everyone shouted rather than spoke and hurried from one stall to another though a final purchase couldn't be rushed. The buyers stood at each stall for as long as it took to obtain a reasonable price. Sellers tried to stay calm as the heat beat down on them. There was no shelter so they burned in the sun, praying for the food to stay fresh and for them to make fast sales so that they could count their money and take themselves home until the next market day.

No one noticed as Rose tried to make her way to the ship, weaving in and out of the crowd in the most insouciant manner she could adopt. She stood a short distance from the ship by a tall glory cedar, trying to avoid meeting the gaze of anyone she knew who might comment to her mother that they'd seen her there. A few of the sailors were already busy preparing to sail back to Grenada. None of them wore that same tatty shirt with the rip in the pocket or the hat with a drooping rose attached.

As Rose moved a little closer, she saw two sailors drinking from a brown bottle and laughing loudly. Neither had the smile she remembered her sailor having. She stood for several minutes, pretending to be interested in the comings and goings of the locals, until she gave up hope. Raphael had not come on this ship, and Rose decided that she must head home. The yard would not clear itself. Her head bowed, she took slow steps.

'Miss! Oh miss!' Rose turned around. He had no shirt on that day. The smooth brown skin on his torso glistened with a sheen of perspiration. He wore his loose trousers like a person who had not eaten in days, and on his feet was a pair of old sandals.

'I really wanted to call you by your name. Rose. It is such a beautiful name, but I don't have your permission.' His hat was in his hands. He fiddled with it as he waited for her response.

'You have my permission—to call me Rose.'

'I waited three weeks to hear you say that. Here.' He took a wilted red rose with a short stem from his back pocket and held it out.

'It look like you waited three weeks to give me that, too.' Her smile was bright as she looked at the rose in his hand.

'I'm sorry.' He looked bashful. 'The flower was in my hat, but the others teased me. I wanted to give it to you, so I keep it somewhere safe.'

'And you let the other sailors tease you? I didn't realise you are just a little boy.'

'Not true. I look young but I have twenty years.' His cheeks grew hot and she grinned at him. 'Oh, you teasing me, now.'

'Yes, just teasing, Raphael.'

'You call me by my name.'

'Well, is your name, isn't it?'

'Yes, Rose.' He looked, unblinking, into her eyes as he finally handed her the flower.

'So, Rose, what you buy today?'

'I didn't see anything I want.'

'And what you wanted?' His full lips swept upwards.

'I don't know—anything that take my fancy.' Rose turned sideways on to him, feeling suddenly aware that he must know that she was there solely to see him.

'Nothing take your fancy?' he asked, moving a little closer.

'Hmm, no, not really.'

'So, maybe next time, you might have more luck?'

'Maybe,' she said.

'So, until then?'

'Yes, until then.'

They faced each other without speaking. Rose, now lowering her eyes, spoke first.

'When is next time?' she asked.

'I will come in two weeks.' His posture changed, straightening and puffing his chest as if her words had encouraged him. 'Will you be here?'

'I'll be here.'

'I hope you're not leaving already,' he said. 'You know, as there was nothing here you wanted.'

She looked up at him and smiled. Over his shoulder she recognised a woman from church that her mother knew very well. She touched his bare arm. 'Can we move somewhere else?'

'Of course.'

Raphael looked over his shoulder before taking Rose by the hand and leading her along the pier to where there were sailors loading up to leave. One sailor patted Raphael's back, another raised his bottle of white rum to him. Raphael and Rose walked to the very tip of the pier where the sun beat its hottest rays, heating the waves on the sea, reflecting white light that made Rose squint and cover her brow with her hand. The vibrations of the market dulled, and the sailors worked silently to get ready to set sail.

'Your hair is so pretty,' Raphael said after a short while.

She stroked her curls. 'Thank you.' Rose stared into the water and allowed Raphael to take her hand again. They stood like this for a few quiet moments more, watching the waves ripple in towards the pier, bathing the wooden stilts that sank low into the seabed. Someone called to Raphael that they needed his help. It was nearly time to go. The man calling spoke in the patois of Grenada. Although Rose could understand every word, as it was much like her own, his accent was the same as Raphael's. She liked the sound of it.

Raphael turned and said he would be along shortly.

'I shouldn't keep you from your work.' Rose released the hand he held. 'You busy and I have things to do for my mother.'

'Of course,' said Raphael. 'I won't keep you, though I wish I could.'

Rose laughed lightly and shook her head. He closed his hands around the hand she held the flower in. His were large and warm around hers.

'But keep this for as long as possible, and I will bring you more next time. Fresh ones. A whole bouquet.'

'I think you might forget, and maybe you'll be too busy carrying produce to carry flowers, too.'

'You just wait and see.'

'I wish I didn't have to wait,' she said.

He shook his head, lightly closing his eyes. 'Me too.'

'Phayo!' Another of the sailors called loudly to him. 'Phayo Douglas. *Annou alé*!

'I have to go,' said Raphael. 'So, in two weeks then, Rose.' Raphael let go of her hand, his face serious. She stepped backwards along the pier. Raphael followed her until one of the sailors caught his arm.

'Okay, okay, I'm coming,' he said shrugging the other man off.

Rose laughed and carried on until she was off the pier and on the road by the market where the sounds and buzzing filtered back to her and people bumped her as they hurried by. She looked back at Raphael and waved the hand in which she held the flower, then turned and made her way through the market.

As Rose pushed and shoved past the crowd, she could feel Raphael's eyes still on her. The people in the market called out to each other, some carrying loads on their heads and others continuing to bargain. And Rose didn't think that Raphael had turned back to his duties on the ship until she was out of sight.

It was dinnertime. Rose brought in a large saucepan of stew with dumplings from the outside kitchen and laid it in the middle of the table on a folded piece of cloth. The wooden table creaked with age, supporting four tin plates, four glasses of water and the board of hard bread that had been crudely cut into pieces.

'Sit down, Rose. I will serve this up,' Marceline said. 'Also, I have some very good news for you girls.'

'Let us say grace.' Her husband, Dunstan, had had a hard day and he was ready to eat. He quickly bowed his head and started to pray; his offer of thanks for the food was brief. Marceline looked at him sideways, then picked up the long-handled ladle and began to serve her family. Her husband first, then her oldest daughter, May, and then Rose. Marceline's plate remained empty while she sat up tall in her chair, crossed her chubby arms on the table and cleared her throat.

'So. Today I was out. I had some business concerning my cousin and the property he leave behind. I been busy trying to arrange everything, but by the afternoon, everything was sorted out.'

Dunstan kept his head down, scooping stew into his mouth like rapids in a stream. Marceline pursed her lips at him before continuing.

'Anyway, what I'm trying to say is that after a successful trip, all of our affairs are in order.'

'We had affairs?' May tore off some bread and dipped a piece in the gravy of her stew.

'We did. But everything is settled at last. In one week, we moving to the countryside.'

'What you say, Mammy?' Rose had not started to eat as yet. Her mind was elsewhere.

'Dunstan, mind you don't choke.' Marceline tutted before turning to her daughter. 'I say, darling, we moving to the countryside. I get the news for certain today.'

'But since when we have plans to move to the countryside?' Rose dared to ask.

'Since your mother decided that living in the capital is too boring and she want a more lively life in the countryside,' said Dunstan. He had come up for air but went back to his meal when Marceline indicated, by manner alone, that she was doing the talking and had no time for sarcasm.

'What you looking so worried for, Rose?' said Marceline. 'You knew your father and me talked about leaving Roseau. We just moving north. A little further inland maybe, but the country air will do us good.' Marceline began to serve herself.

'It's not the air, Mam. This is our home. What about my friends, my life here? Why no one tell me we going to move? What they have in the countryside we don't have here?'

'Rose,' said May, shaking her head at her younger sister. 'For weeks Mammy been talking about the house in the countryside that fall for us since Cousin Basil die. I don't know what your mind has been on lately.'

Marceline put the ladle down abruptly. 'Anyway Rose, you are a child. You only have sixteen years, so you just do as you told. Now eat your food before it get cold. You already skinny. You need some meat on your bones.'

'I don't understand,' Rose pleaded. 'You can't just tell me I am a child and I must do as I'm told. I don't feel like a child. I feel like my life is ending.'

'Now, Rose. The house we moving to is not a palace but it will be ours. No more renting. You and May will have a bedroom. No more sleeping on those old couches in the corner there. This is our inheritance from my family, and we going to make the most of it.'

'But Mama!'

'But Mama, nothing. I say eat your food and don't give me any backchat.' Marceline's voice had risen in volume. Rose flinched at its unbearable pitch.

'I'm not hungry.' Rose got out of her chair and started for the door.

'Just you sit down.' Marceline got up. 'Be grateful to the Lord that we have food to eat. You haven't taken one bite. Now sit.'

Rose felt her cheeks burning red. May looked at her as much as to say, 'How do you think you can get away with that in this house?' Rose picked up her spoon and took a small mouthful of food and chewed. The lump in her throat would make her choke, she was sure.

Their little house in Roseau was small and beyond repair. On stormy days, the house shook and let in water through the cracked window frames. Marceline would stop what she was doing and pray in a loud voice for the house not to be swept away. In reality, it needed to be swept away and a new one built in its place. Rose had no real sentimental attachments to the house; she complained about it as much as her mother did, though now she had every reason to want to stay. But how to make her family understand? Her father would disapprove of the sailor and his appearance. Her mother would want to choose the man, time and place that Rose married, and it would certainly not have been to a poor sailor from another island.

As for Rose, since leaving Raphael's side earlier that day, she had already worked out exactly what she was going to say when she saw him again. She had planned what she would wear. She might even have done her hair in a special way. There had been no doubt in her mind that Raphael would be true to his word and that he would be standing amidst the bustle of the busy port, smiling and holding a whole bouquet of roses for her in just two weeks' time. She would not have minded in the slightest if there was no bouquet, that he'd be holding just another withered flower, as long as he was there. She might even have hidden on the ship and sailed back to Grenada with him if he'd asked.

After dinner, Rose stood beside the wooden house and heard the familiar creak of the corrugated iron roof as the night wind blew. It was a gentle breeze that disturbed no one and left her almost trance-like as she washed up the dinner utensils in a large tin pail balanced on a plank of wood.

Her father had come back from his usual walk along the path towards the river. Rose sometimes accompanied him as he walked slowly, taking long, steady puffs on his thin wooden pipe before turning back for home with the pipe drooping from his lips, hands in his pockets. His was the familiar scent of tobacco that had the neighbours, from their single-storey wooden shacks, calling, 'Goodnight Mr Dunstan,' as he passed by their windows.

On his return, Rose still had her hands in the dishwater.

'You not tired, Rose?' Rose was startled and pulled her hands out of the water, wiping them on the front of her dress.

'You'll spoil your dress. Come, let me throw that for you. You finish wash-up?'

'Yes, Daddy.'

When Dunstan came back from emptying the water along the side of the road, he smiled at his daughter.

'Don't worry about leaving here, Rose. Your mammy right, you know. We lucky to have this house to go to. Own land, own house. No more working for next to nothing all the hours God gives. My back is breaking here, and I still can't buy you a new dress for church.'

'I don't need any dress, Daddy.'

'No, you need to thank God for small mercies. You'll see how you will love this house. You will see how you will make friends. Both you and your sister. Trust me, Rose. There is nothing here for you.' He climbed the two steps up to the house, smiling at Rose before entering. She looked up into the blackness of the sky, and when she could no longer resist the prickling of tears that had threatened to fall since dinnertime, she closed her eyes and allowed them to warm her face.

It took the family no time at all to pack their belongings onto the old wagon and drive their tired ox in the direction of the mountains. They had said goodbye to their neighbours, and as they travelled the pebbly road out of Roseau, they were waved off by any of the townsfolk up early enough to see them leave. Once outside Roseau, they started the rocky coastal road to Goodwill. The mountain range on their right looked impossibly high. The sea to their left was far from calm that morning. Rose sat with May at the back of the wagon, and could see their old town becoming smaller; the spire of the cathedral making hardly an impression now, the tiny cross on the convent of St Mary and the Angels vanishing.

Their destination was the small country hamlet of Moore Park. May had laid out their mother's plans to Rose the week before the journey: Marceline had sent word to a family friend to meet them at the Indian River in Glanvillia, about forty kilometres from Roseau. He would take responsibility for the old ox as it would not be able to pull the wagon any further.

By the time they got to Glanvillia, they were hot and hungry. Their friend took possession of the ox and wished them a safe onward journey. The family rested under the shade of a tree just off the road where Marceline brought out a much needed lunch from a large basket. She placed a cloth on the grass, shooing away the flies that began to congregate as soon as their food was laid out.

'We don't mind a few flies,' said Dunstan. 'We hungry.'

Marceline tutted as she handed her husband a serving of fried fish and bread fruit in a cloth napkin. Dunstan began eating, while his wife stared at him from under her brow, frowning.

'Oh. Grace,' he said.

Rose felt May prod her with her elbow and turned to see her father contemplating spitting out the food in his mouth. Instead, he decided to swallow it whole, eyes bulging as he did. May laughed to Rose, who so far, had spent the morning packing, loading and travelling as if she were an observer with no real attachment to her actions, remaining stony-faced all journey. With his legs crossed, resting his food between them, Dunstan said a few words of prayer. Marceline punctuated it with an Amen and made the sign of the cross.

Once they'd eaten, Dunstan went on foot to the house of Jack Benet whose horse Marceline had arranged to buy. She hadn't seen the horse or exchanged any money for it, according to May. The negotiations had all been done by word of mouth. Marceline knew a man from Roseau who was a friend of Jack's and who often met him in Glanvillia for a glass of rum and a game of dominoes. Marceline had agreed to the sale, and the deal was done.

Dunstan walked back to the women with Jack Benet leading the horse by its rein. Rose and May sat patiently waiting in the shade, their backs to the tree, legs outstretched, crossed at the ankles. Marceline fanned herself with a napkin before wiping it between her breasts. She asked a sullen Rose to help her to her feet. Rose leaned on the tree watching her parents negotiate with Jack.

'Boy, is a shame to give up this beautiful creature,' Jack Benet said as Dunstan tethered the horse to his wagon. It was a beautiful horse, tall and chestnut brown with a thick black tail. But as Dunstan secured the reins, the horse's breathing became laboured even though it had only been a short walk from Jack Benet's house. The horse shook flies away from its face and swished its tail. Marceline came up closer to inspect the horse with a screwed brow. There was a lazy look about his eyes. Jack rushed up to pat the animal energetically on its hind.

'A fine fellow, a fine fellow indeed,' Jack exclaimed.

'You think this thing can pull us up that mountain we have to climb?' Marceline rested her plump fists onto her hips and walked the length of the horse.

Dunstan stroked the horse's face. He did not seem amused. His back was soaked from the morning's effort of steering the wagon, probably wanting desperately to be up at the new house and out of the blazing sun.

'Of course he can.' Jack backed up his statement with another pat on the horse. 'Up you get and see for yourself!' His face beamed as the family climbed back onto the wagon. Rose and May at the back, Marceline and Dunstan on the front bench. Dunstan took up the reins.

'In a few days, I'll come up to Moore Park and collect my money. You hear me?' Jack Benet was still animated. Marceline leaned across her husband from the passenger side, her heavy bust weighing against him.

'Listen, Mr Benet. You come to my house to collect money *only* if you hear we make it to Moore Park in one piece. As God is my witness, you won't get not a shilling from me if this animal you calling a horse don't fall down in a heap before we reach. You hear *me*?'

'Loud and clear, Ma Dunstan, loud and clear. Mind how you go.' He banged the side of the wagon. Dunstan pulled on the reins, clicked his tongue and they trundled off onto the mountain road that crossed the north-east interior.

Rose could not begin to count the shades of green that veiled the deep forests, covered the mountainsides and carpeted the pathways that led the way to hidden rivers and waterfalls. She craned her neck upwards, squinting into the bright sun but could not see the tops of many of the trees and recognised only a few.

They came to a very sharp bend in the mountain road. Rose gripped the side of the wagon as it stuttered, looking at May who had concern on her face. Her parents were silent. Without warning, the horse slowed pace on the sharp incline. The wagon began to groan as the weight tipped and the contents on the top shifted. The sisters jumped down and tried to hold boxes secure, not looking over their shoulders where a sheer drop waited. Rose, straining to keep their property balanced, saw Marceline dip her head. She heard the mutterings of her mother's prayers under her breath. Dunstan cursed and clucked his tongue to the horse as it came to a complete stop.

'But—what the hell?' Dunstan exclaimed.

'Dunstan. Mind your language!' Marceline bellowed and bent her head swiftly to continue praying in an anxious whisper. Dunstan jumped from his seat, pulled the reins over the horse's head and guided it around the bend, walking backwards up the sloping road. Under his breath, he cursed. Under *her* breath, Marceline continued to pray.

The family continued in this way, Dunstan pulling the hesitant horse, the girls walking behind the wagon and securing any of their property that might fall and Marceline, eyes closed, praying to God the Father for safe deliverance up and around the unforgiving bends in the road.

They had taken another rest and had eaten some more food. Dunstan had fallen asleep, snoring loudly while Marceline prodded him, saying, 'Wake up,' every few minutes, but he slept on longer. When they neared the hamlet, the sun had already set and the palette of greens and browns was now hidden by darkness. All they had for guidance were the few oil lamps burning by the windows of the sparse plot of houses of the subsistence dwellers of Moore Park. Every now and then, a voice could be heard from a wooden house, calling, 'Good evening,' and Rose and her family would respond accordingly.

Theirs was the last house along a dirt trail. It stood on stilts deeply planted into a slope in the landscape. The wooden shutters were closed, and the bushy trees to one side of the house grew so wildly, the leaves prevented the windows from opening. Marceline climbed the three steps leading up to the front door. They bowed and protested under her weight.

'Something for you to fix, Dunstan.' She pointed at the steps, but Rose's father had his nose in a container, muttering about trying to find the oil lamp. She too wanted to see exactly what they had got themselves into. When Marceline tried the front door leading into the main room, it swung open and bashed into a piece of furniture, the only chair in the place. There was a smell of damp and the mild scent of a herb that neither Rose nor her family could identify. Dunstan held up the oil lamp as the family stood in a huddle by the door, looking around in silence.

The room was not much bigger than the family room in their old house. As well as the high wooden table that stood in the middle of the room, there was an old couch in one corner and a rusty saucepan in another. Two rooms led off from this one, both containing a double bed with no bedclothes. One of the rooms had a wardrobe with no doors on it.

'Home sweet home,' Dunstan said.

Marceline kissed her teeth. 'You all, don't stand with your mouth open,' she said. 'Go and bring everything in before they steal it like they already steal what was in this house. They take everything worth taking. Let me go outside and look for the kitchen. See if they don't already root it out from the ground and carry it away. We need to pray, eat and go to bed.' Marceline kept on muttering to herself as she left the house with a lamp to inspect the kitchen. Dunstan and May went to the wagon as Rose sat on the chair.

In one week, Raphael would be at the port in Roseau and so, she said to herself, would she.

It was still dark when Rose trod carefully through the main room. May slept soundly in their shared bed, her mouth open as she inhaled and exhaled rhythmically. Her gentle breaths were no match for the loud snores emanating from their parents' bedroom. By now, Rose knew exactly which floorboards creaked. She knew to offer to lock the front door for the night, only to leave it unlocked, putting the key on the windowsill so that it wouldn't make the rattling sound when she opened it later. She took a long stride to avoid the first two steps outside the front door because they both creaked. In her pocket, she hid a piece of chicken from her meal earlier, to bribe the neighbour's dog and stop him barking and waking his master, who was sure to look out of his window.

Rose had already wrapped her yellow dress for church in a bundle and hidden it under a rock at the foot of the tall tamarind by the stream, only five minutes from her house. In the dark, she made her way to the tree and stood beside it as she changed out of her nightdress. It was now four o'clock in the morning. The journey back to the capital, mostly by foot, could take hours. She hoped to get a ride from anyone passing with a wagon, ox or horse. If she was lucky, there might be someone driving a motor vehicle from Portsmouth along the coastal road on its way to Roseau.

Glints of sunrise tried to fight through the darkness but only enough to create indigo shadows. The trees were tall unrecognisable objects, the bushes hiding unseen dangers and harbouring unknown creatures. Rose walked with caution along the road as it wound downhill towards the Windward Coast. A gusty wind made the skirt of her yellow dress flap against her calves and she shivered. A curious wailing sound reverberated around the mountains, one she'd never heard, but then she'd never been this far from home in the dark while everything but the elements were asleep.

Her heart had beaten rapidly since she'd climbed carefully out of her bed earlier. She hadn't slept at all, worried that she'd not wake early enough and miss her opportunity to escape back to Roseau so that she could see Raphael. Her pulse rate doubled. She'd been excited during the planning stages of this adventure; now she felt afraid. She looked back over her shoulder to get an idea of how far she'd come, but it was impossible to make out a distance because there were no indicators. She knew the way to go even though she couldn't quite see it, so she kept her gaze ahead. Further along, the road was less steep and the ground felt smoother under foot. A lot more comfortable for the flat shoes she wore: tiny pebbles had felt like large rocks under her soles. Something told her that she should hurry now.

From nowhere, she heard a familiar sound, a person on horseback approaching from behind. She stopped and stood to the side of the road, squinting into the half-light, the oncoming shadow becoming clearer.

'Hello!' Rose called out by way of a question. She waved her hand, waiting for the rider to notice her.

'Who is there?' The rider slowed the horse as he drew closer. It was Jack Benet's son, Albert, who also lived in Moore Park.

'Rose Charles,' she called. Albert pulled on the reins.

'Rose? What you doing out at this time? You don't know bad weather coming?'

'No. My daddy didn't know when he send me by my aunty that the weather would be bad.'

'Where your daddy send you?'

'Colihaut.'

'Right at Colihaut you going today?'

'Yes, sir.'

'By yourself?' His tone elevated with each question.

'Yes, I have a message for my aunty.'

'You can give me your message and go back home. The weather will get bad. You didn't see the sky yesterday? Your father should have known.'

'But the message very important. I staying in Colihaut until the bad weather pass. I coming back tomorrow.'

'Get up here. I can take you to Dublanc only, but we have to be quick.'

He pulled Rose up onto the horse. He had no saddle, and Rose sat sideways on behind him and put her arms around his waist. Albert was recently married and lived not far from Rose and her family. He told Rose that he had set off early because he knew the storm was coming and wanted to make sure his elderly mother-in-law was locked in tight. He would wait out the storm there to give his wife peace of mind.

'You lucky you meet me,' Albert said over his shoulder. 'I can't believe your daddy would send you on an errand all that way. He could have ask me to go.'

'Yes, but is a private matter. A family matter, and it couldn't wait.'

'But this weather, Rose. Can't you feel it?'

She shivered under the light cardigan and the thin dress at the mention of the weather. The sun hadn't begun to rise fully though it should have by then. Clouds were dark and as angry as the wind, raging all the more intently as the horse trotted on. The temperature would normally have been warmer at this time, but nothing was as it should be which included a girl being out alone when a storm was brewing. She leaned away from Albert, worried that the thunder of her heart might give her away, that he'd realise she was lying and send her home. Luckily, he wouldn't be going straight back to Moore Park; he wouldn't be able to tell her family that he'd seen her, and by the time he'd returned home, it would be the next day and Rose would already have spent the day with Raphael. A day her parents couldn't take away from her. She was prepared to apologise and be punished on her return. But all of that could wait.

Colihaut was just two towns further on from Albert's destination of Dublanc. He had no idea that she intended to continue even further south, and she prayed that when they reached Dublanc, he wouldn't try to find someone to take her back home.

At Dublanc, Rose and Albert dismounted, but the winds had picked up, rain had started to fall and Albert urged her to stay at his mother-in-law's with him just to see what the storm would do.

'Please, Rose. You need to be inside. Your father should never have send you out today. It's a madness, a madness I telling you.'

'I will be fine. Go on Albert. Don't worry. Look, a wagon already coming,' Rose said, brightening. The sun had risen fully yet struggled to make any difference to the darkened sky. Albert spoke to the driver of the wagon.

'Can you take this girl to Colihaut? She need shelter from this storm.'

'No sir. Just down in Bioche I going. A hurricane coming —is not any ordinary storm.' He looked incredulously at Rose whose teeth had begun to chatter. 'Best you turn back or stay put here, young lady.'

'Please sir, let me come to Bioche with you,' Rose pleaded. She angled herself to climb aboard the wagon, but Albert placed a hand on her shoulder.

'He's right, Rose. If your mother know I let you go when a hurricane coming, she will kill me.' Rose gently removed his hand and squeezed it before climbing up on the wagon. She looked down at Albert, saw the concern on his face as if he might cry for her. She smiled as she buttoned her cardigan.

'It's all right. I'll be all right. I'll see you up at Moore Park when you turn back. You'll see.' She turned to the driver whose brow was now as lined and worried as Albert's.

'*Annou alé,*' she said. 'Please, let's go.'

The driver shrugged and hit the horse's back with the reins. It trotted off gently with a snort.

'Rose!' Albert called, but the wagoner had given the horse another flick of the rein and had told it to hurry. Rose rocked and rolled in her seat as they trundled along the coast road.

By the time the wagon came to a halt in Bioche, the winds were blowing harder and faster than before. The sea was rising and falling in wild waves that beat hard against the coastline and did not relent. Only now did Rose begin to doubt her decision. She looked at the man; his eyes told Rose that he feared for her safety.

'Miss, you still want to go to Colihaut?'

'I have to. Someone is waiting for me.' Rose looked at the sea again; even at this distance she could feel the spray on her face.

'You can stay with me and my family,' urged her driver. 'Just up there we are. You want to?'

'I need to keep going.'

'Well, if is go you going, you better do. Go fast as you can to whoever waiting and don't stop until you get there. I'm sorry I can't go no further.'

'I will run all the way. I might be able to get another ride.' Rose tried to run quickly along the roadside but the wind slowed her pace. Grey and white clouds swirled uncontrollably. The wind howled like a sick animal, and Rose's heart raced on. She leaned into the wind that pushed her sideways, bowing her face to stop the rain whipping into her eyes. Very soon her clothes would be saturated. The vibrancy of her yellow dress already dulling with dampness. She'd wanted to look pretty in her church dress, but she knew Raphael would understand that the weather had denied her that.

Rose hadn't made much progress in her journey, the wind stopping her from running any further. She looked up, narrowing her eyes to see how far she had to go. She saw the coastal village of Colihaut in the distance, but the movement of the sea rooted her to the spot. The waves rose too high, far higher than the houses along the beach. Blinking against the wet gusts of wind, Rose saw a great wave roar upwards and crash into several of the houses. It pulled each of them into the sea in an instant.

On the open road, she was too exposed—she needed to find safety. She looked back the way she'd come, hoping the man on his wagon might have taken pity and come to find her. There was no sign of anyone. No one would be out in a wagon or vehicle in these conditions. Both men had warned her not to go on, but it was only the weather and its furious warning that she listened to. It was impossible to continue, impossible to be brave.

Rose ran up a slope towards the woods. She saw a sturdy-looking tree with a gnarled, wide trunk and hoped that by clinging to it, she would be safe. Before she could reach the tree, she was hit by flying branches and twigs and fell on her knees by a small clearing. Soaked to the skin, she landed by the long vines hanging from an old tree. Lying on the ground, she wrapped the vines around her wrists. She prayed under her breath the way her mother did, but the wind began to pull her upwards; closing her eyes, she fought to hold on to the vines. She struggled to keep herself close to the ground, but the wind was too strong—it was pulling the vines off her wrists.

The wind rolled her onto her back, and on opening her eyes, she realised that it was a tall rough-looking woman unwrapping the vines. She wore a long brown dress, and her hair and clothing clung to her body. Without a word, the woman lifted Rose by the waist and pulled her towards a nearby wooden shack. The woman threw open the door and pushed Rose into a small room where she stumbled onto the floor. Rose looked around; it was dim and quiet inside apart from the soft bleat of the goat tied to the dresser and the chickens with their claws tapping the wooden floor as they walked towards Rose.

The old woman shooed them and angled them towards a single metal-framed bed by the wall. The windows of this one-roomed dwelling were boarded up. The only light came from an oil lamp and the cracks between the wooden boards across the windows, not that there was much light to be had from the outside. Like the wind and rain, the darkness had drawn in quickly, altering the look and feel of the countryside. The woman sat on the bed in her wet clothes, exhausted by the efforts of rescuing and carrying Rose. She didn't change out of her soaked garments but sat and stared at Rose, her face stern. Rose scrambled along the floor on her hands and knees, squeezed herself into a corner and cried with her hands over her face, stifling the sounds of her sobs.

Rose awoke to find the woman staring down at her. She blinked several times, feeling the soreness of her eyes from crying: the tears had lulled her off to sleep.

'Here, take this.' The woman handed Rose a cup of milk. She was wearing another long brown dress, the other spread over the back of a chair. Her hair was bound by a dull yellow scarf, tufts of grey showing in the tight bunch of curls on her forehead. 'I can put sugar in it, but I can't light a fire in here to make tea. Everything too damp.'

Rose took the milk, holding the cup in two hands to keep it steady.

'The hurricane pass?' Rose asked.

'Yes, it pass.' She stepped back to size Rose up. 'And where you were going today of all days?'

'To Roseau.'

'Ro-*seau*? What business you have there?' The woman crossed her arms, deciding instead to hitch both fists onto her bony hips and lean towards Rose. 'Ro-*seau*? You mad?'

'I didn't know there would be a hurricane.' Rose, still on the floor, had her knees up to her chest. She stared into her milk and spoke quietly. 'I am going to meet someone there. I must go.' She got up and held out the cup. 'Thank you but it must be late.'

The woman ignored Rose, sat at the table and picked up her own cup of milk. 'That road will be down. Where you come from?' She took a sip from her cup.

'Moore Park,' said Rose.

'Is best you go home to Moore Park, my dear. But you have to wait for this rain to stop and for someone to give you transport.' The woman got up, shaking her head as though she were talking to a drunk.

'But I have to get to the ship that land in Roseau this morning,' muttered Rose, feeling the life tingling back to her legs. Unsteady on her feet, she placed the untouched milk onto the table.

'Which ship you talking? Not today. No ship could land in Roseau today.' The woman kissed her teeth and shook her head again. 'Anyone fool enough to come in a ship on a day like today is bound to be lost at sea.'

1896

The Masquerade Ball thrown by the Laudiers was the grandest that any of the French planters had seen in Dominica. The French pretty much kept themselves to themselves since the British invasion, and then, if they kept up their tax payments, the English pretty much ignored them, too.

One or two of the English attorneys had accepted their invitations to the Masquerade, as they had the year before. Preparations for the ball were causing a commotion in the Great House a whole two weeks before *J'Ouvert.*

Madame Laudier frowned at Antoine, who moped around the house. He was an only child and being male, his father had been disappointed by his indifference to the successful coffee harvest that year or the new mill that was in operation, which promised yet another good year for the family. His mother was disappointed that at aged twenty, she had still not found him a wife and was considering sending him back to France or to their cousins in Canada.

'*Qu'est-ce que tu fais*?' she asked her son. 'People will be arriving and you are not dressed. Go and put on the silk shirt —the silk shirt. *Vitement.*' Madame Laudier looked doubtful her son would do anything quickly and hurried off to make sure the new Negro housegirl was pulling her weight. Bette, the cook, had already been complaining, and this evening had to be the best Masquerade party from there to Roseau.

By about midnight, the black boys in their cut-off trousers and shabby shirts had all the candles lit on the patio and they had raced off to join the others, up in *La Cou*, whose night off would be just as colourful and certainly more raucous than that of their French employers. The French revellers stepped onto the patio with their champagne glasses and looked out across the lawn, past the pulping mill, where on the *glacis*, the black workers played music and danced. The *glacis* was usually used for drying coffee beans that had been washed after the milling process, but tonight, the platform was a place to dance. The musicians playing in the hall indoors heard the *tambou* rhythm from outside and played in time while the younger black boys danced around the patio, hoping for tips from the rich estate owners.

'Look how lively.' Madame Laudier pointed a silk-gloved finger at the dancers on the *glacis*. The singer raised her voice and the man on *la peu cabrit* beat louder than ever. 'Antoine? Do you see?' she asked her son.

Antoine had fixed his eyes on the *bele*, the two dancers in the middle of the bright ring of plantation workers, who clapped energetically. The man wore a bright orange shirt over his Sunday trousers, and the girl held a green and yellow parasol over her head. The *glacis* was lit by a circle of torches, flaming high above the dancers and sending tiny sparks into the black sky. The girl had her skirt tucked into her waistband, and her bare legs stamped and stepped in and around her male counterpart. He followed behind her, his face close to her backside that rose from side to side, and the crowd on the patio, as well as on the platform, laughed with joy. The girl's legs were cinnamon brown, and her low-cut top of pale yellow silk revealed a firm breast that drew Antoine's attention to her more closely. As she threw her parasol and removed her bright red headscarf, he noticed her hair was worn in thick black ringlets and she had silver brooches clipped at each side. He was moving closer and closer to the drying house without even realising his feet had left the patio.

'What is that boy doing? He was always running around with the Negroes when he was a child. I told him, "If you get too close, you will turn into one," but it never stopped him.' His mother was quite drunk now, her voice fading with each step he took.

When the dancers in the circle stopped, another group of four or five took their place. Antoine stood opposite the girl dancer. 'You dance beautifully,' he told her. And in her broad Creole accent she replied, 'You come to watch *les negres danse en glacis*?'

'I came to watch you,' he said shyly, lowering his eyes. He looked up quickly when she said in perfect French, 'I hope you liked what you saw.' She flapped her headscarf by her long and slender neck. A thin trail of perspiration ran the length of it and into the crease of her bosom. Her nose shone and firelight reflected off her hot skin.

'Your French is impeccable,' said Antoine. 'Not pigeon, like the other Negroes or in their patois. Your master taught you well.'

'My father taught me to speak French.' She stopped fanning her face, her smile slipping as she tied the scarf around her neck, ready to walk away.

'Your father?' Antoine sidestepped to stop her leaving.

'Yes. He is from Martinique.'

'So your father bought his freedom, then?'

'We were never slaves, sir. My family owns one of the cocoa plantations a little further inland. DuPont.'

'I beg your pardon miss. The way you were dancing, I…'

'I have Africa in my blood, why should I dance any differently? But my parents forbid me to dance or talk to our workers, so I came here to escape. Now, I have to find my things and hurry back before I'm missed.' She started on her way as another heated drum rhythm commenced and the stamping footsteps of dancers began to vibrate. Antoine followed and was at her side.

'I will walk with you,' he said.

'I can manage by myself.'

'Miss, there are a lot of people on the road who have had a lot to drink and I fear for your safety. Please, I insist.'

They both stopped and faced each other again.

'Then I must know the name of my escort,' said the girl, her smile returned.

'Antoine. *Et vous*?'

'Nanette.'

Chapter 2

It had been two years since Rose disappeared that stormy day in August. In that time so much had changed, not only for Rose, but for her family, too. Trying to establish a good crop of food and fixing up a house that needed greater repairs than they'd expected, meant scrimping and saving and having to sell their horse and cart. Rose was convinced that her running off to meet Raphael in Roseau had been the catalyst to the family's run of bad luck. The day after she'd returned from the house of the old woman who had sheltered her during the hurricane, she'd stood at the door looking battered and sorry for herself. With no time for an explanation, her father, eyes bulging, had pulled her inside, unbuckling his belt so that he could beat sense into her, tears in his eyes. May had watched the first lash being delivered across the back of her sister's legs. She'd shouted, 'No, Daddy,' and had rushed to protect her sister, holding her tight and cradling Rose's head to her shoulder. Dunstan had then dropped his belt, held a shaking hand over his eyes and wept like a child. Marceline had been prostrate on the floor, crying uncontrollably throughout this incident. Rose, having returned exhausted, scared and hopeless since her disappearance, knew that Marceline would not have stopped her continual praying, except to goad her father for being too soft on the girls, probably blaming him for Rose being so bold that she could run away like that. Shortly after Dunstan had dropped the belt, Marceline stood, walked over to the girls and hugged them both—Dunstan wrapped his arms around all three women.

Marceline had gone to warm up some soup for Rose, a thin consommé made from chicken stock and laced with hot peppers to bring the colour back to Rose's face. While the soup was heating, May had put an arm around Rose and walked her to the bedroom.

'Sit down, Rose,' May had said. 'You look frozen and the sun is blazing out there.'

Rose didn't utter a word.

'Why did you leave?' May had asked as she undid the buttons of Rose's cardigan and slipped her dirty shoes off her feet. There was grit in between her toes which May wiped away with a towel before pulling on a pair of socks that Rose had worn to school as a child. May unzipped the yellow dress Rose had been wearing and pulled it off her shivering sister. She rubbed her shoulders and pulled a heavy cotton shift dress over her head, fastening it for a lifeless Rose and helping her into her own cardigan, the new one she'd bought for teaching.

'I'll draw you a bath later,' May had said. 'Wash your hair. Your hair is too beautiful to be left like this.' She'd pulled Rose to her, and Rose happily leaned her head on May's shoulder. Soundlessly, Rose had let the tears slip softly down her cheek and May had wiped them away.

'What is it, Rose? Why did you leave like that?'

Still Rose refused to speak.

'It's all right. The important thing is that you are back and safe. Were you hurt?'

Rose shook her head.

'But frightened. I know.'

May had led Rose back to the family room and sat her at the table where Marceline had set the bowl of consommé down with some dry crackers.

'Eat, Rose,' her mother had whispered. 'Eat and we'll talk later.'

Marceline had talked late into the night, at her daughter rather than with her. Her anger and frustration were not quelled by a silent Rose who chose to shake her head in answer to every question her mother aimed her way. Feeling her mother's irritation, Rose had cringed when Marceline got up, leaned across the dining table on her fists and buried her gaze into Rose's soul.

'A boy who make you do this. But which boy and where the hell you meet him? Tell me, I am your mother.'

'Mama, why you have to shout?' May had protested. 'You can't see your daughter tired? Why you don't let her go to bed and let her talk in her own time?'

'In her own time?' Marceline had stood up, put one hand on her hip and waved a forefinger at Rose. 'From now on, you won't have any "own time" Miss Rose. From now on, you don't go anywhere unless is me or May who take you and bring you back. If is a boy you running around with, he will have to warn himself and stay away from my yard before I set your father to run on him. You hear? I will not allow you out of my sight.' Then she'd pointed a finger across the room. 'Now go to bed.'

For two years, Rose had been under lock and key. She had to be chaperoned everywhere, mostly by May—the sensible one. May tired quickly of the responsibility because she had finished her training and was hoping to take up a teaching post at the new school in Thibaud. She allowed Rose to go where she pleased when they were down in Portsmouth shopping for their mother and arranged a time and a place to meet up after May had run all the errands. May had friends from the college in Portsmouth and met them for fizzy drinks and ice cream or mint tea and biscuits in one of the café bars in the small town by the sea. Later, she would look for Rose where they'd agreed to meet and find her sister sitting there sadly, not talking to anyone and not interested in any thing.

'Oh, Rose.' May would take her hand, and they'd look for some transport to get themselves home.

Since the family moved to Moore Park, Rose had fascinated some of the country folk because of her skin colour. They wanted to know why Rose was so high-colour, why she had a white man nose and why her hair looked like Carib hair. Once, when she and May had gone to the river to wash clothes, a group of teenage girls had gathered at the riverbank and stood and stared for a long time.

'Hey, you,' one of them called to the sisters, who were knee-deep in the river, skirts tucked into their waistbands as they rung out the bedclothes. 'You. Sis. With your yellow skin. You look like a white woman to me. What you doing with that black family? Where you come from?'

'Just ignore them, Rose,' May said. 'We're nearly finished here.'

The girls continued to hiss to get the sisters' attention.

'Too high-colour to talk to us? So where you come out from? You can't speak?'

Rose turned around and began to cuss with the words she had heard the youngsters using so freely with each other when there were no adults in earshot.

'Rose!' May scolded. 'Don't lower yourself to them.'

'Lower myself? I couldn't get any lower than these dirty-looking, foolish young nobodies who have nothing better to do with their time they have to come and waste mine. I say move off!' She scooped a double handful of water and splashed it in the girls' direction. When they didn't go, she kept on splashing, moving closer and closer to the girls who ran away screaming about having been half drowned.

The nosy teenagers made up a song in patois, as they often did to tease anyone, called *Girl Who Your Father?* They whistled the tune when Rose and May walked by; they hummed it by the river when the sisters washed clothes.

Marceline chose to ignore them. The fact that Rose had been given to her as a baby was well known in Roseau. In town, if there was any gossiping to be done, it would happen behind the person's back. But here in the country, the people were relentless, and private business became local news announced by the person with the loudest voice whether the subject happened to be there or not.

Rose had come to realise a long time ago that she was different, but her mother never explained anything about her past. Now that she was eighteen, she considered it time and hoped that Marceline and Dunstan would not find her ungrateful because she wanted to know the truth. She loved them both, and she adored May, her sister and best friend.

'Well, I suppose it's time you know,' Marceline said one evening. They all sat in the main room quite late after dinner. For May, Rose had been the little yellow dolly whose jet black hair she used to brush when Rose was a small child. Marceline and Dunstan had loved Rose from the day she arrived as well as they'd loved little May.

'My goddaughter was a nurse, and she helped deliver you. Your mother died right after you were born, and your father had no job, and he couldn't look after you. Your father was a white man, French, and his family didn't want you, so Cecile bring you for me. You were so tiny when you arrive. A soft bundle with screwed-up eyes and a little cry like a baby goat. Cecile brought some milk and I fed you. You drink all of it all up, and when you finish, you sleep. Cecile said that your name is Rose. Is that your parents call you and it so suit you. It was a happy day when Cecile arrive at the door carrying you. Dunstan and I were so shocked and happy when she bring you come. She know I had wanted another baby, and she know I would love you.'

'I look like my mother?' Rose asked.

Marceline looked at the delicate silver locket Rose wore every day.

'Maybe. If your mother was as pretty as that silver locket your father put around your neck before you come, then yes, you look like her.'

***

In the two years since the hurricane, Raphael's life had taken a new path. Positive that Rose would understand why his ship did not sail that day, he had arrived in Roseau two weeks later with a rose in his hand expecting to see her waiting at the port.

Raphael had stood on a low branch of a tamarind, looking through the crowds in the marketplace. It was almost time for his ship to set sail and still Rose had not arrived. He had jumped down from the branch and walked desperately among the crowds, asking if any of them knew Rose, describing her, trying to describe her sister, pointing in the direction of her home, but no one had been able to help him. Finally, a young girl of about Rose's age pulled at his arm.

'Rose Charles? Is that who you looking for?'

'About so high, slim, light brown eyes, skin like a buttercup and hair black to here.' Raphael used his hands to describe Rose.

The young girl smiled. 'Yes, that's Rose Charles. But Rose gone long time. Right at Dos D'Âne or Moore Park I believe. Rose is a country booky now. I don't even know if they come to town any more. I don't think so.'

'You know if I can get a message to her?'

'You see that man over there in the brown cap and the big bag over his shoulder?'

'Yes—he know her?'

'Should do, he live up that way I believe. His name is Jack Benet. Maybe he can take a message?'

'Thank you—I'll ask him.' Raphael pushed through the crowd quickly before Jack disappeared into the cluster of haggling people, who were quarrelling and shouting across each other as they did.

'Excuse me. Sir? *Monsieur* Benet?'

'The very same. And you are?'

'My name is Raphael Douglas and I have a message for Rose Charles. I believe you know her.' Raphael began to describe her again, but Jack held up a hand, nodding his head with a smile.

'Yes, yes. I know, I know her. Mother Marceline and father Dunstan. How you know them?' Jack rubbed his chin, adjusting his smiling face to one that appeared businesslike.

'Well, to tell the truth, I never meet the mother and father but I know both the daughters.'

Jack straightened. 'Is that so?'

'No, sir, not like that. I mean, I meet them at market some weeks past. I spoke to Rose and she agreed to meet me here a couple weeks ago. But that was the day of the hurricane and I couldn't come. I don't suppose she was here but we never get to make any arrangements to see each other again, so I was hoping…'

'Well, young man?'

'You see, my ship have to come back in three weeks. So, I wonder if you can tell Rose that Raphael was here and I looked for her. Will you tell her, please, that I will be waiting here again in three weeks?'

Jack grinned and patted Raphael on the shoulder. 'Seem like you really like this girl. Maybe you might change your mind when you meet her mother.' Jack bent forward as he laughed, hands on his thighs, shaking his head.

'Please, Mr Benet, I have to set sail now.'

'Yes, yes, of course. Sorry.' He cleared his throat. 'I live in Glanvillia but the message will reach her. Don't worry, don't worry. Leave it with me.'

Hurrying his way back to his ship, Raphael looked, once, over his shoulder to wave to Jack only to find he had lost him in the crowd.

Jack Benet took the message as far as Glanvillia. Five days later, he passed the message on to his son, Albert, who lived close to Rose and her family. Albert greeted Marceline with a good afternoon when he arrived on his horse at her front yard. She had been weeding the small flower bed beside the mango trees and stood rubbing her back before waving to Albert who dismounted the horse.

'And how is that wife of yours?' Marceline asked.

'Oh, very well, thank you.'

They'd exchanged pleasantries in the usual island way. Asking after everyone before going on to explain all the ailments they were suffering.

'I have a message from my father,' Albert said. 'It's from a young Grenadian sailor he met in Roseau. He asks if he can meet with Rose. He'll be there in two weeks by the port market day.'

'A *sailor*?' Marceline forgot the sore back she'd been complaining about, stopped rubbing it and stood up, rigid. 'My daughter has no business with a sailor.'

'I'm only passing the message.' He lifted his hands in supplication.

'Well, that's kind and thank you, Albert. The message is safe with me.'

Gripping the gate and feeling the flaking wood in her palms, she watched him walk the horse the rest of the way home.

Raphael returned in the ship with the crew from Grenada as he'd said to Jack Benet, having set sail a little later than usual. Raphael stood on the bow looking out across the calm blue expanse, waiting urgently to see the mountain ranges of Dominica, the port coming into view, Rose waiting on the pier. The other sailors teased him. They knew he was planning to see the light-skinned girl with jet black hair, whom they had all thought was beautiful, telling Raphael that he was wasting his time: someone so lovely as Rose was not taking him seriously. He didn't want to entertain their thoughts; he only thought of Rose's clear eyes, flecks of green in hazel brown, and his smile grew with each of the 190 nautical miles.

The ship berthed at the pier, the sailors busily unloading cargo and beginning the ceaseless negotiations of produce that was not yet on display. Raphael was busy, too, but he continuously looked over his shoulder, craning his neck for signs of Rose. The captain grew angry when Raphael dropped a whole crate of limes across the decking. They rolled across the planks, and the children playing on the pier grabbed for them, having games of catch while Raphael tried to gather them, asking if he could have them back. Some of the limes rolled into the water, making tiny splashes as they sank briefly and then bobbed up to the surface. The children were giddy with laughter.

One of his shipmates shook his head. 'Is useless you look for her. She must have marry by now.'

The weeks of not seeing Rose were accumulating, and Raphael was impatient to see her. He wondered if there was any truth in what the other sailors said: that Rose had moved on, that he was wasting his time.

Two hours later, Rose had not appeared and the crew would be setting sail shortly. Rose had to come a long way, and she may have been delayed. But if she wanted to see him, she'd know his time was limited and she would have made an effort to be there by now. If she arrived now, there'd be no time for a conversation and barely enough for a kiss. For two hours, Raphael had been occupied with looking around the market and over his shoulder, selling very little produce at all.

'Please,' he pleaded with a woman who had a rack of notebooks, writing pads and pens on display outside her hardware shop. 'How much for a small piece of paper and a pen?'

'I can't sell just one page. You must buy the whole book.'

Raphael searched through his pockets for the money he'd made at the port. He passed some coins to the woman and used her counter to write a hurried letter. The horn for departure of his ship sounded; he had minutes to scribble a note to Rose in the hope that someone would take it up to Moore Park. He thought to ask the woman in the shop if she knew anyone who might be going to Moore Park, but she was already vexed by the brazen way he'd treated her counter as his writing desk and discarded both the pen and the writing pad once he had finished.

Raphael stopped five people in the market square before he found a man who claimed to know Rose and placed the folded sheet of paper into his hands.

'Leave it with me,' the man said.

'Thank you,' said Raphael, bowing several times. 'And your name is?'

'Me? I'm Wilfred Dennis.' Wilfred tucked the letter into the front pocket of his shirt and patted it.

Raphael rushed away and leapt aboard the ship just as the anchor was being heaved from the seabed.

***

The Catholic church on the top of the hill was newly built. The priest had it painted white, and the wooden window frames were deep red. The roof was high so that the sound inside was cavernous and grand, his voice, the music, the singing, all reaching up into the rafters. When the congregation sang, their voices floated out of the open windows and down to the houses, mostly empty because everyone was either at the Catholic church on the hill or the Protestant one down in Paix Bouche. The pews in the

Catholic church were close together as if to accommodate a hoard of people, but there were not enough inhabitants in Moore Park and the two neighbouring villages to fill it.

Every Sunday at the foot of the hill, a group of youths congregated after the service, laughing and joking and catching up with each other before going home to have breakfast with their families. When Rose had first attended Mass, two years ago with her family, she had heard the crowd of youths chattering. The loudest of them all, she later came to know, was Wilfred Dennis. She had worn a pretty yellow dress, a little on the short side and passed down to her by May a few years before Rose's sixteenth birthday. She had glanced at Wilfred, only briefly, to see what all the commotion had been about. Marceline had promptly cleared her throat, and Rose had shifted her eyes front and kept on walking up the hill. All the boys fell silent when they saw Rose. She came to realise, very shortly after seeing Wilfred, that he must have interpreted her cursory sweep over the young men chatting at the foot of the hill as interest in him because he had never stopped trying to get her attention whenever they happened to pass each other. He was bold, she thought, because he would bow his head to her, smile at her even though a member of her family was at her side.

Rose had only had to endure what Marcleine called Wilfred's sweet tongue, briefly after their arrival at Moore Park because after that she was being chaperoned everywhere. Having escaped his sweet tongue for two years, Rose had noticed his dry eye which rested easily on any passing pair of breasts, hips or bare legs he saw.

For the first time since Marceline had insisted that Rose be chaperoned, she was allowed to run an errand one morning. Her mother had asked her to take some leaves to a neighbour so that she could brew a tea to relieve her of her tingling fingers. Rose, desperate to show that she could be trusted on her own, had her head down, focusing on the small pebbles along the side of the road and the safe delivery of the leaves. Someone called her name and it broke her concentration. She had got used to the solitude and not having any friends other than May. She hadn't had a full conversation with anyone when she was on her own in a long time. It wasn't that she coped with her loneliness but that she had become her loneliness. She'd spent hours of every day since her failed trip to Roseau wondering what her future would be like if she never saw Raphael again. Rose had accepted this new way of being, a precious jewel that had to be protected from grabbing hands and people who would keep her from shining. She'd accepted her punishment and hadn't tried to run away again or complain that she needed her independence.

She hadn't told anyone, not even May, that she thought about the rough-looking sailor with his workman hands, dried and cracked in the creases. She missed Raphael's softly spoken voice, the gentleness in his eyes, the courteous way he treated her. He was proud, too, as though his tatty clothes didn't matter because they were more to do with his circumstances than the man he was inside. Though Rose smiled and got on with her chores, she thought about Raphael and hid her sadness. Living instead in her dreams and imaginings of how her life could have been. Rose's mind was always occupied with her daydreams of Raphael, even when she was reading a book and fiddling with the silver locket around her neck.

Her mother's voice in the back of her mind reminding her to come back home straight after making the delivery was the only one she'd expected to hear, so she was shocked to see Wilfred Dennis standing at the side of the road, grinning at her as she walked towards him.

'So, where you taking yourself in such a hurry?'

Rose looked up at Wilfred, nodded her head briefly and carried on walking.

'Miss Rose and your lovely face. You going to town, nuh?'

Again, Rose ignored him.

'If you going to town, I going, too.' He tucked the tail of his shirt into the back of his loose-fitting trousers and hurried to catch her up. Rose's skin prickled with anger. This was bound to get back to her mother. She would never let her out alone again if she found out. Rose halted abruptly, swung behind Wilfred and crossed to the other side of the road. He stopped for a moment and laughed as though as few crumbly rocks and pebbles couldn't keep him away. He continued to walk behind her for a short while. She had her hair piled high above her slender neck, pinned and covered with a silky headscarf. Her hips swayed slightly under her floral skirt.

'Rose, Rose, Rose. You hear how I love to call your name? One day you will call mine, too.' Wilfred stopped following her and she heard him say, 'Yes, sir, you have to call my name one day.'

***

Raphael was packing a cloth bag with his personal items. He was already in his uniform. His father stood at the bedroom door, agitated, trying to reason with his son.

'Can you just stop what you doing for one minute and look at me?' His father—who had been shouting at Raphael since seeing him saunter into the house in the British Army

52

uniform—had a calm voice now. 'Raphael, son, please. Tell me why you go and sign yourself up to this regiment?'

'Because there is a war and the British need us.' His voice was flat, and he kept his eyes on the bag.

'You don't see the amount of soldiers come back from all over the world on crutches? Blind?'

'No, I don't see them, Daddy.'

'You don't see them because you don't want to. Raphael, this is a white man's war. It's not for us. What we care if those people have time to stand and kill each other? What difference it make to us?'

'Look, in the army, I'll get paid. When I come back, I'll have a pension. I will have something to do with my time besides sit here, no money, no future, no hope.'

'And no Rose?' His father sat down on Raphael's bed. 'Look, son. It's brave of you to volunteer, but it have to be for the right reasons. Don't run away from your problems. Face them.'

Raphael said nothing but shook his head. His mother had gathered herself from a slumped position on the sofa where she'd collapsed earlier after she'd seen her son in a uniform, and stood in the bedroom doorway. It had taken her a few seconds to realise he'd signed up to the British Army; his mother had cried 'No' so many times, Raphael lost count and had gone to his room to gather the few possessions he had. His father had leapt from the table demanding to know how his youngest son could break his mother's heart.

When the war broke out in Europe in 1914, Raphael had ignored the newspapers, he was uninterested. When a year later, and the first West Indian Regiment had set sail to fight for King and Country, Raphael thought it laughable that West Indians had fallen for the promises of free land at the end of the war. He couldn't believe that they'd allowed themselves to be coerced into signing up because from where would all these supposed plots of land be obtained for so many men and not one of them had anything in writing. He had heard of the number of West Indian men who had fallen, the number of families who had lost their sons. The returning soldiers had so far not received land, and there had not been a single mention of the West Indian soldiers who hadn't returned in any of the lists of the fallen.

Now, two years since the war began and just months after finding and losing Rose, the call from the generals on the radio and the posters displayed in town made Raphael begin to think differently. He had sent out messages in a bid to find Rose. When the second message failed to reach her, he had sailed to Dominica and had gone to Moore Park himself, only to meet with the same young man who had promised to deliver his letter just three weeks before. After being told emphatically by this man that Rose's family had left Dominica and gone to Guadeloupe, Raphael felt hopeless. Rose was gone. She didn't come to the port, she left no message to say she was leaving, that she'd changed her mind about him. No goodbye. Losing Rose felt like losing his future. Signing up to the army would take his mind off her. Rose and the thought of what they could have had had filled his every waking moment.

Standing in his uniform convinced him that he was moving on. On the way home from collecting his uniform, children playing in their yards had saluted him. Adults nodded their praise for his courage, though some shook their heads. But it was when he saw his parents' reaction that his resolve to move on weakened. Had his father been right? Was he just running away from his problems; had he given up on finding Rose too easily?

'Daddy, I have to do this.'

'Is it too late to change your mind?' His mother pleaded from the doorway.

'I will write to you, Ma, when I know where I'll be stationed. I will write regularly and I'll come back.'

It was a bright, sunny morning when he left Grenada. He never looked back when his mother called his name from the front yard, but he'd heard the ruffle of her skirt and the thud of her knees on the front lawn, and the image of his father shaking his head while tears poured from his eyes, stayed with him until he reported for duty.

***

The subsistence workers from the countryside arrived every Saturday morning at the marketplace in the coastal town of Portsmouth in the north-west of Dominica. A heady morning of waiting, bartering, selling and honing their sales patter on the townsfolk made them weary and wanting to be back up in the mountain villages. But they had to make their money first. When they headed back, their wagons, carts and trucks would, hopefully, be empty as they bumped up the mountain roads, heaving sighs of relief and shrugging off the frustrations of the day. Most farmers did well. Most enjoyed their day. It was a time to catch up with the other farmers, form working partnerships, make friends, find lovers. Many stories could be had from the relationships that had been struck up on market day.

Come Saturday evening, a comfortable chair, a warm meal and a good night's sleep were well appreciated. Sunday was a rest day and, for most, a day of worship and a day to eat well and relax because when the sun rose the next day, normality returned. Mostly that meant backbreaking work in the gardens, extra jobs on the side like cleaning, cooking and mending. Then Saturday would arrive. Starting before sunrise, wagons would have to be loaded with ground provisions, dairy goods and meat, and the cycle for the week would begin again.

Having proven to her mother that she was not about to run away in the night, Rose, now approaching nineteen, was responsible for the journey to the market in Portsmouth to set up the family stall on her own. She sat on a low stool, goods displayed on the ground in front of her on a waterproof sheet, and sold all she could before the morning was over.

Each Saturday she would share Albert Benet's wagon. He picked her up and they chatted all the way to Portsmouth. He never once mentioned the time before sunrise when he'd met the sixteen-year-old Rose on her way to the coastal road on the western side of the island, just as a hurricane was brewing. Albert's wife was pregnant again, and he talked to Rose about his first child and how he looked forward to the new one being born.

It was late morning and Albert had set up his stall of dasheen, yam and tania, still mucky with soil. He was chatting to another of the traders, the fishmonger to the right of him, when a young boy tugged at Albert's shirt and wouldn't let it go. Breaking from his conversation, Albert looked down at the boy pulling his sleeve. He had a sheen to his cocoa skin and large sorrowful eyes.

'Son? What happen?' Albert screwed his eyebrows together.

'*Monsieur* Benet, your wife making her baby. They tell me to call you.' Before the boy could finish the speech he had rehearsed for the twenty minutes he'd been running, Albert had begun to gather his ground provisions. Several heads of tania rolled on the ground as he loaded the wagon and started for home.

Rose was in the middle of a sale when she noticed him go. She relied on Albert for a ride home and ended the conversation she was having with the woman bartering for limes rather abruptly.

'You want my money or what?' the woman was saying as Rose watched Albert crack the reins on the horse's back and disappear up the road.

'Oh, I'm sorry,' said Rose. 'Take the limes, my gift.'

Her mother would balk at the idea of giving food away, but Rose was wondering why Albert had rushed off home and not stopped for her. She had no way of getting home.

Trading ceased by about midday. Rose gathered up her unsold provisions and the waterproof sheet and put them into her box and rested her empty basket beside them. Then she hopped from stall to stall like a butterfly, asking if anyone could spare her some space. She was happy for anyone to take her as far as they could, but no one seemed able to accommodate her. She walked back to the empty stall space, crossed her arms and shook her head. That walk to Moore Park in the afternoon heat would kill her. She would have to stop so many times it would be dark before she got home. There was one last person she could ask, but she had avoided meeting his gaze as she'd hurried around trying to make at least one person take pity.

Wilfred Dennis stood a short distance away in the thinning market square long after he'd packed up a wooden box of unsold goods and loaded them onto his father's wagon. Rose hitched her basket over her shoulder and stooped to pick up her box.

'Rose, Rose, Rose.' Wilfred sauntered over to her. 'Look like you have yourself in a situation. One I can help you with.' The smile on Wilfred's face turned her stomach, but she knew she had no other choice.

'Here, let me help you with that.' Wilfred took the strap of her empty basket off her shoulder. His touch lingered on her fingers as he relieved her of the box. With a smirk, he carried her things over to the wagon and placed them in the back. She followed slowly, dreading the idea of a ride home with him but knew she should be grateful.

'Thank you,' she said through tight lips.

Wilfred offered his hand, placing an upturned palm under her nose to assist her up onto the wagon, but she ignored it, climbing up in a very ungainly fashion because of the height. Wilfred laughed and jumped up, too, sitting closer on the seat to Rose than was necessary. She faced away from him but expected he'd be grinning like a fool when he clucked his teeth and steered the horse off.

The journey would take the best part of an hour, and Rose wondered how much she could tolerate of this irritating man. He didn't speak at first, whistling three bars of the same tune incessantly and turning and grinning at her as though he were keeping her entertained. Rose either kept her eyes straight ahead or turned away, pretending to admire the scenery. Mountainsides, trees and trails which she'd seen a thousand times before.

'That is a pretty locket you wear, Rose,' Wilfred said. She touched the chain but said nothing. 'Yes, very nice, very nice. Where you get such a nice necklace? You don't have to say—I imagine is from a nice young fellow. Maybe someone from town, someone special you meet before you move up here?'

Rose shifted in her seat, adjusted her headscarf and looked back at her box. The unsold ground provisions rolled noisily about as the wagon ascended the steep slopes.

'Don't worry,' Wilfred assured her. 'We won't lose anything. I know these roads. I know these mountains just like I know about women.'

Rose let out a cough as she tried to stifle a laugh.

'You may laugh, but I know a lot of women who would agree.'

'Yes, I know what kind of women you mean,' retorted Rose, immediately regretting giving him an opening and recovering the stern look she'd held for most of the journey.

'Rose, you think you know me. I know you do. But you don't. It's not my fault if women want to throw themselves at me. I can't stop them. They think if I make a baby with them, I will marry them.'

'And so you should.'

'When I marry, it will be for love, Rose. As soon as I find the right one.'

'Well, you looking very hard for the right one, Mr Dennis. You not tired yet?' Rose could see that Wilfred was amused by her witticism when he turned to face her.

'I don't tire easily,' he said. 'Besides, I think I know who I choose.'

'Well, you better tell her quickly so all these others can stop throwing themselves at you.'

Wilfred pulled up the reins. The horse stopped and shook its mane.

'Why we stop?' Rose looked from side to side and then over her shoulder. Of the villagers on this road from Portsmouth, they were the last in the trail. Along the way, though it had frustrated her, Rose noticed that Wilfred had been slowing the pace, and they were a good few minutes behind the drivers ahead of them.

'My horse tired,' he said and jumped from the wagon to undo the harness on the old nag. Without speaking, he led the horse into a shady wood.

'Wilfred!' Rose called to him from the wagon. 'What you think you doing?' She jumped down after waiting several minutes, intending to chastise Wilfred for this ridiculous behaviour. Wilfred had led the horse down to a shallow pool where he let it stop for a drink. He'd sat down and rested against a tall tree, his legs stretched out in front of him, hands crossed behind his head and closed his eyes. Rose realised how much dimmer it became in the wood the closer she got to him. It was cooler, too, and she crossed her arms to keep the chill off them.

'Wilfred. Come on. My mother waiting for me. What you think you doing? I haven't got time for games.'

Wilfred did not answer but tilted his head to one side as though he had fallen asleep. Rose lost patience and marched up to him.

'I taking your horse and I going myself, alone.' She knelt next to him when he still did not move. 'Wilfred. I vex, *oui*, as you see me there.'

As quick as a flash, Wilfred rolled towards Rose, pulled her by her shoulders and pinned her to the dry grass. Leaves and twigs scratched her arms and legs as she fought to be released from his grip. All Wilfred could do was laugh. He did not try to kiss her, he just held her by her wrists to stop her scratching, his weight preventing her from wriggling away. She stopped struggling for a moment.

'Wilfred, I going to tell my father on you. He'll kill you. You hear? Now get off me or I will scream so loud a policeman will come and throw you in jail.'

'So, what is it to be?' Wilfred was giggling like a child.

'What?'

'Your daddy going to shoot me or the police going to arrest me?'

'Wilfred, this is madness. Get off me!'

'Well, as you ask so nicely.' He rolled over onto his back and started to laugh out loud. Rose immediately got up. Dirt and leaves stuck to the back of her dress, some of them floating off in her wake as she raced to the roadside. At the wagon, she began pulling her basket and the box containing the remaining ground provisions off the back. Her eyes were red but she did not cry, the anger swelling inside her like a pressure cooker about to explode.

'You think you strong enough to carry that all the way by yourself?' He was behind her now, still laughing, one hand in his pocket, the other leading his horse back to the wagon. 'It will get heavy in no time.'

Rose tipped the box up, letting every last item of food fall to the ground. She turned and began walking in the direction of home. Wilfred secured the horse to the wagon, jumped up and started after her.

When he caught up with Rose, she was holding the box so tightly the skin on her fingers were stretched and her fingernails dug into the wood. Her eyes bore a deep trench in the road ahead of her. The sun shot hot, dazzling rays through the trees lining the road, and Rose started to perspire. It was only then that she realised her headscarf must have come off in the scuffle. A thick strand of hair fell from the bun on the top of her head, but she refused to stop and fix it. She heard the wagon rolling up closer to her until it was just at her side.

'Rose.' Wilfred's voice was soft, apologetic. 'I pick up your food for you. No need to worry. Any time you feel you want to rest your legs, just jump on.'

She glanced swiftly at him. He wasn't grinning but shaking his head at her as if she were a child. She felt like one now. May would tell her she was cutting off her nose to spite her face. There was a long way to go, and she could feel the beads of sweat building above her lip, the empty box feeling as though it had been refilled. This is a game for him, she thought, chasing yet another girl was such fun.

He rode along slowly. Just the idea of his presence incensed her. How serious was he being in his pursuit of her? He'd looked earnest enough when he'd spoken about only marrying for love. Had he fantasised about her since she was sixteen? The girl he thought would one day look his way. The only girl he could ever say he loved and mean what he said? Or was she merely a girl he wanted to seduce and his fantasies about her going no further than just hot and empty dreams in his bed at night? She grimaced at the thought.

'Rose,' he called. 'I sorry. I just thought—I don't know. It was just a joke. I can see you too serious for foolishness, and I don't know what I was thinking. Look, you take the wagon, I will walk if you don't trust me.' Rose stopped but did not turn around. Wilfred jumped down. 'Look, take the reins. I'll walk.' He strolled on, hands in his pockets, head down.

'Wait,' she called after him. 'Take the reins, man—I don't know how to drive this thing.' Rose climbed aboard the back of the wagon with the produce. She sat where she could keep an eye on him but would be ready to jump off if he made one wrong move.

Wilfred returned to the wagon and they set off once again. They remained silent all the way to Moore Park. Rose, trying hard to quell her rage, did not notice that her treasured locket was gone.

***

Since arriving in France for his first tour of duty, Raphael hadn't yet held a rifle in his hands. He had not expected an easy time of it. This was a war. Soldiers fought, people had to die. He might be one of them, but nothing he'd done so far had been anything like he'd imagined. So far, he had not learned how to use a gun and he had not been trained how to disarm the enemy. All he and the rest of the Caribbean soldiers of the British West Indies Regiment, 4th Battalion, had been engaged to do was clean latrines, dig ditches and be on call night and day for all the back-breaking and risk-taking tasks the British Army could throw their way. Raphael never knew, when he sat on that ship to Europe, if he would be capable of killing a man, but without a weapon, he was defenceless and that made him afraid. The enemy was close by, and neither he nor the other black and brown men were armed like their white counterparts, who were fighting and dying around them or coming back to the base, blood spilling from them, limbs lost, nerves frayed to shreds.

The black Caribbean soldiers slept in their small tents, set up in such a tight cluster they could hear the men from the next tent breathing. Some lay on the grass, looking up to a darkening sky, their bodies aching, their minds numb and their ears pounding with the sound of enemy fire from earlier that day.

'But why we have to lay telephone lines?' one soldier from Trinidad was saying. 'So much trenches we did dig this past week. The Tommies want to ring up the Boche and invite them to dinner?' There was a ripple of laughter among the men, tired and strained, but laughter all the same.

'Well, the hofficer dem have fee contact each other to draw up plans and tings. Dem have fee know what orders fee give.' Eugene, a Jamaican, was very young. Eighteen, but so fresh-faced, he could be four years younger.

'They don't need telephone lines to know how to give orders. Those white NCOs give plenty orders and I never see them on a phone,' added Delroy, Raphael's countryman.

'You all talking rubbish, man. You complaining, but what we doing here is just as important as kill people,' suggested David, who was from Barbados.

'Yes, but what we doing here, no one will ever remember. No one will ever know we was even here.' Delroy closed his eyes.

Raphael had had enough of listening. He crawled into his tent to get some sleep. The next day there would be frontline action, and he and his battalion would be right there, loading ammunition for the white soldiers, running backwards and forwards with supplies in those mud-filled, narrow and deep trenches, and with no word of thanks from the soldiers calling for the darkie to load them up.

George was already in the tent. He'd told Raphael all about Barbados and how he couldn't wait to go home. Raphael felt the same, but wasn't sure that Grenada was home any more. After the war, he would move on. He might even stay in Europe, live in France and start his own farm in the French countryside. He'd seen the cottages. Many of the farms were deserted now, but on several lonely and cold days, he pictured the countryside—sunny, warm, a French wife and crops of his own.

Odette hadn't been scared or run away when she'd seen him, walking up to her farm where she was hanging sopping cotton sheets on a low clothes line, so heavy they hung almost to the tufty grass below them. She'd said something in French that Raphael hadn't understood. She'd mimed 'eat' and 'drink' with hand gestures. He'd nodded happily and followed her into the stone cottage which stood isolated in a wide field. The others, both black and white, had gone into the village for beer, but Raphael had wandered away from them in pursuit of quiet.

In his solitude, his mind took him to dark places, remembering the still bodies at his feet, men younger than him. Boys. Their people back home would cry for them. He heard his mother crying. Sometimes, he had thoughts he couldn't fathom. He only knew that the thoughts left darkness which buried itself into his very soul. Sometimes, he had a feeling that he was searching for something and he pictured a brown-skinned girl with light eyes and silky hair. She haunted him. He had begun to think of Rose as a dream when he pictured her. He couldn't remember how many curls she had, how slender her wrists were. He only knew he missed her and hoped to see her again, but not as a dream.

It was the only day off his regiment had had. The sergeant must have taken pity on the black soldiers when he allowed them time away from camp with the white soldiers. Raphael's regiment thought it was a wonderful thing, even though the white soldiers rode to the village in jeeps and trucks while they walked.

Inside the stone cottage, the French woman turned, put her hand on her chest and said, Odette. Raphael, making the same gesture, revealed his name. They tried to communicate during the early evening supper and only ended up laughing as one tried to teach the other how to speak their language.

When the sun fell, Raphael wondered about the time and if his curfew had begun. By then, he had drunk so much wine he was drowsy with sleep, the morning's work having tired him so and the afternoon sun having sapped him of even more energy. Odette's naked body wasn't something he wanted to leave, whether he was in curfew or not. The sheets on her bed smelled of lavender, her skin had the fragrance of working under a hot sun, but it was soft and full and he couldn't stop himself sinking into her as her thick legs wrapped around his waist.

She was sleeping when he left. He brushed a kiss to her forehead and left the house.

'Mr Raphael, you tired too?' George asked on the other side of his tent.

'Yes, I tired. Tired of hearing stories. Tired of being hungry, wet and cold, tired of the noise, the smell...'

'Yes, man, you sounding tired to me,' George cackled. His laugh was shrill, feminine sounding. But George liked to laugh, and Raphael had to get used to it. George carried on talking, but Raphael's eyes began to close; soon, all he could see was a warm beach, palm trees rising high above him and clouds, brilliant white and dancing in a deep blue sky. A child was playing and threw a ball that landed on his shoulder. He threw it back to the boy who caught it and threw it back even harder against his shoulder. It surprised him and he shouted to the boy.

'Don't you yell at me, Darkie.' The soldier was prodding Raphael in the shoulder with the butt of a rifle. 'Take this and get your carcass in them trenches. Now!' The soldier left the tent, dropping an Enfield rifle at Raphael's side. Raphael could hear the sound of endless gunshot. Flashes of light broke through the entrance to his tent, and he could see the legs of men running frantically in all directions. He crawled a few inches on his knees, saw his hat and made a grab for it. In his left hand, he held the rifle. As he stumbled to his feet outside the tent, he saw George ahead and ran after him.

Down in the trenches, the gunshots were deafening. The enemy fire was getting louder, and when Raphael turned to his right, he saw a German soldier jumping into the trench just a few yards away. A voice bellowed directly into his ear.

'Let 'im 'ave it, Darkie!'

Raphael charged at the enemy, thrusting hard with his bayonet as he ran at the soldier. He heard a prolonged groan and felt the body fall away from him as he pulled the gun out of the dead soldier. The large face of another German soldier was approaching him at speed; Raphael swung the butt of the gun hard and fast into his target's throat, then hit him again directly in the forehead. Stumbling backwards, Raphael aimed his rifle upwards, firing and hitting the arm of another enemy soldier invading the trench. Pulling back the action, his next bullet entered someone's face. Raphael walked backwards, deeper into the trench, still with his rifle high. More German soldiers came. He took aim, the way he'd seen the British soldiers do, firing, pulling back the action and firing again and again until the explosive sound stopped. A sudden cracking sound sent Raphael tumbling forward, face first into the mud. The last thing he remembered seeing was Rose running towards him on the beach.

'Raphael, Raphael.' A voice he recognised was close to his ear. Raphael blinked several times but saw nothing at first. Then the colours came. Stone, shades of brown, beige. The faces became clearer. Identifiable. He saw his friend George; Raphael whispered his name.

'Yes is me. Man I take you for dead.' George's high-pitched chuckle brought Raphael round.

'What happen?' Raphael asked.

'What happen? What happen? I tell you what happen, you were a champion out there. A hero. You fight like a mad man and you shoot like some big old crazy killer, like I never seen before in my life, man.' George's laughter was cut short.

'On your feet, soldier, if you can stand.' The sergeant's voice was loud and cold. 'You want to take that rifle of yours, make sure it's loaded and get over there and guard the POWs. There. With Collins.'

'Can you stand?' George whispered into Raphael's ear.

'I think so. Help me though.' Raphael saluted his sergeant when he finally got to his feet. The sergeant nodded briefly and went back to the officer's hut, followed by the corporal who eyed Raphael before taking his leave.

Collins was a thin red-haired boy from Liverpool. He got up and saluted when Raphael came to join him. Immediately, from behind the tall wire fence, three or four of the German prisoners got up and looked sternly at Raphael. Their faces were bloody and caked thick with dried mud. Their eyes were bright like bits of sky lost in dark earth and pools of red. They said something in their language then spat on their hands and started to rub the dirt off their faces. They pointed and laughed at Raphael.

'I think they wonder if your colour comes off,' Collins said.

'I know what they think.' Raphael looked down the barrel of his Enfield and walked towards the fencing between him and the prisoners. He made quick, long strides despite the searing pain in his head, then made an elaborate action to show that he could fire his gun whenever he chose.

***

'That boy, Wilfred, is by the yard talking to Daddy. He asking him for permission to marry you.' May had jumped off the truck where the road split and walked the narrow leafy lane leading to Moore Park. She looked tired after coming back from the school and had spotted Wilfred and her father chatting in the yard just after passing the row of sleepy houses at the end of the lane.

Rose didn't care to hear anything about Mr Dennis. 'My stomach hurts,' was all Rose said. She was lying on their double bed on her front, reading one of May's history books.

'What you have? You want I get you something?' May was concerned.

'Is that Wilfred Dennis that making me sick, May. I hate him.' She rolled over and sat up, fuming.

May sighed a laugh as she shook off her jacket and shoes. 'So why he coming here asking about marriage? What you say to him?'

'*Nothing.*' Rose's lips were drawn into a thin pink line as she shook her head.

'Well, you want me to go and tell the boy to stop wasting Daddy time? He talking all sorts of rubbish about how he

69

going to start growing limes and make more money than anyone else in Moore Park, Paix Bouche and Dos D'Âne put together.'

'Let him talk. He won't get past Mam. She knows what that boy is really like.'

'Yes, Mammy just stand up and watch him at the side of her eye. She not saying *anything*—and that says a lot.' The two girls squealed with laughter as May imitated her mother. They only just heard the timid knock from their father on the door.

'Your mammy just chase a boy from the yard with a broom. Come and have your dinner, she say.'

The girls came and sat at the table, Dunstan relaying how Marceline shook her broom at Wilfred all the way from the yard to the top of the road to the laughter of the neighbours, who had stopped to listen in on Wilfred's great claims of acquiring a big house very soon. By the next day, they would make up a song about it. Rose knew how furious Wilfred would be. He had a lot of pride and, as far as she was concerned, stupidity. He would never win her over, he must have known. Thoughts of marriage had only ever been associated with one man. She had no chance of ever finding that man again, so there was no likelihood of her ever marrying.

***

We dig the ditches blind by sweat
For hours we work and don't sleep yet
Without a rifle to hold up high
My troops all fall, their mothers cry

None of the soldiers of the British West Indies Regiment ever knew who wrote those words, but this was their lament during the misery they encountered every day they were on duty. Their only comfort came when the war ended. Armistice Day could not have come any sooner for them, and as the troops prepared to demobilise, eight battalions of Caribbean soldiers stationed in France and Italy were called to the Italian port of Taranto.

At Marseilles, Raphael and the remainder of his battalion were joined by soldiers from Mesopotamia and Egypt. These soldiers had seen action. They were battle worn and they had stories that some of the soldiers stationed in Europe had never heard. Raphael remembered the reluctance the British had to arming the black soldiers, but a time had come when there was no choice. Cleaning, cooking, building, fixing and mending was no good to a regiment who was under fire. The coloureds and darkies could be of better use with a gun in their hands. A man from a battalion mixed with black and white soldiers sat beside Raphael on the ship to Taranto. A scar closed one of his eyes, and there was little movement in his neck as they sat drinking water from an old barrel on the top deck.

'I don't know what I remember of home,' he said to Raphael. It was obvious that this man had had little to eat: his jacket looked several sizes too large, he smelled of months without bathing. Neither had he combed his tufty hair that grew unevenly and he scratched his head with a fury to settle the head lice.

'You will remember everything, and everything you went through will be nothing,' said Raphael, wondering how bad his own odour was and what he must look like.

'I will remember all of this,' said the soldier. 'I remember before we set sail and got to the military camp back home, they tell us they have no guns for us yet. Some men run and find knives, blades, chains and share them. How we can go in a war and not have weapon? Just one day after we land, the Germans come and it's the knives we bring from home we use to hold them back. Only that let us last the day and allow us to remain in the war. Otherwise, we would be long dead.' He scratched his head and got up to tear off a chunk from a loaf of bread that was being passed around across the other side of the deck.

It took a whole week to sail to Taranto that winter. They arrived in Italy sick, injured and lacking sleep. The British had told them they were going to stop in Italy before home and talked about 'demob'. No one Raphael spoke to was actually sure what it meant. Chat and rumours were going round, but all Raphael wanted to do was get back to Grenada. He hoped that this demob was one last thing before he could return home.

Not long after they landed, unrest among the West Indian soldiers began. They were quickly tasked with cleaning latrines and cleaning boots and uniforms for the British soldiers.

'That is what we good for now?' One West Indian soldier kissed his teeth.

It was time for them to go home. They had served long and hard beside their white peers, and these latest duties were an insult. From England, ships arrived loaded with ammunition. The job of unloading the ships and loading the ammunition onto trains to be taken further up the line fell on their shoulders alone. It was heavy and gruelling. The West Indian soldiers worked hard in the harsh conditions with only their dirty jackets to keep them warm, wiping shining brows with the backs of their freezing hands, shaking sweat from their eyes, the salt stinging and the wind blistering their skin.

Raphael helped one of the soldiers to carry a heavy box of ammunition from one of the ships to a truck parked at the entrance to a sparse woodland. An angry conversation near the trucks had begun. The West Indian soldiers, though speaking in whispers, were boiling to the brink of scalding someone with their anger. Raphael knew it was something to do with conditions, money and the endless work, but he hadn't taken part, just caught snatches as he went to and from the ship, his dirty boots feeling as though they were full of grit as he heaved boxes along the pier.

'It's true. I read it with my own eyes. Kitchener give all the white soldiers a pay rise and none of us going to get a copper more.'

'That can't be true,' George exclaimed. 'That's not fair.'

'What is fair about how they treating us? What is fair about it?'

The soldier's skin was mahogany, shining from heavy lifting though his lips were chapped and white from the cold. His arms had been battered in combat, but somehow he found strength in them. He marched towards his commanding officer who was standing a short distance from the pier. He was reading through a bulletin and didn't notice the angry soldier who, in one smooth motion, picked up a rifle leaning against a tree, unattended by a private smoking a cigarette. He fired point-blank into the officer's head, watched the man drop and let the rifle fall to the ground. For two seconds, no one moved until another rifle shot was fired from somewhere and all the soldiers began to run for cover, taking up arms and firing; British troops attacking each other, black against white.

Raphael pulled George behind a line of trucks. 'Just keep your head down and don't get involved in this,' Raphael shouted.

Bullets were flying past them and they needed a safer position. On their elbows and knees, they shuffled along the ground towards a row of trees and rolled down a slope where three young white soldiers huddled on the ground for protection. One of them was armed with a pistol. He got to his feet and aimed his gun, his hand shaking fiercely.

'Fuck you!' he shouted.

'We're not armed.' Raphael raised his hands, shaking them excitedly above his head. The young soldier pulled his trigger. Raphael heard the bang and felt a cold whistle blaze past him. He was deaf for a second, colder than he'd ever felt as if there was no blood in his veins, just ice. The young soldier aimed the gun at Raphael, his hand still trembling until one of his compatriots put a hand over the barrel and lowered it. Raphael turned to George. He had gone. How did he run so fast without him noticing? Then, at his feet, he saw a pair of legs sprawled awkwardly, one twitched and stilled. George lay flat on his back with a bright red trail seeping from his head into his open eyes. Blood soaked the knees of his trousers and stained his hands as Raphael got to the ground to hold his friend George in his arms.

1896

They left their respective homes with practically nothing. Antoine had a small sum of money that his grandmother had given to him when he went to her bedroom to say goodbye. She was the only one he'd told that he was leaving.

It had been an impossible situation. He'd been lying and creeping around like a criminal just because he wanted to see Nanette. She was beautiful, intelligent, kind but his parents would never approve of her. He knew how they felt about the blacks, and regardless of her family wealth, Antoine's family would never allow him to marry Nanette. His mother would die, slash her own wrists so that she wouldn't have to live with such shame.

The one time he quizzed his father to gauge how he would react to his seeing Nanette, he hadn't really been surprised at the tone of the conversation.

'Do you remember anything about the night of the ball, Father?'

They sat on the same patio, where the revellers stood a few months ago drinking champagne, chatting drunken nonsense. They had abandoned the classical orchestra who had been touring in Montreal, and whom Madame Laudier had hired especially for the evening, in favour of the drums and excitement of the black workers.

'How could I forget? Your mother fussed so much I thought she might combust. I think she drank too much in the end.'

'But you saw the dancers over there?'

Antoine and his father watched their staff engaged in the labour of producing coffee. It was early afternoon and some of the workers were drying coffee beans on the *glacis* which had been their dance floor the night of the Masquerade Ball. Previously, the work had been done by slaves, but since emancipation laws had been employed, their staff worked even harder, growing food on the plots of land they now rented from the Laudiers.

Antoine had been very young when the Laudiers owned slaves, never getting a true idea of their trials, though hearing whips and guns and screams in the night. He remembered his grandmother holding hands with the little black children, saying please and thank you to the house slaves and taking cake out to the drying house when the men and women took their breaks. She was the tolerant one, the accepting one who saw fellow humans working hard in the sun to keep the roof of the grand house over their heads.

Antoine looked out at the workers, at their laboured movements, but his thoughts turned to Nanette, the night of the ball, the way she moved, her rhythmic actions and the deep concentration as she placed each step. She hadn't missed one.

'Those women have grace about them,' he said to his father. 'Some of them. Very wise women. Some can be very engaging. They know a lot even though they cannot read. Some of them.'

'Boy, you will come to know that there isn't much that goes on in their minds. Full buttocks, breasts and hips. Great for bearing children, hard work and … well, you know what else.'

'But Grandfather used to treat them badly. He raped some of them.'

'How the hell would you know a thing like that?'

'He bragged about it, and I think when I was a boy, I think I witnessed something.'

His father waved a hand before picking up his china cup of strong black coffee.

'They are used to it. It isn't a sin.'

'But you shouldn't speak of women like that, Father. And they work so hard—'

His father cut him off. 'If you can't see these people for what they really are, then you have not finished your education. Your mother used to shout at me because I didn't stop you playing with their children. They will never be your friend. They resent you, and they would sooner cut your throat and steal your money than become your ally. It's time you learned your place and theirs.'

'Father, not all black people were slaves.'

'They were born to be, son. They were born to be.'

Antoine bit his tongue. Quite literally. Tears misted his view, the taste of metal filled his mouth and he couldn't say another word. How could he tell his father that he was in love with Nanette? His father would kill him if he knew.

His grandmother had already retired to bed on the night he decided to leave the family home for good. She'd been sleeping, so he sat beside her on the satin bedding and waited a while. He touched the silken skin of her hand and she woke up. His grandmother was still weak from a heart attack, and he struggled to decide if it was wise to say goodbye or to make up a reason for wanting to see her. His mother insisted that *Grand-mère*'s heart attack had been brought on in part by Antoine's refusal to settle down and allow his mother to search for a good wife for him in France.

'*Mon cher.*' His grandmother's voice was low and hoarse.

'I'm sorry, I didn't mean to wake you.'

She smiled, her thin lips stretching and highlighting her high cheekbones. She had been a beautiful woman. Only sixteen when she married Antoine's grandfather in Marseille and moved to the colonies at age nineteen.

'It's a nice way to wake up,' she said. 'Is it late?'

'Not too late,' said Antoine, shifting closer. 'I think everyone is about to retire.'

'And you? Off somewhere again?'

He blushed and smiled at her.

'I assume there is a young lady you are courting. Your mother thinks as much.'

He lowered his gaze; his grandmother didn't know the full story it would seem. His mother had been digging lately. She'd found out about Nanette and told his father who had raged at him to drop his foolish nonsense. This girl was good for one thing and that wasn't marriage. He would be disowned if Antoine didn't give her up immediately. He had a matter of days to come to his senses, and if he didn't, he could say goodbye to his inheritance and the roof over his ungrateful head.

'You are in love.' His grandmother's smile grew wider, her eyes glistening. 'It's good to know. And who is she, this girl?'

'Someone they don't want for me. They never will accept her as part of the family.'

'Well, tell me who she is.'

'She's a very kind, gentle and beautiful girl I met at the end of the ball.'

'Oh, your mother mentioned she'd invited the usual eligible girls but I thought you'd dismissed them all. She isn't one of those, then?'

'She is someone new. An island girl. She comes from a good family, a rich family, but she is not one of *us*.'

His grandmother closed her eyes and nodded. Her smile vanished, and when she looked up at Antoine, her eyes were wet with tears.

'I know what it is to love, *mon cher*. I didn't marry the man I loved because I was not permitted. If you feel you love this girl, then you must follow your heart. You are young—you deserve to be happy. Always.' She shifted in her bed and stared hard at Antoine through cloudy, grey eyes. 'What is it, my love? I think you have come to say goodbye … haven't you?'

He nodded.

'It's all right, don't you worry one bit.' She looked over at her dressing table and pointed to it. 'Over there, I have a jewellery box. A wooden one with a brass lock. There is some money in the lower compartment. Take it all.'

'No Grandmama, I didn't come here to ask for anything.'

'No, you came to say goodbye and this is my gift to you. I can see it written all over that beautiful face of yours how sad you are to leave. I could always read everything in those eyes. Large pools of love and innocence, I always said. Love is innocent, love is pure and it shouldn't be stamped out, not ever. I stayed in this godforsaken place all my adult life without any love in my heart. Until you came. You are my heart, Antoine, and I want you to take it and allow it to be happy. Now, open the jewellery box.'

He rose slowly from the bed and picked up the box. It was carved in walnut, varnished so it shone, the key in the lock.

'Lift out the top shelf and you'll find the money.'

Antoine gasped. 'Why have you so much cash in here?'

She snorted a laugh. 'For rainy days.'

'But you don't mean for me to take it all. Surely? This is too much.'

'Foolish boy—what is an old woman to do with it? There is no more rain in my life, but you might encounter plenty. Think. Both of you are used to a certain style of living. It will be hard for you both to go from this,' she waved a gentle hand at her surroundings. 'To nothing at all. It will help you for a while, but it won't last forever.'

'*Merci Grand-mère, merci*. I will pay you back one day.'

'You will repay me by staying safe and happy. That is all I wish from you.' She pulled her wedding ring from her crinkled finger. It came off easily. She put it into Antoine's palm and closed his fingers around it. 'I have no need for this either, but you might. Now go. I need my rest.'

Antoine placed a warm kiss on his grandmother's forehead. She closed her eyes and immediately fell asleep.

Antoine met with Nanette by the mouth of the river—the place where they had been meeting secretly for six months before their respective parents became suspicious of their comings and goings. Antoine was known to go into Roseau for beer and cigars and to chase loose women, as his mother called them. But his dear Nanette had found it extremely difficult to keep anything from her sister who followed her and questioned her, until Nanette finally gave in and admitted there was a boy. From then on, all her sister did was quiz her about who this mysterious boy was and why she couldn't introduce him to her mother and father. They had said that at nineteen it was time she married, anyway. Her sister quickly realised the boy was someone their family would not approve of, but by then, Nanette's mother had begun keeping a very close guard over her.

At the river, Nanette arrived, carrying a bag with a few personal items: some clothes, a bible and wearing her silver locket.

'Was it difficult?' he asked her.

Nanette had told Antoine about how strained the atmosphere had become when the truth was out. She had suffered just as much as he had. When she'd finally admitted the truth to her parents about her love for Antoine, they'd wanted to keep her under lock and key. Her father said Antoine's family were white devils and had no right to still be here. Common decency dictated they give up their land and sail back to France: they'd have more than enough money to set up in a palace in Europe.

'Father, Antoine is not like the rest of them,' she had pleaded. He had stomped up and down the hallway, frightening the timid maid who was dusting the porcelain ornaments on the small table. Nanette's mother had tried to calm him down.

'They are all the same.' He'd exploded again. 'He is using you, and he'll impregnate you and leave you on the side of the road. That's what his kind do to brown girls like you. Are you that stupid to think he actually cares about you? You can love him all you want, but he will leave you when he has used you and tires of you.'

Nanette had rushed to her room; her sister had tried to soothe her, tell her to reconsider seeing this boy. She would find another love. But, as Nanette had told Antoine, he was the only one she would love in her life and she was ready to sacrifice everything for him.

'Oh, it wasn't easy. The atmosphere in the house has been explosive. And when I went to say goodbye it was like a fire blasted through the whole place. I couldn't wait to get out and breathe at last. My sister waved from the drawing room window and I burst out crying. My mother cried the whole time I was packing, and my father, well, my father had a lot to say. He would not relent.'

'Because I am white.'

'He might have been able to forgive you that, but in the end, his stance on status was clear. Without your family, you have no money. You are no one according to him. I am a disgrace to my family because I want to marry a man with no position. I hate my father.'

'Don't say that, Nanette. You love your family. That is why you have been crying.' He took her bag and held her hand. 'I will find work,' he assured her. 'Then we will sail to Guadeloupe or Martinique and live happily ever after.'

'Is it that easy?' She smiled at him.

'Everything is easy when you have love, Nanette. And I love you.'

With his grandmother's money, they took a room in a guest house in Roseau. It was intended to be a temporary measure while Antoine set about finding a job so that they could have enough to rent a small house. They talked about buying one outside of town, maybe by the sea, perhaps in the mountains or the country. Anywhere that was away from their parents' estates, anywhere where they could live together and be happy. Free from the pressures their families put on them. For Nanette and Antoine, anything seemed possible as long as they had each other.

They walked in town, holding hands, stopping to eat fried fish at the tavern with uneven cuts of bread and large jugs of beer and tumblers of rum. It was a rough place but they ignored their surroundings, showing up as they did in fine clothes and shoes, Nanette carrying a silk purse embroidered with delicate needlework. It came from Paris, though she had never been there. It was a present on her fifteenth birthday from one of her father's business partners.

They had grown oblivious to the stares and comments made about them behind their backs. Some of the townsfolk stopped and pointed. They called them the young master and his slave bride, laughed at their ridiculous finery and refined way of speaking. So far, Antoine had not been able to find work. His skills, limited only to assisting in the running of his father's coffee company, were of no use to a single soul in Roseau. Unused to thinking about how long their money would last, the couple continued to enjoy their lives and thought nothing about the next day.

Each morning, the guest house was filled with the sound of their lovemaking. Loud, passionate and raw, they rocked the timbers of the rickety guest house, the bed creaking with every move of their bodies, the ornate metal headboard pulsing a rhythm on the peeling wall paper and threatening to pull the whole house down.

Months after their respective departures from their grand homes, they began to notice that Grandmother's cash was dwindling. They had no idea what they would do if they could no longer pay for their room.

Nanette put the rest of their cash into her silk purse and wrapped a shawl around her neck and shoulders before they went out for a walk along the seafront in the early evening.

They were both hungry. Their rent afforded them one meal a day. They could choose between breakfast or supper. Today, they had chosen breakfast and they were wise enough to know that they could no longer afford to eat at the tavern.

As they walked, three young boys—locals who had probably worked their gardens all day—approached them from behind. Antoine and Nanette held hands and hadn't noticed them.

'I think we should eat something, Nanette. I can hear your stomach complaining above the sound of the ocean.'

Nanette giggled and pressed a hand to her cheek.

'I am hungry,' said Antoine. 'Maybe we could buy bread, though I don't think we will find a bakery open at this time.' It had all been a mystery to them, learning how to take care of themselves when they'd been used to servants running their baths, placing large plates of food in front of them at every meal. 'We'll see what we can find further into the town.'

Before they could cross the narrow road, the boys were upon them. One grabbed Nanette's purse and tried to yank the chain handle from her wrist. Antoine reached towards her, but the two other boys pulled him aside, punched his jaw and sent him bent double with blows to his stomach. He panted Nanette's name. She shrieked and called for help, but the boy was able to remove the purse from her with very little force and run away laughing. The other two followed having left Antoine on his knees on the ground.

Nanette knelt beside him. 'Are you all right, my love?'

'I'm perfectly fine, how are you? Did he hurt you?'

'Not at all, but they took the money, they have everything.'

They rose slowly to their feet. Nanette dusted Antoine's clothes.

'Leave it, just leave it. We'll be fine. We'd better just get back to the guest house.'

'But Antoine, what will we do? We cannot pay.'

'They won't know that. We'll be discreet as we come and go, and by the time they realise, something will show up. I don't know how much it is worth but there is always Grandmother's ring. Though I wanted it for…'

'I know,' said Nanette. 'One of these days we will get married.'

One of the first things Antoine had done was propose marriage, but the time and opportunity hadn't seemed appropriate and it still wasn't, now that they were faced with the matter of keeping a roof over their heads.

'Wait,' said Antoine. 'Your locket.'

They stopped in the road leading to the guest house and Nanette put her hand on her throat. She pulled at the shawl and checked her neck; the silver shone in the twilight as Antoine took her hand.

'If they'd seen it, they would have taken it, too,' said Nanette. 'Oh Antoine, I'm afraid. For the first time since we left, I'm actually afraid for our future. I don't want to go back.'

'Never, we never have to go back. I promise you, we'll find a way. Don't cry, Nanette. We will be fine. I know we will.'

They continued walking. They held hands, not uttering a word more as Nanette tried to stop herself sniffing. She wiped a tear away and looked down at the red marks on her wrist before touching her hand to her locket and covering it once again with her shawl.

Weeks passed with no change. There were no jobs that Antoine could take and the couple were surviving on one meal a day, barely going out and using as many excuses for not paying their rent as they could concoct: Antoine was awaiting an inheritance; Nanette was expecting her aunt to arrive with money they were owed; Antoine had done a job for a man in Du Blanc and it was merely days before he was to be paid; they were going to sell some jewellery but hadn't got a good enough price. They made for far better liars than they would have liked, but it was the only option they had until they devised a plan to either find money or a place to escape to without trace.

Nanette washed her face in the porcelain bowl on the stand in their room. As she patted her skin dry, she thought about the expensive pots of cream and bottles of perfume on her dressing table at home. She looked into the mirror. Her hair was lifeless, and without her rags, she was unable to set it in ringlets. She tired of wearing the same clothes but then shook her head at the idiocy of those thoughts. There were far worse issues to consider, and with each passing day, a solution seemed harder and harder to find. She buried her face in the soft cotton of the towel and shook her head.

'Nanette.' Antoine got up from the bed where he had been lying on his back, gazing up at the ornate flower on the ceiling from where the light was attached. The ceiling was high, the rooms in the guest house were large and the furniture old but of high quality. The house had been a very fine one in its day, probably owned by a rich landowner before the town became divided by narrow roads, congested with people and traffic and so loud in the town centre that the couple could hardly think. He hadn't been thinking, he'd been dreaming of a place where he and Nanette could feel safe and happy. He hadn't noticed at first how desperately she cried into the towel, muffling the sound. He put his arms around Nanette, pulled her head into his shoulder.

'It will be fine, we'll find a way to overcome our problems, you'll see.'

'That's just it, I don't see any more. I'm not myself here. I'm weak and restrained. We're going to have to leave here, Antoine. You know that.'

He nodded and kissed the top of her head. 'I know, but until then, we have to be brave.'

'I'm trying.'

He held her tightly in his arms as their naked bodies sealed close, the movement of their bed more than likely waking anyone in the house from sleep.

Downstairs, Mrs Bellamy, the owner of the guest house, giggled as she washed plates and pots in the kitchen sink. Her husband shook his head.

'Did they pay their rent this week?' he asked.

'Not this week or last week, either,' his wife said, lowering her head. 'They have not paid for several weeks.'

'And you said nothing up until now?'

'Give them a chance, they're young and wet behind the ears. They say they have money coming.'

'They could tell you anything and you'd believe them.' He rose abruptly from his chair and took long strides to the wide front door, pulling on a jacket from the hat stand. Mrs Bellamy crossed her arms.

'Where on earth are you going at this time, in the dark.'

'Not far. I need to make arrangements.'

'With whom?'

'Never you mind. I'm not having these young socialites taking advantage. They come from money, Marie. Lots of it. And if we can't see any of it, then we shouldn't be giving them the easy ride they've grown accustomed to their whole lives.' He slammed the door and left the house on foot.

In the early hours of the following morning, Mr Bellamy rushed up to the young couple's room and threw open the door. Nanette sat astride Antoine, her fingers sinking into his chest. When they became aware of Mr Bellamy standing at the open door with flame red cheeks, Antoine sat up quickly and Nanette leapt up and crouched beside the bed, bending low enough to be out of Mr Bellamy's sight.

'*Monsieur.* This is an outrage.' Antoine pulled the sheet up over his middle.

'What is outrageous is that you have not paid your rent. Now, where is it?' Mr Bellamy fixed his eyes on Antoine who blushed furiously. Nanette looked up over the side of the bed at Antoine. Mrs Bellamy came to the door.

'They have no money,' she said and looked with pity at the pair. 'I already told you.'

'So,' Mr Bellamy bellowed. 'Get up. Get dressed, pack your things and come with me.' He charged out of the room.

'What is he going to do?' Antoine asked Mrs Bellamy.

'I don't know but you best do as he says. Come on—get dressed.'

Outside, the couple saw that Mr Bellamy had rigged up his wagon. They climbed on board with their belongings, and Mr Bellamy drove them south to Soufrière. He explained on the way that he had a cousin married to a man named Lafferty. They owned the Hudson estate and they needed some new domestics. Mr Bellamy had sent a message to them the night before saying he had solved their staffing problem and that help was on its way. Assuming that the message had been received, he set off with Antoine and Nanette, having assured his cousin that they were husband and wife, that Antoine knew how to keep a garden and that Nanette would make a good house servant.

Antoine and Nanette entered the house by the kitchen to find what looked like a complement of staff having breakfast around a large table before Mr Bellamy ushered them along a dark corridor. He signalled for them to wait while he sought his cousin.

'Can she cook, too?' asked Mrs Lafferty as she stood sizing up the pair.

'She's a fast learner,' he said. 'Very courteous, the pair of them.'

Mrs Lafferty probed them about their families. They spoke as honestly as they could, leaving out anything that might put them in a bad light and allowing Mr Bellamy to make up for the things they had no idea how to answer: where had they worked before, how long had they been in service.

'Very well spoken,' said Mrs Lafferty, crossing her brow. 'For servants, I mean. But at least I can understand you. I can't pick up on that Creole the other servants use. Very good, off you go and report to Charity. She'll appoint your duties, both of you, and show you your quarters and the rest of it. You'll be given your wages at the end of each week after my husband has done the ledger. Well, off you go.'

Mr Bellamy stayed to chat with his cousin for a while as the couple tried to find their way back down to the kitchen. They held hands tightly and followed the sound of chatter, the chiming of crockery and silverware and the smell of poached eggs and fresh bread. Their mouths watered as they entered the kitchen, finding their luggage had been moved into a corner. They stood looking at a row of six expectant faces.

'And? You are?' A fat woman with skin that was blue-black lifted herself from one of the low-backed dining chairs and approached them slowly. She asked for names, their business there and what they expected her to do with them, arriving without warning. Her Dominican accent was broad and drawn out, flowing from her thick lips like a song from church.

'They told us to ask for Charity. We work for Mrs Lafferty now.' Antoine squeezed Nanette's hand. She placed her other hand on her locket.

'Oh-hoh? Well, I'm Charity. And what work you come to do?'

'I'm to work in the garden and Nanette is to learn to cook.'

Charity looked them up and down, then over her shoulder at the others: three other women and two men.

'Well, before you bend and break, you better come and have some breakfast.'

The staff, who had all fallen silent, began to chat again, making space at the table for Antoine and Nanette, lighting the stove, setting water to boil, slicing bread and poaching four eggs for their breakfast.

'You drink your coffee and then I'll get you settled,' said Charity, tapping Nanette's shoulder before giving out orders to the others. Antoine and Nanette ate busily, smiling to each other, cheeks bulging with food as they sunk gulps of coffee. Charity cut slice after slice of bread, loaded their plates with cold meat and slices of tomato and cut off healthy portions of a fruit cake and placed those beside their coffee cups which she refilled continuously.

'My, my,' Nanette exclaimed. 'I think we will burst.'

'There have plenty food. As long you can eat, then you eat. You are thin like my little finger.' She waved a chubby finger and began to laugh at the way they devoured every morsel.

'You just rest a while,' said Charity. 'I'm going and sort out the shopping list with the madam and then I will tell you what needs to be done.'

The youngest girl on the staff, her skin as light as milky coffee, washed up all the dishes and cleared their plates when they'd finished eating. She looked at Nanette when she collected their coffee cups and giggled. She looked over her shoulder at Antoine as she carried those to the sink and giggled even more.

Half an hour later, Charity returned and flopped into a chair opposite the couple.

'Audrey, stop your nonsense and go and collect the linen from upstairs to wash,' she said in a stern voice to the giggling servant.

'Yes, Mrs Charity.' She rushed out of the kitchen giggling again after tapping Nanette on the shoulder.

'Don't mind Audrey. She is simple but she has a heart of gold. Now, young man.' She turned to Antoine, who immediately stood and told Charity his name. 'You see the high-colour man who was here a while ago?'

'The tall man?'

'Him. He is in the front lawn, fixing the garden. You go and tell him Charity send you and you have come to help.' She gestured to the door with her eyes. Antoine excused himself, kissed Nanette on the top of her head and left the kitchen.

'Your husband?' asked Charity.

'Something like that but not officially.'

'The madam told me you were husband and wife.'

'I think Mr Bellamy wanted to make sure she, the madam, would employ us.'

'Very saintly, the Laffertys. Very God-fearing. You better remember that and maybe find a priest to marry you as soon as you can. I won't say a word. But you better mind yourself around here.'

'I will.'

Charity looked Nanette up and down again, taking in every detail of the silk dress she had on. It needed a good steam before being rolled flat, but it was obviously not the dress of a servant. Antoine looked dishevelled, too, although his clothes had been handmade in Paris and shipped over as was most of his wardrobe.

'I suppose the madam didn't ask too many questions about where you from. Lucky,' said Charity looking at Nanette from under her brow. 'She might have been surprised that she was hiring a girl who look like she have more servants than she.'

Nanette lowered her eyes.

'You don't have to tell me all your business, but I know neither of you has worked a day in your life. Am I right?'

'Well, Antoine supervised the workers in the coffee mill and I did have responsibility for the maids … under Mama's supervision, of course.'

'Giving orders and taking them are two different things.' Charity stood and beckoned Nanette to do the same with a movement of her fingers. 'You're coming to buy some essentials for the madam's house and then we can make her lunch. First, I need to find you a dress. No lady goes shopping for her mistress, only the servant girl. Come, servant girl. This is your first day of work.'

Nanette accompanied Charity in the wagon driven by the skinny boy who had been skulking in the kitchen earlier. He hadn't quite finished his breakfast before Charity clapped her hands and assigned them all to their respective duties. He grinned at Nanette as he helped Charity into the seat on the wagon. When he helped Nanette into the back, he made a comment about clothes making a person look like they should. He was referring, of course, to Nanette's cotton dress, a simple garment with no frills, no lace and only three plain buttons to fasten it at the back. Otherwise, it could be a tube of fabric wrapped around her, no flattering lines and no petticoats to make it stand out. She brushed down the skirt as she sat, pulling at the hem to cover her lower calves. Charity had made her remove her stockings, and she was feeling naked under the driver's constant staring over his shoulder at her.

'Barnabas, watch ahead before this whole contraption don't tumble down,' Charity declared. 'We need it for all the errands. And make no mistake, we have a lot of errands.'

Nanette turned her gaze to the road, the tall forest trees that lined it rolling past like a canvas of jade, emerald, lime green, yellow, rich red and brown. All of these colours had shown themselves earlier when Nanette arrived on Mr Bellamy's wagon, but she hadn't noticed them, too afraid of what her fate would be.

She worried about their future, hers and Antoine's, and wished all the way to the village market that one day they would be shopping for their own house, carrying it through their own front door and sitting around their own table to eat the food they'd prepared. Now she would be cooking for someone else, something she'd never done, serving instead of being served. She was willing to make the sacrifice, willing to wait for the day when this part of their journey would become something they could laugh about, talk about in years to come without the anguish. One day, they would forget just how many steps it took to achieve her dream, though for now, there were many miles to go. The important thing was that they would be together.

Antoine and Nanette worked for the first time in their lives. It wasn't easy. Not only did Antoine learn all about the herbs, plants, flowers and trees that he usually took for granted every day, he also experienced back-breaking work out in the fields. The Laffertys' groundsman, Charles, sent him to join the fieldworkers about half a mile away in the food garden when there was not enough work in the gardens around the big house. Antoine wondered if it wasn't some perverse sense of justice that Charles could order Antoine to work the fields, sweating and toiling with the black men rather than sitting back and being in command. From a distance, Antoine could be one of the field hands, his skin burning brown, a golden hue that made him blend with the other men. He learned their patois and they called him *Nonm Blan*, White Man, until the foreman told them to stop, that all the workers were equal and they all had work to do.

Charity taught Nanette how to cook while Audrey taught her how to turn down beds and wash clothes, though she giggled so much that Nanette could not get a conversation out of her. The other two women, Margaret and Mallie, taught her how to clean, watch the children and serve at the table. She had to make sure she wore a clean dress in the dining room, tied her hair away, had clean fingernails and never spoke until she was spoken to.

The first time she encountered Mr Lafferty was at dinner. She reached to place a bowl of freshly made bread rolls on the table beside him when he grabbed her wrist.

'You,' he said without once looking up from his plate. 'You're new, aren't you?'

Nanette looked at Margaret who nodded for Nanette to answer.

'Y-yes, sir. I am.'

He looked up at her then, holding her thin wrist between his large thumb and index finger. He stared into her face, but Nanette lowered her eyes. All the time, Mrs Lafferty kept on eating and Margaret went to stand with her back against the dresser.

'You have a name, I suppose,' Mr Lafferty went on, sounding bored.

'Yes, sir.'

He turned his body to face her. 'And is it a secret or do I have to guess?'

'I'm Nanette.' She glanced at Margaret and quickly at Mrs Lafferty, neither of whom regarded her.

'Nanette, Nanette. Sounds a bit French. Your family had French masters.'

'Sir, my family were not slaves. They own land in two territories and—' She stopped when she saw Mrs Lafferty look up and Margaret turn to her, large eyes warning her to calm her emotions.

'Feisty little thing, whoever you are.' Mr Lafferty turned and picked up his wine glass. He took a large gulp before launching into his roast chicken.

'That will be all, Nanette,' Mrs Lafferty said, her fingers on the tall crystal glass, green eyes piercing Nanette's skin.

She left the room quickly, a tear eagerly waiting to spill. Margaret caught her up and put an arm around her shoulder as they hurried to the kitchen to prepare dessert.

'You good for yourself, girl,' Margaret whispered.

'I said too much,' Nanette whispered back and dried her tears.

Nanette and Antoine shared a small room in the dim servants' quarters. Four of the others lived in, too. Mallie in one room and Charles, whose family lived in Antigua, in the one closest to the larder. Audrey and Barnabas each had box rooms off a door in the kitchen and down the end of a narrow corridor that led to the stables.

Antoine lay on their single bed, fully clothed, his arms crossed to support his head. A sliver of moonlight lit the room from the narrow window and illuminated the side of Nanette's face. She hadn't wanted the lamp on: she hated the way her headscarf flattened her curls and how the efforts of the day made the front of her hair frizzy and wild. She would sit and brush her hair and braid it but she couldn't lift her arms after beating out the rugs and hanging up dripping wet clothes near the herb garden.

'Is this really our lives now?' Nanette asked as she removed one of the two simple dresses she had been given to wear.

'We'll work hard and save a few shillings so that we can leave as soon as we can.' Antoine sat up and watched as Nanette removed the last of her clothing. The silk petticoat she wore under her dress revealed the lady she truly was. He took her hand and pulled her towards him. She stroked his hair off his face. It had grown long, wild. He had a fluffy beard that would probably make him unrecognisable to his family. Antoine traced a small pattern around the dark circles of Nanette's breasts with his tongue, trailing an invisible line from her nipples to her stomach where he rested his cheek.

'Why have we left it so long before we married,' he whispered. 'I asked you months ago.'

'I know, there just hasn't been time for it.'

He looked up at her. 'I know you want something lavish, but I think that might be a way off. Let's do it. Now.'

'Yes,' she said and bent down to kiss him.

Three weeks later, Antoine and Nanette stood at the altar of the small church on the grassy mound overlooking the sea. The early morning Mass had been delivered by *Père* Lamont, the kindly, diminutive priest from Belgium who had agreed to marry them that evening. With the four servant women as their witnesses—and the only guests—Antoine placed the ring that his grandmother had given him onto Nanette's finger just as the sun, glowing warm and yellow against the crimson sky, sank into the sea.

Chapter 3

There was something about the girl that Elise La Fleur found striking, setting her apart from the others in the market square. It could be that her complexion was like the light sand on the beach, distinct from the blacks and browns of the locals and different from the milky brown of her own skin. Of course Elise stood out, too, a tall, elegant, middle-aged woman in a silk dress. Most of the women wore headscarves, but her hair was uncovered, neat and tidy and twisted into a bun at the top of her head. Long gold earrings, dangling at the sides of her kind face.

For a moment, Elise wondered how this girl would fit into her household. Her girls in the past who came to keep house and serve as her companion had proven to be liars and thieves. Those girls must have thought her foolish and that she would not notice a small pin brooch or a pair of pearl earrings disappear. Or how a gap was left in the cabinet every time a crystal glass had supposedly broken when the girl was dusting. She had had to let them all go.

Rose sat chatting to the customers and to the other market traders. She laughed easily and people seemed to warm to her. Elise obviously had done, too. But maybe that was her charm, and maybe, just like the others, this one would also let her down.

'Mistress, would you like me to carry your bags back to the carriage?'

Elise was deep in thought and her driver had startled her out of her reverie.

'Oh, yes, yes please. Take these and wait for me there.'

As usual, she'd come to the market with no real purpose but to be among people who were not her servants or the odd, stuffy business person who used to know her husband and was dropping in on a holiday to the island. She had tired all too quickly of the greasy estate agent, Mr Bartholomew, who was always after her to sell her house and land because, in his opinion, she was rattling around lonely as a pearl in a shell and wouldn't she like to make a killing before the property bled her dry? She bought mangoes every time she went to market and ate them alone in her dining room, the juice dripping down to her wrists, and she would lick it off like a ravenous child, washing her hands in the bowl her girl left for her. Sometimes she bought spices with the intention of cooking but was brusquely ushered away by her housekeeper, Lucinda, who assumed the mistress coming into the kitchen was her idea of a joke. Thinking herself silly or bothersome, Elise would leave her purchases on the counter and take herself back to the lounge. As soon as she left the kitchen, the lively atmosphere she'd encountered on entering resumed.

She needed company, that much was true. She had been lonely since she lost beautiful Sebastian, her late husband, who had arrived from Guadeloupe the summer she turned eighteen. He'd won her heart, though she'd been reluctant to give it since it had been broken when she lost her sister.

Elise watched Rose who had been laughing so much she had to wipe away a tear. It made Elise smile as she walked across the busy square towards her. She'd need a reason to start a conversation with the girl. Her stall, Elise noticed as she got closer, was a plastic sheet on the ground with her produce laid out on it.

It was the beautiful silk dress that Rose noticed first: the skirt was peacock blue and far fancier than any she'd seen. This woman was too dressy for church, let alone a market. Rose continued to gaze at this lady, at the calf-length dress, straight and loose-fitting around the body with a scooped neck and three-quarter sleeves. Three rows of necklaces reaching her navel hung from her neck which was dabbed with flowery perfume that Rose could detect above the fresh food products of the sellers. The lady wore gloves and stockings which Rose found strange under the glare of a late morning sun. But she was poised and cool, the powder on her nose and her ruby lipstick fixed as if she were a photograph of herself. Her high-coloured skin was flawless save for a few creases beside her slanted eyes, and Rose imagined if she'd allowed herself to smile, the faint lines by her lips would deepen and make her appear less aloof.

'Can I help you, ma'am?' Rose smiled now, realising she must have been staring at the lady for too long.

'Yes, yes you could. How much for the yellow yams?'

'The yams are sweet. I only have two left.'

'I'll take them,' Elise said, and pointed.

'But I didn't give you a price yet,' Rose said, grinning.

'It's fine. They look good. I'm sure you will give me a fair price. But, before you do, I wonder if I could pull you aside for a minute?' Rose looked from right to left at her market trader friends. Matilda on her right shrugged her shoulders, and Benjie on her left shooed her away in the woman's direction. At last, the woman smiled, her teeth gleaming white against her painted lips and Rose began to relax.

'Don't worry, my dear. Is not anything bad I have to tell you. The thing I was wondering is whether or not you could come and work for me?'

'Work for you?' Rose was taken aback. 'But I'm working already. I help my family.' She looked over her shoulder at the stall.

'Yes, you look like the type of person who would help her family. You look as if you're not afraid of hard work. I'm offering paid work. A job working for me, in my house, and hopefully, not hard work at all.'

'I see,' said Rose, though there was a knot in her brow. The request seemed strange. The way the woman was asking and looking at her so closely made Rose want to take a step away, think this offer through. What she could do for this woman, she had no idea. Her sister, May, was the one with the training, the education, and without that, all Rose was capable of was exactly what she was doing now. Hard work in the food gardens and selling at market.

'I have to tell you, ma'am, that I'm not educated past the age of sixteen. I don't know what you want of me, but I can't do very much.'

Elise held up a gloved hand. 'You can probably do more than you think. You must know how to cook and clean,' she said. 'Keep house?'

'Well, I know everything my mammy teach me.'

'Well then, I need you to do everything your mammy teach you but at my house, and I will pay you for it.'

Rose turned to look at her friends. Both Matilda and Benjie stood together in front of her stall, their faces close as they stared with curiosity in Rose's direction.

'Talk to your mammy. You have a father, too?' Elise asked.

'Yes, ma'am.'

'Well, tell them I will need you from Monday to Thursday, living in for those days, and your weekend is free to do whatever you please. My man can come and collect you and bring you back home.'

'But ma'am, is right at Moore Park I live. Your man can find me there?'

'That's not a problem. My name is Elise La Fleur.' She removed one glove and put out a delicate hand for Rose to shake. Rose took it. Mrs La Fleur had not had to dig gardens or wash her clothes on the rocks of a river in her life. 'When can you give me an answer?' Elise asked.

Rose said nothing at first. She still held the lady's hand and was transfixed by the almost black wells of her eyes and the clarity of the whites that surrounded them. Not one hair on her head was out of place, even in the breeze that blew up from the sea.

'Young lady, what are you called?'

'My name is Rose. Rose Charles. I will be at market next Saturday, and I will have your answer then.'

'Good. Well, my man, Cuthbert, will come and you will speak to him. If you are agreeable, then he will collect you early on the following Monday morning, so have your things packed. Of course, Cuthbert will return you home on Thursday and pick you up each Monday.'

The woman walked away, now, without the yams, without a sales transaction, only this offer of a live-in job which Rose couldn't imagine her mother agreeing to even if she wanted it. She wasn't sure she did, but there was something about this woman that intrigued her. Though she had seemed standoffish at first, there was kindness and softness within the look of concentration she studied Rose with. How strange that she had propositioned Rose for this job, to stay at her house and to have her servant come and fetch her for work without even knowing who Rose was. All the same, it did give her a feeling of importance. Her father would want to know how much she would earn and that was something she should have asked about but had been so taken aback that she'd forgotten to.

Matilda and Benjie were beside her, guiding her back to her stall by her arms.

'You know who is that?' asked Matilda.

'Just a lady who want me to work for her.'

'She isn't just a lady, she is one of the La Fleurs. Her husband have an estate in Picard. but he dead now and she live there by herself. They say, though the husband die, she still have plenty money.' There were very few estate owners left on the island. The large houses were owned by anyone wealthy enough to be able to keep one, but most of the land surrounding these estates had been sold off to subsistence farmers, all traces of the big plantations now gone.

'Well is pay she want to pay me,' said Rose.

'What for?' asked Benjie.

'What you expect? Cook and clean. She want me there half the week and her driver will bring me come.'

'True?' exclaimed Matilda. 'Well, I know she is very particular about who she hire. They say she like to have a lady's maid who just sit and talk to her. I think she get rid of the last one. You must be the replacement.'

'I don't know why is me she ask.' Rose crossed her arms and looked off in the direction she'd seen Elise Le Fleur boarding the small carriage by the pier and watched it trundle up the road.

'Because of your straight nose.' Matilda playfully slapped Rose's shoulder, and she and Benjie went back to work.

Rose was once teased about being adopted and having a white daddy. She didn't think Elise would choose her because her father was white, there was more, and if she was permitted to take the job, perhaps she'd find out.

***

When Raphael left European shores, it was under armed guard. The remaining West Indian soldiers who had not had to serve sentences after the mutiny in Taranto were shepherded away onto waiting ships. No chance of taking part in victory processions and no chance of receiving any medals of valour just as they would never find their stories of valour written in the history books.

Raphael had heard the gunshots fired when the rebel who started the mutiny was executed in front of the troops. He had refused to watch, choosing instead to collect the belongings of his deceased friend, George, so that he could deliver them safely to his family in Barbados. In the camp just off the port, Raphael knelt to pack and fold away the few things George owned: letters from his family not replied to because there had been no time for Raphael and his troop to write to their loved ones for several months. Raphael had finished pushing clothes, letters and a prayer book into the backpack when he found a picture underneath the Italian newspaper that George kept, not because he read the language, but because there was a photograph of an actress whom George claimed was the most beautiful woman he'd ever seen. He'd claimed that if he got back to Barbados and couldn't find anyone there as beautiful, he would return to Italy for her and ask her to be his wife. Raphael hadn't laughed as the others had done, teasing George about how he'd be too short for her, too simple for her, too black.

'These people hate us as much as the English,' someone had said. 'They just need to get to know us, who we are,' said George, and put the newspaper under the mat he slept on.

Raphael spotted the hope in George's eyes, a dream he had that he wanted to follow. Then he'd thought of Rose. Still only a dream to him, still unobtainable. Even more so because of time and distance. Could he also go back home, look for someone as beautiful as Rose? *No*, he'd thought, *it could only ever be Rose*.

He held the picture which was of George standing outside his tent in Marseilles, laughing out loud because the white soldier taking it had at first forgotten to remove the lens cap. Raphael would never hear George's high-pitched laughter again; he'd told George he'd be glad when they went home and he didn't have to listen to it. Words he'd regretted when he'd held George's limp, thin and bloody body in his arms and looked up at the soldier who'd shot his friend. His eyes cried, '*Why*?' And in the soldier's, there was no answer. They had dug a communal grave close to Taranto for the West Indian soldiers. The British had refused to ship any of them home.

Raphael's ship docked in Jamaica. He had a few shillings left in his pocket and pushed some change towards the barman in the smoky hut. He'd stopped there for a while to get his bearings and find out when the next vessel would be setting sail for Grenada. It was late afternoon and he hadn't expected to see so many men drinking at that time.

He took a seat with his shot of whisky: the barman had made it a double when he saw his uniform under the heavy jacket he was wearing, a souvenir to remind him of the European weather.

'Soldier boy.' A Jamaican man called to him and beckoned him over to a table where another three men were drinking and smoking unfiltered cigarettes. 'You come from foreign?' the man asked him. As Raphael pulled up a stool, he noticed that the bottom half of the man's leg was missing.

'You been fighting, too?' asked Raphael.

'Yes, boy,' the man said. Raphael thought the man had looked in his forties from across the bar through the fug of smoke. Closer up, he could tell he was nearer to thirty. 'Been home a year.'

'Here's to you, then.' Raphael raised his glass and took a sip. The strength of it burned and he spluttered.

'I know,' said the man. 'They don't make booze like this over there. This one will put hairs on your chest. This one's the real thing.'

'I just haven't had a drink in a while.' Raphael took another sip, slower this time.

'But glad to be back, I can tell.'

'Oh yes, this war did nothing for me.'

'And not for any of us, neither.' The man drew a circle with his finger to include the men around the table. All of them ex-service men, Raphael could see it now. Flashing explosions reflected in their eyes, fear and worry in the lines that surrounded them. Fatigue and pain in their posture and diminished hope hanging over them like a cloud heavy with rain.

'The war don't do me nothing,' the ex-soldier went on. 'I'm back here just the same as when I leave. No money, no job. I been asking an asking for me pension but no dice. Me house brock down—me cyant fix it up. Me leg brock up, too, an is me wife have fee do everything for me.'

'So, nobody don't give you no free land like they promise?' Raphael asked.

'No money, no land. To say I just the same is a lie. I worse than before.'

In the morning after sleeping with his head on his bag and with his arms wrapped around George's backpack, Raphael boarded a large boat to Grenada. The Jamaican soldier, Hubert, had invited Raphael to his home and offered him a meal after their drinks the evening before, but once they'd got inside the door, Hubert's wife quarrelled constantly about the state her husband was in. On leaving the bar, Raphael had looped Hubert's arm around his shoulder to get him home, supporting his weight because somehow he'd lost a crutch and no one knew where it was. The whole afternoon at the bar had been hazy, their words and ruminations about the war years and their lives evaporating into the damp timber of the walls and floating out of the open window with the smoke and their boozy laughter. From the corner of Hubert's living room where Raphael had tried to settle down for the night, all he could hear was the angry voice of Hubert's wife rumbling from their bedroom and their dog barking back at her from the yard. He'd left in the dark and staggered back to the dock.

His back was racked with pain as he sat on the boat to Grenada, glad to be on his way but not knowing what to expect when he got home. He'd been away for almost three years. Just feet from his house, he spotted his mother standing just as he'd left her in the spot where he'd hugged her goodbye. She was talking to a woman he recognised, a busybody who had lost a son in the war.

'Mercy me,' Raphael heard her say as he approached the yard. His mother turned to him. She looked stunned as she walked towards him. Raphael stood, hand poised on the gate, motionless apart from his throat as he swallowed a deep breath. His mother pulled open the gate; Raphael dropped his bags and stepped towards her. She sighed and rose onto her toes to pull him into a hug. She squeezed his neck and wouldn't let go. He closed his eyes as tight as he could to stop the tears. They would expect him to be strong, brave, but the truth was he'd missed his family, his old life. He took in the familiar scent of his mother's hair oil, the food she'd been cooking on her apron. He looked at the front door and saw his father, leaner, more grey hairs, a smile spread upon his face, brows arched in joy and pain combined.

'Babs, I have to go, my son is home and I have to be with him.' His mother barely regarded her neighbour: her eyes were trained on Raphael's face as she led him by the crook of his arm into the house while his father rushed to carry the bags in.

'You look thin.' His mother fussed around him after sitting him at the table and sending his father out to light the stove. 'There is some breadfruit from this morning, I'll go and warm it for you.' She left the room just as his father appeared carrying some cold coffee for his son. Raphael stood to attention when his father came to the table.

'What you doing?' his father said and laughed. 'I'm not your general. Sit, sit.'

They both sat now, pensive: the buzzing and fuss his mother created had left with her and the two men sat quietly across the table from each other.

'You have changed,' his father said after a long pause. 'How you feeling, son?'

'How am I feeling? I don't even know. Happy to be home. A bit, well, a bit lost. Like I have no ground under my feet and I don't know what ground is anymore.'

'You are not lost, you're home.'

'I know, Daddy, but…I wish I had the words to explain. I know this is home, but I don't feel like I'm home yet. Like something is pulling at me, calling me.'

'Like how? Son, don't tell me. Is it the girl? Still? After all this time?'

Raphael pondered his fathers questions, getting an answer straight in his own head. When he'd signed up, he had told himself that he could forget Rose, that he could move on. Just days after arriving in France, he'd told himself that if he survived the war, he would look for Rose. Search everywhere, search every land he could find on a map. Then the days and nights and the noise and agony that he and his men endured told him he was foolish, that if he could withstand the war, then he could overcome a broken heart. It would be nothing in comparison. But when his heart didn't heal, years later, the gruelling time spent in Taranto told him that he didn't want to live without her. Was home with Rose? Is that why after every hard mile he'd travelled to return to Grenada, he was still not home? Still lost?

'She means a lot to me. But there are other things. Daddy, I have to build a life. Be a man who can stand on his own two feet. If I ever found her, I'd have to have something to offer. I would also need to be strong on my feet if…'

His father nodded. 'Yes, it's a long time. She could be married and have children.'

Raphael's eyes sank to his hands that twitched at the table. His father reached over and held them.

'You will find your way.' They sat in silence before his father spoke again. 'A lot has changed here in Grenada.'

'Changed?' Raphael straightened. He hadn't even asked after his parents let alone the country he had been away from for nearly three years.

'You know that things were changing even before the war. Trouble was brewing.'

His father was referring to the wave of political and social awareness that had been developing among the working class people. He told Raphael that while he'd been at war, there had been a number of strikes and rebellions. Workers were no longer prepared to sit back and accept low wages and bad conditions. Raphael was in disbelief at first. He remembered after reading about the rumblings of unrest that there had been a lot of lethargy about it. People not taking action but rather standing in groups and discussing it as though low wages and bad conditions were a *fait accomplis*. Had something happened to his people? He wondered if they were stirred up by the war.

'This world has always been a world for the rich, but the workers here, the real working classes, are unsettled, unhappy. You say you feel you have no ground under your feet. Son, this is what you have returned to. No one know their feet and where they going to land from one day to the next.' His father said that the strikes were becoming violent. His mother returned with a plate of warm breadfruit, a pile of tiny sardines fried crisp as he liked it and hot tea. He hadn't yet touched the coffee, but the smell of fish reminded him of how hungry he was.

'They had guns, Raphael, the police and the bosses, their security. They fire into crowds. The workers were full of anger, you see. They kill some of them.'

'And why is this you find to talk about when you see your son for the first time?' His mother squeezed his arm and Raphael began to eat. 'Let him eat in peace. I can draw you a bath, Raphael.'

'He needs to know everything,' said his father, shaking his head as his wife signalled for him to stop talking. 'He needs to know about Detroit.'

Raphael stared from one parent to the other. He put his cutlery down. 'You have to tell me.'

His father heaved a big sigh before continuing, his face softening as he looked into the eyes of his weary son. 'You see, with all the unrest and the uncertainty, your brother... Well, your big brother went to Detroit last year. He married Marlene and they have a baby boy. We did write to the address you send but we didn't hear back.'

'Getting and sending letters wasn't easy, I'm sorry. So what happen to my brother?'

'Nothing, apart from he have a good job. Plenty money, a nice house. They set up really well. We have pictures.' His father was about to get up and show Raphael but his wife's expression implied that this wasn't the time.

'The thing about it is your brother is worried about how it is here and he's sending for us to come stay with him in Detroit. Is useless he send money here for us because we don't have nothing to spend it on. This place is going to ruin,' his father said. It was quiet around the table until Raphael picked up his cutlery and began to eat again.

'I understand,' he said after his parents exchanged a series of glances. 'So you and my mother going to America?'

'Well, we thinking about it but we haven't decided to tell you the truth. What you think? You think that you would come? Imagine us all there.'

'America is not for me. It's too big. This island will be fine when we can govern it ourselves. That's all it will take. People who know the people and what they need.'

'You sounding just like the newspapers.'

'Well, Daddy, the Representative Association isn't there for nothing, you know. But I don't know how long I can stay without work. There is talk and there is talk, but I need money to survive. I don't know how long these meetings can go on before something change.' Raphael made little impression on the vast amount of food his mother had set out for him.

'Raphael.' His mother looked at him lovingly but as though she were looking for the man called Raphael. She seemed to search his face as if she wasn't seeing him clearly enough and perhaps didn't recognise him after all this time. He had been a fresh-faced boy when he'd left. Clueless, yet hopeful. Carrying the burden of a broken heart but capable of finding love again whenever he chose to let go of a memory. Now, as he sat across from her with a strengthened frame and eyes that told the story of too much pain for one man, he could tell that she no longer knew the man she saw.

'We would go in America but I love where we are,' his mother said. 'I would miss the sun and Detroit have cold. But I not going anywhere until I know you settled, happy. I want you to tell me, what will you do?' His mother's eyes were damp with tears; she tried not to let them fall.

Raphael rested his hands on the table. 'I'll find something, Ma. I will. And soon. First, I need to make a trip to Barbados to visit the home of a friend. I have his belongings and I need to return them to his family. Then I'll see what I can make of myself.'

'We'll be here for you. Waiting to see.' His mother blinked away her worry.

'You take your time, son. We not rushing anywhere.' His father nodded several times.

'Please don't worry for me. I think you done plenty of that. I respect any decision you make, and I know I need to make my own.' Raphael smiled, nodding assuringly to both parents. 'It's time to fly. I have wings now.'

***

'Your duties are very simple, Rose. You have to bring my tea in the morning. At my bedside. Seven o'clock. Lemon tea with a few drops of honey. I will take breakfast in the dining room shortly after. I have lunch at midday and I would like you to sit and eat with me for that meal alone. I take a cup of coffee and some fruit loaf at three in the afternoon, and I read the newspapers quietly or one of my books. Supper at seven in the evening but nothing too heavy —not like a country diet. You understand?'

'Yes, ma'am.'

'You can call me Madame La Fleur. Monday is washing day and general cleaning of the house. Lucinda, the housekeeper, will show you. Everything else you will pick up as you go along. I've had my breakfast already, so now is time you start the washing for the week.'

'Is you alone I cooking and washing for?' Rose asked.

'How you mean, Rose?'

'I know you don't have no husband but you don't have no children, nothing?'

'No, is me alone who live here.'

'In this big house all by yourself?' Rose raised her eyebrows and looked up at the high ceiling and the elaborate

113

chandelier that needed a polish. The rugs had been beaten recently, but there was a thin layer of dust on the oak tables and on the low wall cabinets with their ornaments and vases that also needed some attention. Elise La Fleur sat in a high-backed chair with oak armrests; her back was supported by two raw silk cushions, and her slippered feet were resting on a well-padded footstool.

'If you must know, Rose, and I'm sure you'll find out, God never grace me with any children and my husband die just three years ago.'

'But you can marry again.' Rose felt her cheeks redden as she said this. She was being too familiar with her new employer. She should be more respectful. Her mother had warned her as much. Elise let out a little laugh.

'I think maybe I am a little too old for that. I have come to enjoy my own company. I have cousins. I travel to visit them once in a while. One here and two in Guadeloupe.'

'I'm sorry, Madame La Fleur. That is your own private business.' Rose bowed her head.

'Rose, as you well know, in Dominica one's private business doesn't stay private for long. I have no secrets. Anything you don't know, I'm sure the local baker or the gardener's wife would be happy to tell you.' Rose did not raise her eyes from the floor.

'Off you go, Rose. The washing is in the side room next to the kitchen, and anything else you need you will find there. The river for washing the clothes is easy to find if you follow the little path in the garden at the back of the house.' Rose turned to leave. 'Oh, and Rose,' Elise called. 'Some of the girls trample my flowers to get to the path quicker. I don't appreciate that at all. I love my flowers.'

'Yes, ma'am. I mean—Madame La Fleur.'

***

It was good to be out of the uniform. Raphael wouldn't be keeping it—neither for sentimental reasons nor a sense of honour for the country he had fought for. He felt as if his life was starting from scratch but with one main thread that needed to be rewound onto the spool or cut loose from it. He remained anxious about following the thread only to find that Rose had cut all ties to their brief interlude.

His first trip was to Barbados. It was easy to find George's family. Though he'd never been to the island himself, George had described it so well on those cold, wet nights in the trenches and on the windy evenings by the tent. Raphael was able to locate the school he'd mentioned, the Baptist church and the bend in the road leading to the house with the wild dog in the front garden. George's house was the one just beyond the lemon grove. A man with a face like George's, only altered by furrows of maturity and worry, walked to the gap in the bougainvillea bushes along the path from the door and smiled at him. This had to be George's father. He held out an arm to welcome Raphael inside. Raphael wondered how he knew his was the house Raphael was looking for until he noticed how intensely the old man eyed George's backpack, which hung at his side. When George's father looked at Raphael, he could tell immediately that the family must have received the news about George. He had been dreading, the whole time that he would have to be the one to tell them. He doubted the army had done their job but could finally allow the weight of this worry to leave him.

Raphael reached out to shake hands. 'Mr Lewis,' he said. George's father pulled Raphael towards him. Heart to heart, he patted Raphael on the back and stepped away.

'Come, come. Come inside. My wife is here and my daughter, too.' It was a Saturday afternoon. It was as if they had been expecting him on that day and at that time.

It was bright inside the house: there were windows on both sides of the low narrow building. Furniture tripped over itself with lots of wooden side tables in various corners and under every window. On each was a framed black and white photograph of family members propped onto starched doilies. He shook hands with George's mother, short and round and who smiled at Raphael as if he were a close friend she hadn't seen in a while. George's sister, Marylin, looked a lot like George. She was heavily pregnant, her own house not more than a ten minute walk on the road opposite the lemon grove, she told Raphael. He knew already that this was a close-knit family and that George was an uncle to twin boys. He would never meet his new niece or nephew.

Mrs Lewis handed Raphael a tall cup of coffee and asked him to join them for dinner later. He wanted to stay as long as he could. George's family reminded him so much of his friend: their warmth, their friendliness and the ease in which they welcomed him into their home.

Raphael handed the backpack to Mr Lewis. 'I thought you would want this.'

On the sofa opposite him, the family opened the bag, pulling out each of George's belongings and looking them over. With each item, their eyes welled more until their emotions spilled onto their cheeks. Smiles of nostalgia reflected in their eyes, no signs of anger for losing George in that way. Raphael had been filled with it. Anger had consumed him for every moment of his incarceration since the arrests after the short and bitter mutiny.

Mrs Lewis picked up the photograph of her son laughing and held it in front of her husband and daughter. Her body sagged for a second, and with clenched eyes, she shook her head from side to side and a teardrop landed on her husband's hand. He guided her head to his lips and kissed her brow. Involuntarily, Raphael's body curled forward. He had to excuse himself and leave the house. He walked blindly into the front yard, found the stump of a tree and sat down. He had not cried so hard since he was a little boy and lost his grandfather in a boating accident. The years of overwork and debilitation during the war, the pain, blood and hardship he'd experienced flowed heavily and painfully out of him. His shoulders shook with grief and his sobs were loud, mournful and beyond his control.

In a little while, Mr Lewis came and stood beside him. Raphael held up a hand in apology for his outburst. His demeanour was at odds with the peaceful garden. It was rich in colour and there had been birdsong until his sobs hushed it. He tried to gather himself, Mr Lewis calm and patient at his side.

'Son, I'm so happy my boy had a friend such as you.'

'I tried to save him. I tried to tell them we not armed, but they didn't want to hear. War was over. You should have your son back, not a photograph.'

'Yes, but in that photograph, my boy is happy. And that's how I will remember him.' He stooped beside Raphael and rested a hand on his knee. 'Come and sit with us. When you ready. Tell us how George get on over there. He wasn't a great one for letter writing.'

Raphael wiped his face with the back of his hand. He sniffed until the sobs subsided and turned to look at George's father. 'I will tell you everything, from the day I met your son to the day I told him goodbye, as best I can.'

Raphael stayed in Barbados for a whole month. He boarded at the Lewis house and with Marylin's family and one of their friends from the church. At each, he paid for his board by working around their houses and on their land. He looked after the children and animals and walked for miles into forests and mountains. He was becoming himself again. It didn't pain his heart to laugh any more, and he had not found any reason to want to cry, not even when he thought of Rose.

The season changed and so had Raphael, and it was time to decide where to go. He was tempted by the call for workers in the oil fields in Trinidad. But then, just by chance, he heard a radio announcement saying that there were jobs at the lime factory on the island of Dominica. Raphael recalled the lush island. He knew Rose had long since left there and gone to Guadeloupe, but he wasn't quite ready to begin his search for her. He had not built a life for himself. Besides, he was still overwhelmingly afraid of finding her married with children and to have forgotten all about him. In the battle between love and fear, it was the fear that he gave way to. The job in Dominica would pay well. He would be closer to making something of his life, closer to having something to offer her.

***

'You asked me once why I never marry again.' Elise sat at one end of the long dining table with Rose just to her side.

118

Elise had insisted that Rose stop setting her place for lunch right at the other end of the table.

'Yes, Madame La Fleur, but that was not right of me. I apologise.'

'Oh, don't apologise Rose. This time *I'm* doing some searching.'

'Madame?'

'I wonder if you have a young man. How old are you?'

'I just turn twenty. But I don't have no young man.'

'But why is that, Rose?'

'Well, Madame La Fleur, the truth is there is no one who...'

'No one good enough?'

'Something like that. People say I am too proud, but I can't love just *anybody*.'

'But you already love before.' Elise smiled.

'How you know?'

'Just a feeling. I'm right. I knew it. And what happen to this man?'

'He gone back to Grenada and I never see him again. He forget about me.'

'But you never forget about him.'

'Never.'

'But Rose, if he gone away, then you have to try, otherwise you won't find space in your heart for anyone else.'

'Unless I find someone who make me feel like he did, then I don't care if I don't find no one. My sister never marry yet. She older than me, and she say she don't see anyone she like. We will grow old together in our little house in Moore Park, and we will be happy enough. We will keep each other company.'

Elise stopped eating. She rested the delicate silver cutlery onto her plate, her eyes dimming, her eyelids looking heavy.

'I'm sorry, Madame La Fleur. I talk too much. You want I clear up the plates?'

'No, you finish eating first, Rose. I'm going upstairs to decide what to wear for dinner tonight. A good friend has invited me.' She slowly left the dining room.

Rose had decided weeks ago that her employer must be lonely. She saw how she sat at the grand dressing table in her bedroom doing nothing more than looking through her things, her jewellery, fine handkerchiefs, combs and perfumes. Moving them from place to place, sometimes trying on a necklace or pair of earrings and then putting them away again. Filling in time with nothing in particular until she retired to bed by nine o'clock. Having Rose lunch with her was the only time she indulged in conversation. Otherwise, she was giving orders to the driver, the gardener or the housekeeper. Rose noticed that their lunches lasted up to two hours these days and that it was Madame La Fleur doing most of the chatting.

Once Rose had cleared away after lunch, she went up to Elise's bedroom and knocked gently on the door.

'Would you like any help picking out a dress, Madame La Fleur?'

'Oh, yes Rose, that's very kind of you.'

There was always the aroma of flowers in the bedroom. She insisted that her bedlinen and her underwear were washed delicately and left to soak in cool water filled with added coconut water and a potpourri of blossoms and sweet spices. She always wore scent, and her hair oils were perfumed with bergamot and lavender. It was like walking into a garden but without the flowers, only silk, lace, lush rugs and jewels sparkling from the afternoon sun.

They spent an hour looking through the gowns in Madame La Fleur's large wardrobe until she finally decided on a burgundy and cream organza dress.

'My friend will say I'm over-dressed, but I don't care.' Her smile made her look playful and young, but when Madame La Fleur wasn't smiling, stern lines appeared which, now that Rose knew her better, belied a harsh exterior. 'Now for a necklace. Rose, you never wear jewellery. Why?'

'I don't have none. I did use to, once, a necklace I loved, but I lose it one day and could never find it again.'

'I'm sorry to hear that, Rose. Was it special?'

'Very. But let me help you pick something out.'

'It's late, Rose, Cuthbert will have the wagon waiting.'

'Yes, Madame La Fleur. I hope you have a nice time.'

'I will.' Elise walked over to her dressing table. 'There is one particular necklace, a locket, I might wear and that I haven't in a long time. I'll look for it now. My father bought one for me and an identical one for my sister when we were both very young. I've a picture of my sister in mine. I kept it in her memory.'

'Your sister died?'

'A long time ago now.'

'I'm sorry.'

'It's fine Rose, but you should go. I'll see you on Monday.'

***

It felt like home in some ways, though Raphael had decided that he officially didn't have one yet. He would decide where he belonged when he was ready. For now, he was content to travel anywhere and leave the second he felt it was time. He had been in Dominica for all of twenty minutes, having disembarked from the passenger boat at

Roseau and stopped to get his bearings. If he was right, the lime factory was a little further west. Roseau wasn't the largest capital he'd visited, but now he'd get a chance to know it better than just the port and market square that he'd frequented in his days as a merchant sailor.

He was dressed in a short-sleeved white cotton shirt and loose-fitting cream trousers, tapered at the ankle. He carried a small suitcase with an off-white blazer tucked over his forearm. He had a fair idea of how to get to his destination but needed to check with someone. The first person he came across was someone he recognised from over three years ago. He could not mistake the tall, arrogant, young man with the grey eyes, who spoke a lot with little to say. He remembered that this man had worn his straw fedora so far back on his head, he thought it might fall off.

The young man was standing by the side of the road with the bonnet of his Ford pick-up truck open, staring at the mechanics. The truck had rusted in several places, and there was a smell of burning coming from the engine. Before Raphael could open his mouth, the young man stepped in front of him.

'Tell me what you know about motor vehicles.' He was still as brash and cocky as Raphael remembered. He'd also remembered shuddering at the condescending way he had looked at Raphael's shabby attire, as if he could be contaminated if he stood too close. Now it was he whose brow shone and whose collar was damp and dirty from a morning of labouring, clearly exasperated by the failed mechanics of his truck. Despite his state, he showed no humility at all, demanding of a stranger for assistance in this way. He hadn't recognised Raphael.

'To be honest, I know very little,' Raphael replied. 'Tell me what has gone wrong with it and maybe I can help you.'

'I drove all the way down from Moore Park with it. It was fine. I left it while I did some business, and now it won't start.'

'It don't smell right to me.' Raphael put down his case and looked at the engine, too. 'When last you change the oil?' Raphael asked.

'Not long I have this truck,' the man said. 'I buy it from a fellow just off George Street, but I think he sell me a can of rubbish. I going and get my money back.' Furious, he slammed the bonnet shut.

'Well, good luck, but I don't believe he will give you your money. You need an expert to look at the engine, and I know there don't have many good mechanics in Dominica.' Raphael was shaking his head, sorry for the poor man. Of the little he knew about motors, he was aware how expensive it was to get parts. If this young man was as short on cash as he was, then he'd be back to using a horse and cart like most other trades people. Raphael would be surprised if buying a vehicle hadn't already bled him dry.

'Well, good luck,' Raphael said as he went to take his leave. 'I wonder if you can point me in the direction of the lime factory.'

'You walk straight up this road. You can't miss it. That's where I just come from.'

Just before Raphael left, he turned to the man one last time. 'I recognise you but you don't know me, do you?'

'Should I?' he was puzzled.

'Well, it was a long time ago. I came to Roseau, and I asked you to carry a letter for Rose Charles. I came another time, right in Moore Park, and you tell me she gone to Guadeloupe with her family.'

'Oh, yes.' The young man quickly wiped his hands on an old cloth which he threw onto the passenger seat of his truck. 'I do remember you. From Grenada, right?'

'That's right.' Raphael nodded.

'You still looking for her?'

Raphael shrugged. 'I came here to work. I decided to settle here and see what your beautiful island have to offer. Somewhere here I have relatives, distant ones, and I have instructions to search for them by my mother.'

'I don't know no Grenadians here. You might not want to stay on this beautiful island, as you call it. I'm afraid you won't find she has very much. You might be better off taking your little case and your second-hand suit and go back to where you came from. Everyone here trying to leave.'

Raphael shook his head, amused by his arrogance. 'You trying to leave Dominica, too?' he asked.

'One day. Yes. I've had enough of this place. So, is Roseau you staying then?' The young man walked around to the driver's door.

'Yes,' said Raphael.

'Well, is the best place. You won't find work up in the country.'

'No, I don't suppose. Anyway. I best be going. I hope you fix your vehicle. I don't think I ever knew your name.'

'My name?'

Raphael couldn't help notice that the man was becoming agitated again, bad tempered even and keen to get away.'

'Wilfred.' He locked the car door and walked hurriedly in the direction of the port without a farewell. Raphael watched with curiosity before making his way to the factory.

Elise La Fleur had taken a great interest in Rose. For months she had been encouraging Rose to pick out books from her bookshelves, helping her to improve her writing skills, calling her to listen to news reports on the radio. Some afternoons, they sat in the garden and drew pictures of the scenery. Elise promised she would bring back some paints when she next visited her cousins in Guadeloupe. She had employed a girl for Mondays to take over Rose's housework and laundry duties. Her name was Jane and she took an instant dislike to Rose who tried to show her how the mistress liked things to be done.

'And what you will be doing?' Jane asked the first time Rose walked her down to the river path to take the laundry.

'Why you ask me that?'

'Well, I see you looking so pleased with yourself and you are just a servant girl like me.'

'I know that.'

'The only reason she favours girls like you is because you have high colour.'

'She likes me and she trusts me. That's all.'

Jane huffed and threw all of Madame La Fleur's clothes into the water.

'Not like that,' Rose exclaimed. 'You have to take care and you have to be gentle with her things. They expensive. Some come all the way from America and even France.'

'Clothes are clothes. You can go now. I know what I'm doing.'

'But you need to know how Madame likes her delicates to be soaked.'

It was with half an ear that Jane listened to the instructions, and Rose was reluctant to leave the girl alone with the responsibility. Rose had taken great care to make a good impression on Elise. It wasn't so she could keep her job but that she'd come to like her employer a great deal. To Rose, her relationship with Elise was one she treasured. Elise didn't have to be so generous with her time, her education and to tell her so much about her personal life, but she did, and Rose was convinced that Elise had the same amount of affection for her as she did Elise.

Every Monday, Rose looked forward to hearing Cuthbert pulling up in the wagon and was usually already in the yard with her shawl around her shoulders, a cloth bag in her hand with her clothes and personal items for the next four days. She had left a few things in the room at the top of Madame La Fleur's house which was hers for the part of the week she stayed there. Her mistress had fresh flowers cut especially for the glass vase on the table by the window, and they'd be waiting there when Rose arrived to get ready for work.

Just two weeks into Jane's employment, Rose came down from her room on the Monday morning and saw Jane on the same landing as their mistress' bedroom.

Rose hurried down the stairs and asked Jane to wait. 'Why were you upstairs?'

She startled Jane who gripped the bannister rail and whipped her head around, the sullen look she always had for Rose spreading on her face.

'I was looking for the laundry,' Jane replied and carried on down towards the kitchen. Rose looked at the closed dining room door, beyond which Madame La Fleur would be sitting, waiting for her breakfast to be served. Rose pulled

Jane back by her arm and blocked her before they entered the kitchen.

'Lucinda always has the washing ready for you in the basket by the kitchen door.'

'I didn't see it.' Jane crossed her arms, her face daring Rose to pursue the conversation.

'What were you doing upstairs?'

'Look, I don't answer to you. Lucinda give me my orders and is she who send me upstairs to make sure everything collected and she never drop nothing on the way.'

She barged past Rose, allowing the door to swing closed behind her before grabbing the laundry basket and heading out of the kitchen to the river.

Lucinda looked up at Rose as she entered the room. 'What that girl have this time?' Lucinda asked, shaking her head.

'I can't say a thing to her, she rude as anything to me.'

'Not just you. She's the daughter of a friend. Madame ask me to find someone and is she I could find.'

Rose prepared Madame La Fleur's tray and brought it in to the dining room, a wide smile on her face as she shook off the bad feeling she had about Jane.

By the afternoon, Rose had forgotten about the ill-tempered girl. She and Madame La Fleur walked barefoot in the garden eating their lunch of fried sprats on thin slices of bread. The afternoon wind was fresh and Elise wanted to be outdoors. For a change, her hair was loose and hung to her shoulders in thick, wild waves that she ran a hand over in a carefree way. Rose had thought how much like a young girl she seemed. On a rickety garden table, Rose had laid out their lunch. Her mistress had wanted it to be light and simple, so Rose had sliced cucumbers and tomatoes, made a jug of lemonade and fried a plateful of sprats. Elise wanted to sit on the grass rather than at the table, so Rose had to plate up her lunch and carry it to the deep lawn bordered with purple and yellow allamanda shrubs where Elise sat, hands supporting behind her, legs outstretched in front. Elise had insisted they use the silver goblets from the cabinet, so Rose filled two of those and handed one to Madame La Fleur. Rose told her she was being too extravagant, but Elise had laughed this off, inviting Rose to join her for a walk around the grounds and to carry the rest of their food because she felt restless and didn't want to sit still. It was odd to see her mistress with greasy fingers from the fish, no napkin, rubbing the oil into her palms as they walked towards the limits of the grounds where they sat on a high mound with views out to sea.

'So, tell me what you will get up to this weekend, Rose, apart from selling at market.' Elise rested backwards on the grass, supporting her weight with her elbows before reclining even further so that spiky grass framed her face.

'Madame Le Fleur, you will have all kinds of insects in your hair.'

Elise laughed at Rose. 'I thought I was supposed to be the bossy one.' She shielded her eyes from the sun and turned to face her lady's maid. 'Tell me, Rose, what does a young girl like you do with her weekends, anyway?'

'Well, the church has organised an excursion,' said Rose, sitting cross-legged and pulling out a blade of grass which she wrapped around her index finger. 'On the way down from Moore Park just before we reach town, there is a lovely little river. I'm not sure it have a name, but there is some woodland, too, and a good place for a picnic. I not really sure I want to go.'

'But why?'

'My sister not going, and these days, I don't know which of the other girls I can call a friend.'

'What make you say that?' Elise sat up, but Rose made no attempt to answer. 'They are jealous of you, Rose. Because you are beautiful and because you are good.' Elise lay back on the grass. 'I've had a lot of girls come and work for me, and out of all of them, is only you I find are the most honest. You are a pleasure to be with. Apart from that, I'm sure you have a lot of young men looking your way, whether you show interest or not. This kind of indifference is what keeps them keen, and with that the other girls believe you think you are too good for them. They don't allow you to come close because the boys won't see them with you around. Too much competition when all they want to do is catch one fish out of the many you already toss back into the sea.'

'Madame, you flatter me. A lot of girls my age already marry. Some have jobs. They can spend money on nice clothes, shoes. They are the catch, not me.' She tossed the blade of grass and it vanished among the rest.

'Believe me, Rose, you have admirers, and until you get married, you might never make a friend of those girls.'

'Well, Madame La Fleur, if is true they jealous, then really they don't have to worry. There is not one of those men I would want, anyway.' Both women laughed.

'Rose?'

'Yes, Madame La Fleur.'

'Please—call me Elise. I would much prefer it.' She sat up and smiled affectionately. 'Listen, Rose, I want to ask if you would like to accompany me to Guadeloupe on my next trip.'

Rose sat to attention. 'You really mean it?' She joined her hands together as if she were praying.

'Yes. I wouldn't say it otherwise. You are good company for me, Rose. I would love for you to come with me. I have to arrange the passage for two weeks on Monday. I thought as it is a work day, anyway…'

'I would love to come with you. It would be an honour. Thank you.'

Elise laughed at the girl's enthusiasm. 'Better to ask your parents and tell me what they say.'

'Oh, I'm sure they will say yes.'

'Well, if they do, Cuthbert will come as usual, if not, I will send him the following Monday. It's less than two weeks away. Maybe that is short notice, I don't know, but I only decided last minute.'

As Elise spoke, Rose's enthusiasm for the invitation was quickly diminished. Elise rested a hand on Rose's lap.

'My dear girl, why you look so sad?'

'I was silly. I shouldn't have said yes. I'm not sure if is a good idea.'

'But why?'

'Because, look at me. I will shame you, Elise. I have only one good dress and that is for church. And that one is even too short for me now.'

'Don't worry, Rose. I had an idea you might say something like that. When you come on Monday, we will go to Roseau and see if we can buy you a few things.'

'But Madame La Fleur—I mean Elise. I cannot afford to buy anything in Roseau.'

'You won't need money, my dear. Think of it as a little present from me,' she said, but Rose shook her head. 'No, Rose.' Elise put up a hand. 'I insist, and you will insult me if you refuse.'

'Well, if is that you saying, then who am I to be insulting?' A sly grin crept over Rose's face and the two women laughed, long and loud, into the afternoon breeze. They chatted until it was late. Rose rode back to Moore Park in very high spirits, chatting endlessly to Cuthbert—long after he'd stopped listening—about ideas for a new dress, what a young lady should wear on a ship and wondering what language they spoke in Guadeloupe. Once Cuthbert pulled the wagon to a stop at her house, Rose ran straight inside to tell her mother about the trip with Madame La Fleur.

The congregation spilled out onto the soft grassy slopes outside the church. Children ran around, playing chase, undoing top buttons, pulling off straw hats. The older crowd chatted in low voices: gossip should be conducted further away from the church, but the service was long and some things just couldn't wait to be said. The young people who were going off on the picnic excursion were finalising plans. Some would need to hitch a ride on a wagon, some organised food and drink, and a time was set for meeting at the river location.

Rose, who had been in two minds about the picnic, was persuaded to go by one of the girls. Luckily, she could hitch a ride with someone other than Wilfred, but he was skilful enough to make sure he was sitting as close to her as possible at the picnic. She had to suffer his tedious monologue about the ins and outs of lime picking. When she found a suitable gap in the proceedings, Rose slipped away, out of sight. Her mind was filled with thoughts about going shopping with Elise the next day and the imminent trip to Guadeloupe.

The river narrowed as Rose walked further downstream. She got closer to the river's edge where the gnarled roots of the trees showed above the waterline and formed an undulating path that Rose carefully trod along. The river trickled slowly, gliding easily past the rocks and stones. She saw two large rocks taking pride of place in the shallow water and climbed carefully onto the larger of the two to take in the view. On each side of the river, the banks were covered with slippery, low-lying shrubs and plants. Wild lantana grew on both the east and west banks, their red flowers bright in the emerald-tinged light. Rose closed her eyes and took a deep breath.

'You looking very peaceful there, Rose. I wondered where you got to.' Rose was startled but did not turn to face Wilfred. She thought if she ignored him, he might go back to the others.

'You know there are several kinds of snake around here,' Wilfred continued. 'What you would do if one jump out from one of those vines?' Rose closed her eyes again. She tried to imagine Wilfred away. 'Rose—I have a big confession to make.'

'I'm not your priest, Wilfred. Go away.'

'I can't go away because my confession concerning you.' Rose kept her eyes shut. Wilfred moved closer to the river's edge and climbed onto the rock adjacent to hers. He stood and balanced there a while. 'You lost your locket, didn't you Rose?'

'Yes, I did.' Rose opened her eyes. 'You have it?'

'That is my confession. I picked it up that day you ride in my wagon after market. You remember that day? When we came into these woods?'

'How you expect me to forget?'

'Well, Rose, I said is a confession, so please hear me. I was only holding the locket for safe keeping. And I even have it fix for you in town. It's like new again. I thought you might ask after it.' He sat on his rock so that he could look into her eyes. 'But a long time pass and you don't want to see me. I forget about the locket until coming here remind me.'

'Wilfred, where is my locket now?'

'I say I have it and…'

'And what, you throw it away?'

'No, no. Of course not. It's at my home—keeping safe.'

'Wilfred, you think I'm foolish enough to come at your home?'

'I would love to invite you but look like you still vex with me. Rose?' He hoisted his leg so that he could place a foot on Rose's rock and lean in close enough for her to have to look him in the eye. 'What I can do to make you like me?'

'Is nothing you can do, Wilfred. I thought you understood that I'm not interested in looking for a man.'

'What you mean is, you not interested in me.'

'You have plenty women to choose from. But Wilfred, you have to understand I'm not one.' She kept her tone as polite as possible when all she felt was annoyance. She'd had enough of replaying this conversation and couldn't wait for the day when he gave up on her. 'All I want is for you to give me back my locket. Could you please just do that?'

Rose stood up, a little shaky on the rock. She needed Wilfred to move out of the way so that she could return to the riverbank. Wilfred did not budge. His foot remained as it had been and she was likely to fall if she tried to jump across him. He looked up at her.

'Well then, fine. You win. I lose. But Rose, I making big money, you know? No one in Moore Park will be rich like me.'

'Wilfred, give me pass. Is time we go and join with the others.' He stood but remained on his rock, eyes burning into hers with an emotion she couldn't fathom. He no longer looked arrogant, his eyes had saddened and she realised she had hurt him. He'd never shown this side of himself; he'd always treated her as if it was a loss to her that she wasn't interested in him. She hadn't meant to hurt him and hadn't realised that she could until then. It was more than clear that Wilfred could not accept her rejection of him; she could see that, for him, she wasn't just another conquest, another girl he could brag about to his friends.

'Wilfred, I'm tired of this. I'm sorry.' She folded her arms, uncrossing them quickly to steady her balance.

'Sorry for what?'

'Every time we meet, we go into battle. I hate it. Please believe that there is no future for you and me. I may well never marry. You understand?'

'I wonder if is because you have someone else in mind.'

'There's no one.' She attempted a side step but lost her footing and had to counter her balance before she could stand straight.

'Here,' he said, putting out a hand. 'Let me help you to the bank.'

If there was one thing she could be sure of with Wilfred, he was stubborn enough to continue his annoying behaviour until she relented and allowed him to help her. He would stand there all day with that outstretched hand. Reluctantly, she took it and allowed him to guide her back to the river's edge. Once she was on steady ground, she pulled her hand away. They walked a short way in silence.

'You can drop my locket up by me any time,' Rose said once they'd got closer to their party.

'I will be away for a while. For work. Meet me at the dance this Friday and I will have the locket for you.'

'Wilfred!'

'No, is not like that, Rose. I hear you say to the others already that you going to the dance and is Friday I coming back. I'll see you there and I'll bring the locket. Maybe I will bring you back a present, too.'

'No. No presents. Just my locket. That's all I need.'

'Well, Friday then.'

'Thank you, Wilfred.'

1898

Margaret had shown her how to bind her stomach. She told her those white people mostly don't see you, anyway, but don't make no fuss. Walk in the room soft, soft, soft. Don't spill nothing, don't make no mess. Nanette wore one of Margaret's dresses but, at six months pregnant, her stomach was hard to hide. Despite what Margaret said, it wasn't true that their white employers didn't notice them. Mr Lafferty, owner of the Hudson Estate, noticed his black staff, particularly if they were girls and especially the ones who looked like Nanette. It wasn't long after she'd been there that Mr Lafferty had caught hold of her wrist one evening as she'd placed a cup of hot milk on his desk.

He'd inhaled deeply and closed his eyes, his face close to hers. She'd tried to leave.

'I haven't dismissed you.'

'You wanted anything else?' she'd said without looking at him.

'Your skin is so soft,' he'd replied, grinning at her. 'And I bet it's as sweet as the cocoa powder you've dusted over this hot milk. Was that especially for me?'

'Margaret make the milk.'

'Indeed. You have such poise and elegance, Nanette. Unlike the usual servant women. Yes they hold themselves strong and proud but you're really quite graceful in your step. You know you remind me of those haughty, rich Creole women at the dinner parties we attend. I have a feeling you are from their class. Surely. As for your husband, the lucky bastard, he comes from money, too. My wife may not have asked questions but I'm very sure there is a story there, a secret.'

'May I go?' she asked, unblinking.

'One more thing. I get restless at night. Walk around my house, even passed the servants' quarters. Late at night, I've heard the sounds that you make in your bed, Nanette. They betray you. Set you apart from the other high-classed women on the island, be they black, brown or white. I love all that wild abandon.'

She had felt dirty when she'd left his study as if his filthy tongue had actually been on her skin.

It was late in the evening, not long after this incident, when he caught Nanette by the elbow and pulled her into a guest bedroom.

'Mr Lafferty, what you think you doing?'

'Why don't you call me "sir" like the others do?'

'Because Mr Lafferty is your name—sir.' Nanette did not look him in the eye. Margaret had told her never to do that. Nanette mimicked her own servants, but Mr Lafferty couldn't be fooled.

'Tell me, Nanette. Where do you come from?'

'How you mean, sir?'

'How I mean? You know what I mean.' Nanette did not reply. 'You have brown skin, you dress like a servant, you fetch and you clean but it's all a game for you, isn't it?'

'Mr Lafferty, I have to turn down the Mistress bed. She going to retire soon.'

'Yes, I know. But not in my bed. My bed is big and it's empty and it's a long time since I had a woman in there to keep me warm.'

'They'll be bringing the hot milk to your study, sir. And the Mistress will complain if I don't go now. Sir, I have a job to do.'

Mr Lafferty laughed. 'You're not fooling anyone.' He shoved her towards the door and she stumbled against it, turning back just once but not daring to look at him.

Nanette hurried to carry out her duties before joining the staff for supper in the kitchen. She was the last to arrive, the others sitting at the table, each with a bowl of dumpling stew steaming on the place setting in front of them.

'You look like you seen a ghost,' Charity said, putting a large round loaf of soft bread in the middle of the table.

'I'm fine,' Nanette said. 'Just tired.'

As usual, Antoine rose from his seat as soon as she entered the door, pulled out her chair and saw that she was comfortable before sitting down himself.

'That is one gentleman you marry there,' said Barnabas, a mouthful of stew bulging at the side of his face.

Nanette patted Antoine's hand and smiled.

'Eat, my love,' said Antoine. He passed a hand over her tummy. 'You need your strength.'

'You haven't long.' Charity looked grave. 'We can all see that stomach you have. You can't keep it hidden and it have to come out one day. When you going to tell them you leaving because you know they not keeping any baby here to stop you from your work.'

'Yes, I know, Charity.' Nanette hadn't started to eat yet. She thought about how close Mr Lafferty had been to her upstairs. If things had gone any further with him, he would have felt her stomach for himself, seen that she was pregnant and she would be out on her ear.

She and Antoine had saved money over the past two years, a small amount. When Nanette discovered she was pregnant they had hoped to find accommodation close enough to the Hudson Estate so that Antoine could keep working there and she could stay at home and look after the baby. But there was no such accommodation nearby which meant their having to leave the estate and hope that their savings would last long enough to keep a roof over their heads until something came up. They knew the Laffertys would not have a servant baby in the house, and they knew the risks they were taking keeping the baby a secret. The deception was grounds for instant dismissal, but they had to bide their time until an alternative showed itself. If nothing came up soon, they might end up having to plead with the Laffertys for time to find somewhere else to live. Perhaps Charity could vouch for them. She was the Laffertys' most long-standing and trusted servant.

'Where there is a will, my old grandmother used to say,' said Antoine. He pushed Nanette's spoon so that it touched her fingertips. She finally began to eat.

'I wonder,' said Margaret. All the servants looked at her as if they all knew what she was about to say.

'Yes?' said Nanette.

'Well, is just that all you have been here for nearly two years. Neither one of you talk about family. Nanette don't tell me nothing but that she lost them. That tell me they dead but so much expensive your clothes you come in must be, I believe you should have money. Like an inheritance from your dead family maybe?' She looked long and hard at Nanette who did not answer.

'And you, Antoine?' said Charity. 'You have all the refinement of a gentleman and all the good manners that Mr

Lafferty will never have. This old grandmother of yours, she can't give a little money to help you now?' Her eyes darted between Nanette and Antoine whose hands were closed around each other by their sides. Charity looked as if she would say more. All the questions the servants held at bay were palpable.

'I used up everything my grandmother gave me,' Antoine finally said. 'There is nothing more. All we have are the clothes we arrived in. All we have is each other and our future and we don't have a past to return to.'

The servants ate in silence and when their bowls lay empty on the table, and the loaf of bread was half eaten, the room grew quiet. Outside, a still night peaked above the yellow half curtains on the kitchen windows. The only thing moving, though it was barely a flicker, was the candle on the table surrounded by the square lantern. The yowl of Barnabas' harmonica broke the silence. No one noticed him leave the table. He stood in the shadows by the larder door and blew louder, making the tune more lively and faster by the second. Audrey giggled and got up to clap. She danced dizzily in front of Barnabas, the others turning from the table to watch her.

'Mind you don't bring up all that food you just guzzle,' said Charity. She tapped a rhythm on the table with her chubby fingers. Charles picked up her beat, tapping it out on an empty tin tray with the handle of his spoon. The two other girls, Margaret and Mallie, got up to join Audrey who had started singing some improvised words to the music being created. In patois, she told the story of the white man and the brown girl who came to Hudson to work and make babies every night in the moonlight. Margaret laughed and pointed at the couple, then pulled Antoine up to dance, too. Nanette looked over at Antoine; she hadn't seen him so animated in a long time. He worked hard in the gardens and when he was sent to the fields. His skin was brown now; any trace that he was a fine, rich white gentleman gone, only the passionate way in which he loved her remaining, unmistakable in their moments alone together in the cramped room or when they slipped out to be by the sea first thing in the morning. They very rarely had a day off and never at the same time. Nanette laughed now, pushing out her chair to get up to join them. She would have loved to strip off the bandages and free her stomach and breasts so that she could dance the way she did on *J'Ouvert*, the night she met Antoine.

'What is this?' A voice from the open doorway halted the night's festivities. Mr Lafferty's face was ashen though his grey eyes blistered his anger into the centre of the dancers.

'Mr Lafferty, I'm so sorry,' said Charity. 'We didn't mean to be loud. We finish now. I'm sorry.'

'I'm surprised you allowed this to happen, Charity. You know the mistress is in bed now, not to mention the children are asleep.'

'I thought, as their bedrooms on the other side of—'

'Well, you thought wrong and I won't have this rowdiness happening under this roof from you people ever again. Is that understood?'

'Completely, sir.' Charity turned to the others who either nodded or mumbled their agreement.

'You,' said Mr Lafferty. 'I want you to come with me.'

They looked from one to the other, not sure which of them Mr Lafferty was referring to. He pointed a finger and directed his eyes. He meant Antoine who in turn pointed at his own chest.

'That's right, you come with me, boy.'

Antoine followed his employer who had already turned and left the room. Nanette pulled Antoine by his arm.

'Be careful of that one,' she whispered.

'Don't worry,' he hurried back in French.

Nanette retired to their small room after helping to clear up the kitchen and say goodnight to the other servants. She sat on the bed, her knees underneath her, biting a piece of skin at the side of her thumbnail. She leapt up when the door opened.

'What was it, what did he want?' she whispered to Antoine who came in shaking his head.

'Mostly for me to help him pull off his boots while he rattled on about nothing.' Antoine sat and unbuttoned his shirt before taking off his own boots.

'Did he say anything?'

'Nothing of importance. He was curious about my accent. Hadn't realised I was French. Of course, he's never said a single word to me since we arrived, so how would he know? Only looks me up and down if ever he passes me. Which is not often, thank the Lord.'

Nanette sat, putting her arms around Antoine. 'I'm scared,' she said.

'What? Of him? Don't be.'

'He just wanted you to take off his boots? Nothing else?'

'He just probed me about my parentage. I said I was a migrant worker from Martinique and I have no family. Don't worry, Nanette. It's nothing.'

But she was worried. Despite how fatigued she was from another day of hard work, she couldn't fall asleep. She looked at Antoine's bare back which she could just about make out in the darkness of the room. He was fast asleep, snoring lightly. She pressed closer to him, her round stomach into his broad back. She felt the baby move and put her hand on her tummy. She must rest, the baby needed her to. She had to keep away from Mr Lafferty, that was all. Bide time until they found a solution to their dilemma. She wanted this baby to be happy. This baby and Antoine were everything to her, and she refused to let the threat of being thrown out by the Laffertys hang over her all night.

Chapter 4

'Calm down, Rose, is only Roseau you going. You not going to England to buy the dress.'

'I know, Mam, but I only used to look into the windows of those shops in town when I was a girl. Now I going and buy a dress in one of them. Not a made one but shop bought.'

'You know homemade is not shameful, Rose. Remember who you are.'

'I do. I don't mean to be disrespectful.'

'And I hope you thank Madame La Fleur enough times.'

'Don't worry, I did.'

Rose did not know what to do with herself. She barely touched her breakfast. She was up before her mother, trying to fix her hair at the small mirror in the living room. Rose had rolled her hair with rags the night before and stood arranging the neat row of waves she'd achieved, checking the way her hair lay from all directions until she was satisfied and then sat and waited for Elise La Fleur's driver to arrive. May came in from picking flowers and set down a large bunch of bougainvilleas on the table where Rose sat, agitated, listening for the rumble of the wagon to take her to Roseau.

'You look lovely, Rose.' May sat beside her. The schools were on spring break and she was taking advantage of not having to get up before daybreak to catch a ride into Thibaud. 'And don't worry about what Mam said. She is happy for you. And so am I. You lucky you getting a new dress and a trip to Guadeloupe.'

'It's not just the dress and the trip. I'll be in Roseau again, and it's a long time since I been there.'

'You mean since you saw your sailor.'

'Don't tease me, May. I know is foolish to think I'll see him after all this time.'

'It's not. But I didn't know you were still thinking about him.'

'Only every other day.' Rose grinned and May put a hand on hers.

'Just don't build up your hopes. Rose, it's been almost four years now. He is older than you are, and by now, he might have taken a wife in Grenada.'

'I know all of that. But we never said a proper goodbye. Even if he has forgotten me, he would at least be kind. Wish me well. That's all I want.'

'You sure?'

'I just know that I have a gap right here in my chest, and when I think about him, the gap feels like a lump that rise up and suffocate me.'

'I didn't know. So all the times we said that we wouldn't get married and live in a house together, it was only because you didn't want anyone else but him?'

Rose looked down. She stopped the rapid tapping of her heel against the floorboards and put her hands on her knees.

'Don't be embarrassed to feel the way you do,' said May. 'Funny how you are the youngest and you're the one teaching me about love.'

Rose looked up at the window, aware that the driver, Cuthbert, had pulled up the wagon at the gate and was stilling the horse. She hadn't even heard him arrive, her mind full of thoughts about Raphael and the morning she tried to get to Roseau to search for him. Of all her memories of Roseau, it was the image of Raphael standing at the pier waving to her that stayed with her. Not the shops and the dresses in the window.

At Madame La Fleur's house, Cuthbert harnessed the freshly groomed horse to the carriage. It was cushioned inside and the cover was up at the back.

'My first ride in a carriage,' said Rose as she sat back and grinned to herself.

'Such a shame it's a tediously long journey and the roads are so dangerous.' Madame La Fleur wore her face powder and lipstick, silk gloves and a linen coat that Rose had never seen her wear before. 'I very rarely go into Roseau. But at least the scenery is wonderful and I have good company.'

They chatted happily for the long journey. When they arrived at the Old Market Square, Cuthbert helped Elise down and she promptly put up her parasol.

'While Cuthbert waters the horse and takes a break we'll make our way to the town square,' she said.

The tall church appeared far more elegant now. Rose had lived up in the countryside for so long the whole of Roseau seemed to have changed. She looked around the square in amazement like an excited child who'd had an enormous treat laid out in front of them and had been told they could have anything they wanted. Butterflies fluttered in her stomach, her gaze shifting quickly from one shop to another. Among them was a craft shop selling straw goods, a tailor's shop with a mannequin in the window, a vendor of leather shoes and bags of all shapes and sizes.

Their first stop was a dress shop owned by a white American woman. Inside, necklaces with shimmering stones dangled from hooks, fancy gloves lay folded on the counter and dresses of a modern design hung on rails from cushioned hangers. Rose wondered who would wear dresses like these. They certainly weren't designed for country girls like her. She'd have nowhere to wear them. She imagined the beautiful women she'd seen riding in carriages in town as a girl, the ones that lived on grand estates. They had lots of money and travelled. They had parties and gatherings, and they had servants, cooks and drivers. Just like Madame La Fleur. She couldn't imagine that there were still so many wealthy landowners in Dominica that would require this number of designs.

Rose thought of her mistress as a young girl, when the Europeans on the island lived in all of the grandeur that their wealth allowed. Elise La Fleur had been just as rich as they were, though coming from a Creole family, they may well have owned slaves themselves. She would have acquired a hefty inheritance from her father, and her husband would have left her comfortably off.

'Look at this, Rose.' She turned to see her mistress beckoning to her. She stood by the glass counter looking in at the trays of bangles and silver earrings.

'So beautiful,' said Rose and traced a finger over the glass.

The American woman smiled at them. 'They are beautiful,' she agreed. 'You just take your time. I'm right here if you need any help.'

Elise took Rose's hand and led her to a row of dresses by the window and asked Rose to take a look to see if there was anything she wanted. Her eyes were alight as she looked through the garments, pulling each away from the last and looking up and down the length of them, glancing back at Madame La Fleur as if to check her offer was still open. Had she an actual rich mistress or had she imagined it all, walking into the shop in a dream state.

Then her eyes fell on a dress. She knew she wanted it straight away without knowing if it was the right size or how much it cost.

'Take it out, then,' Elise said.

'Let me.' The seller in a straight calf-length dress with a drop waistband and several strings of beaded necklaces past her middle, stepped out from around the counter and unhooked the velvet hanger. She held it up in front of Elise, one hand displaying the cut of the dress.

'What do you think, Rose?' Elise asked. 'I think it is just you.'

'Would you like to try it on?' asked the woman. The air around her was masked with perfume, her pale skin caked with powder, her cheeks daubed in blush pink. Rose checked that trying on the dress was acceptable to her mistress.

'Of course, you go ahead, Rose.' Elise nodded with a smile.

'This way,' said the woman, and Rose followed, her hand on her mouth to stop her exclaiming her excitement as she looked quickly back at Madame La Fleur.

The dress was brick red with tiny white polka dots on it. The sleeves were short, it had a small neat collar and the bodice was fitted. The dress buttoned all the way down the front, and the skirt was flared at the hem and fell to just below the calf. When Rose stepped out from behind the curtain covering the small alcove in the wall, Madame La Fleur put a gloved hand to her lips.

'You can look into the glass just here,' said the shopkeeper. Rose turned and looked at her reflection, holding the dress on either side and turning to see the fit.

'Rose, you look beautiful.' Elise beamed.

'Perhaps, Madame, you and your daughter would like to see the new pretty blouses we have in stock?' Rose and Elise looked at each other and grinned. Neither offered to correct her.

Rose left the shop carrying a large parcel. Wrapped in brown paper and tied with string were her new dress, a pink silk blouse and a coffee-coloured cotton skirt. Elise had suggested a new bonnet, but Rose said that she had been far too generous already.

They wandered out of the square and onto the main street. It was hot in the sun. White willowy clouds shifted across the sky and made way for grey ones. Rose remarked on how special she would feel to wake up and find the whole shop had become her personal wardrobe. Elise laughed at her and took the hand that swung at her side as Rose skipped down the road oblivious to her surroundings.

'What about some lunch by the pier? They have a place that does fresh fish and cool drinks,' Elise suggested.

'I would love that...' Rose's voice drifted into silence, her feet halted. She let go of Elise's hand and her mistress walked on a few paces, still chatting. In a moment her surroundings seemed to disappear. The wooden pathway beneath her, the small shops and offices to her right, the distant view of the sea. She was only just aware of her mistress staring back at her, asking if everything was all right. One thing was very clear to Rose, the outline of a person on the corner of the row of shops whom she'd seen cross the road to her side of the street. A, tall and handsome young man had stopped still, staring straight back at her.

'Rose? What's wrong? What happened?' Elise touched Rose's arm. Just then, a shower of rain started. It was the dry season now, and people hurried by, exclaiming and complaining about how unexpected and unwelcome the rain was. Elise backed up under the canopy of the solicitor's office she was standing in front of for shelter. The young man from the corner of the street started to approach Rose. Rose took a few steps forward. The young man was now two paces away from Rose. They continued to stare at each other with warm, full smiles on their faces.

'Rose?' Elise called again. '*Lapli ka tonbé*—take shelter.' Yes, the rain was falling but Rose ignored her mistress who pulled the brown paper bag from Rose and stepped back under the canopy. The shower continued and finally, the young man spoke.

'I can't believe it's you—after all this time. Rose, you look so...'

'How do I look, Raphael—after all this time?'

'As beautiful as the last day I saw you.'

'I've grown up.'

'I see that and I think maybe you're even more beautiful.' Raphael put his arms around her waist and lifted her slightly off the ground before setting her down. Rose rested her head against his chest and closed her eyes. If this was a dream—a rich woman buying her expensive clothes, a chance meeting with the man she never thought she'd see again—then she had better not open her eyes. The world could never be that cruel. Hadn't she suffered enough? Cried enough? Lived in longing for far too long?

Rose could feel Raphael's heart beating fast against her body, but it may well have been her own. Two women barged past them in a hurry to escape the rain, saying under their breath how stupid to be standing there getting soaked. When Raphael finally loosened his embrace and stepped gently back to look at Rose, his eyes were watery. They began to speak in rapid bursts.

'I lost you, Rose.'

'I came to meet you, I tried, that day we were supposed to meet. The hurricane.'

'I know. We never sail that day but I come back weeks later. I look for you. They tell me you gone.'

'I live up in Moore Park now. In the countryside.'

'You live in Dominica still?'

'Yes. Where you expect me to be?'

'I thought is in Guadeloupe you gone. I think by now you married. Children. I don't know what happen, but all I know is I lost you. I came looking for you in Moore Park but then you weren't there.' He grinned, bashful now, and their momentum slowed.

'Here I am,' she said, smiling. 'I don't have husband, I don't have children.'

Raphael touched his hands to Rose's cheeks. He pulled her face gently towards his and kissed her. Softly at first, their lips only brushing. Then full and warm. He put his arms around her, and she wrapped her arms around his shoulders.

'Excuse me—Rose?' Elise coughed. 'Is best you introduce me to your friend and come out from the rain. Look at how your dress is getting wet.' Rose pulled away from Raphael.

'Oh, I'm so sorry, Elise. I must introduce you to Raphael. Raphael, this is Madame La Fleur—I work for her. She just buy me some beautiful clothes, spoiling me, and look how rude I being.'

Raphael bowed.

'Not rude at all,' said Elise, hugging the package to her chest. 'It's my pleasure, now please.' She took hold of Rose's arm and pulled her under the canopy, Raphael following and brushing the front of his shirt which clung to his skin. The secretary inside the solicitor's office peered at them all through the window then shook her head.

'We must all go for a drink,' Elise suggested.

'I have to get back to work,' Raphael said. At that moment, the shower stopped.

'You working in *Roseau*?' Rose asked, surprised.

'Yes, for the lime factory on Bath Estate. I only come down to the port for an errand, but I better get back before I lose my job. But Rose—I need to see you again. Where I can find you?'

'Well, I working at Madame La Fleur until Thursday. But come this Friday, I will be in Moore Park. Ask anyone for me. Saturday, I'll be at market in Portsmouth.' Rose could not take her eyes off Raphael, still afraid that he might not be real.

'Rose—now I find you, I will never lose you again.' He kissed her hand, nodded a farewell to Elise and went on his way, turning back at regular intervals, smiling and waving at Rose until he turned a corner and was out of sight.

'Rose? Should we go and eat?'

As Rose looked back at Elise's smiling face she saw a rainbow over the sky, its end vanishing into the sea ahead of her.

Her mistress could not get a sensible conversation out of Rose for the next few days. With every conversation that she tried to initiate, Rose would bring the subject around to Raphael. How much taller he seemed. How much more mature and handsome. Considering Elise had never met him before and had only seen him briefly, she had nothing to compare this change to. That would prompt the story of how they met, how he seemed to Rose and how her heart skipped a beat when he stood close to her for the first time.

'And what your mother think of him?' Elise asked.

'Oh, Mam?'

'Yes, your Mam. What she think about him?'

'Well, she haven't exactly meet him yet.'

'*What*?' Elise closed the book she had been trying to read aloud to Rose from. 'But you acting like a woman in love. Maybe one who wants to marry this man and your mother don't know him?'

'*Marry*?'

'Yes, marry. And marry quickly judging by the way I see you act the other day.'

'You think he will ask me?'

'If he loves you, yes. He look like he could do.'

Rose drifted over to the big window in the study and looked out into the garden. The hibiscus was in bloom and the flowers swayed gently in the southerly breeze. The gardener was working hard, whistling as he went along, and Rose's mind began to wander. It filled with images of her and Raphael marrying on Elise's huge lawn, the grass long the way Elise liked it, hers and Raphael's bare feet sinking into the cool blades. Behind her, Elise was trying to continue the conversation, but only one or two words filtered through. Only just enough to bring Rose back to reality.

'So, Rose. The first thing you must do on Thursday when you go home is speak to your parents about Raphael. Tell them all about him and don't hide a thing. Honesty is always best.'

'Yes is true. But I scared.'

'Why you scared?'

'They were so angry when I tried to go to Roseau to meet him that day.'

'But you were a child then. Surely if they see you still have feelings after all this time, they might be more accepting of him.'

'I hope so.'

'Me too, Rose, me too.'

It was Thursday evening, the Charles family had gathered together but the room was in turmoil.

'Marceline, calm down!'

'Don't tell me to calm down. Your daughter telling you she serious about a man. A man from Grenada we don't even know and you telling me calm *down*.' Marceline puffed and panted and walked over and across the small rug in the front room with enough determination to embed it into the floorboards.

'Mam, please,' May interjected. Rose had been hoping she would. May was the only one who could appease her mother when she got over-excited. 'Rose is not a child any more. This August will make four years since Rose see Raphael. If after all this time he still want to see her again, then you must give him a chance to prove himself. Rose been good, Mam. You never had to worry about her. And she is a woman now, she working and she working hard.'

'Rose not a woman. She's a girl and she needs to mind me.'

'She do mind you. We all do. She never run away when she see him. She come to you and she explain. Because now she sensible and you must give her a chance.' May went over to her mother and squeezed her chubby hand. Marceline pursed her lips; her eyes held a slight smile in them when she turned to Rose who was sitting quietly on the couch.

'Rose—you think this boy good?'

'Yes, Mam. He working and he look very well presented now. You will like him, I promise.'

'When we can meet him then?' At this, Rose leapt up and hugged her mother.

'Well, he might pass here tomorrow or he might come to Portsmouth on Saturday. If he do, I'll bring him straight up to see you.'

There was so much for Rose to look forward to. Seeing Raphael again, her trip to Guadeloupe just days away and she would finally be getting her locket back at the dance that evening. Marceline had insisted that May escort her. May had reluctantly agreed and hurried Rose up to get going.

'You expecting Raphael to show up at the dance, Rose?' May was oiling down her hair.

'I hope so. But if not, I'm sure he will come to meet me at market tomorrow.'

'You not putting your locket?' May asked.

'My locket?'

'Yes. I don't see you wear it for a long time.' May sat on the bed as Rose knelt to buckle the strap on her Sunday shoes.

'Don't tell Mam, but I lost it for a while. I getting it back tonight.' Rose stood, she was ready to go.

'You lend it to someone?'

'Shh, keep your voice down. No, is that stupid Wilfred playing tricks on me. He coming and give it back at the dance later. Come, let's go. I look all right?'

'As beautiful as ever, Rose.'

They held hands as they trotted off down to the bottom of the hill where the school had been transformed into a dance hall. There was a dance each year around February or March as people got in the mood for carnival, making the most out of the celebrations before the fasting began for Lent.

The music was lively. The band had travelled across the island especially for the occasion, the organiser of the dance having called in a few favours to secure them. The people were also lively. Not much happened by way of dance or music up in the country dwellings, so the events were always well attended. They wore their best clothes, the women styled their hair better than for church, lipstick was worn and face powder was applied. The men shaved and wore ties. Even when the band got hot—and it wasn't long before this one did—they kept their ties on. Trousers were loose-fitting, dresses were tight, shoes shone and so did their skin. By the time Rose and May arrived, they were met with a gust of heated cologne and immediately got swept into the pre-carnival spirit.

Rose watched May dancing with a teacher from the school. The school children would be shocked to see their teacher dancing so rhythmically and they would not recognise their classroom. Rose smiled as she watched her sister having a great time, while keeping half an eye on the door. It swung open and closed with regularity letting in some air, more revellers and letting out the pumping sound and heat. There was no sign of Raphael, and neither had Wilfred shown up with her locket. She kept touching her neck and bending her head to the door.

'Not enjoying the music?' May's nose was shiny and she fanned her face with her hand.

'It's wonderful. It's a wonderful night.' Rose not only faked a smile but had to raise her voice above the music.

'But no Raphael.'

Rose shrugged her shoulders.

'Come and dance with me.' May took both of her sister's hands and wiggled her hips as she moved backwards into the crowd encouraging Rose to dance by moving her arms. At last, Rose gave in and started to sway and copy the action of May's hips. She stopped looking at the door and lost herself in the pulsing vibrations of the room. A few of the men tried to break into the sisters' circle, but May swiped them away like irritating flies.

Out of nowhere, a clammy hand wrapped around Rose's upper arm and wouldn't let go despite her shrugging to loosen the warm fingertips. She looked around and saw Wilfred. His shirt was brightly patterned in shades of orange and red like an announcement of his arrival. This wasn't his Sunday shirt and he wore no tie. He expanded his chest and looked around the room before circling his gaze back to Rose. She and May had stopped dancing, moving off the dance floor with Wilfred close at Rose's side.

'*Ou belle, oui,*' he said. 'Your hair, your dress, very beautiful.'

'You have my locket, Wilfred?' Rose barely looked at him.

'Is in the truck. Come.' He started walking back through the crowd before she could protest.

'What he say?' May shouted.

'He say my locket in his truck. One second, May, I going and get it before he change his mind.'

May shook her head. The teacher she had been dancing with arrived at her side with a tall glass of juice.

'Be quick,' May called after her but Rose was already vanishing into the throng of dancers whom she had to weave around to follow Wilfred out of the school hall. It was pitch dark outside apart from the small area in front of her that the lights in the hall shone onto. Wilfred seemed to have disappeared into the cool night. Trees rustled close by, crickets had started singing and the giggling from a girl at the side of the school building caught her attention until Rose thought she heard a set of footsteps nearby.

'Wilfred!' she called. 'Where you gone?'

'Look me here. By the truck.'

'I can't see you.' Just then, the headlights of Wilfred's pick-up shone brightly into her eyes. She tried to block the light with her hand and followed in the direction of where the beam was coming from.

'Why you have to be like that, Wilfred?' She stood at the passenger side where Wilfred had thrown the door open. He sat in the driver's seat and ignored her, searching inside the glove compartment. He turned off the headlights.

'Jump in, Rose—I'm trying to find it.'

'No, I'll just wait here.'

'Jump in! There have snakes in this grass. They bite. Don't be silly, Rose.' He sounded agitated by her, and she felt childish standing there hugging the breeze away and watching him under the interior light, very obviously looking for her locket.

Rose kissed her teeth and reluctantly jumped up into the pick-up. Wilfred leaned over her and slammed the door shut. He was wearing cologne. Something he must have bought in town. It made Rose cough and hold her nose. He was still leaning over her when the interior light flickered out.

'What happen, Rose, you can't take the smell?'

Before she could answer, he grabbed her firmly by her shoulders, trying to kiss her. With her back pressed hard against the passenger seat, she felt trapped. Rose moved her head from side to side to avoid his wet lips and tried to hit at his arms whilst kicking up with her knees. It was useless. He caught her by the wrists and started to laugh.

'Let me go. I hate you, Wilfred. Get off me!'

'You sure you want me to do that?' He planted a kiss on her neck. Still with his hands clasped around her wrists, he raised her hands to the ceiling of the truck and moved his face towards her breasts. She slid towards the door but Wilfred mounted her and forced her sideways on, putting his full weight on her, his face hovering inches away from her own.

'Wilfred, you will live to regret this,' she said through clenched teeth.

'You will never want me by choice, will you Rose? All I want is a little bit of fun, and then you can have your locket back.'

'Well, let go of my hands, you fool. What you expect me to do like this?'

'You mean…?'

'Yes—if this is the only way I can make you leave me once and for all, then let me loose.'

'Don't try to run away, Rose. When I let go your hand, you undo your dress and stay quiet, you hear? It's one way or the other tonight. Understand?'

'Yes,' she hissed at him. Slowly, he released the grip on her wrists. As soon as he did so, she began scratching and kicking out as hard as she could. Neither had noticed the lamplight beaming across the surrounding area, a searchlight. Someone was looking for Rose.

The driver's side door of the pick-up flew open. Rose saw the horrified look, first from May and then, Raphael. May held the lamp up and Raphael lunged forward, wrenching Wilfred out of the cabin by the belt around his trousers. Despite Wilfred's attempts to kick and hit out, Raphael threw him to the ground and pounced on him. Under the lamplight, the men launched feet and fists at the other, grappling on the ground, grunting, thuds landing on skin, cries for mercy. Raphael pulled Wilfred up by the collar of his bright shirt; leaning on one knee, he raised a clenched fist.

'No, Raphael!' Rose's voice cut into the air. The music from the dance was muffled in the distance. A heavy silence hung over the four people, now as still as if time had held them in place. Slowly, Raphael's fist loosened. He got to his feet, pulling Wilfred up firmly by the collar.

'You!' Raphael exclaimed.

'You know him?' Rose asked.

'Rose, what you doing here with this man? This is the one who tell me all those years ago that you and your family pack up and go away.' Raphael shoved Wilfred hard, back onto the cold grass.

The three of them looked down at Wilfred who was sniffing like a child, touching his face with a shaky hand.

'This man is a dangerous man,' Raphael said. He stepped closer to Rose and held her close. 'How you find yourself out here with him?'

'He have my locket in his truck, and he promise he will give it back.'

'Let me look for it.' May went over to the truck with the lamp as Rose clung to Raphael.

'I didn't think you'd come,' Rose whispered. 'It got so late.'

'I'm sorry, Rose. I get a lift up here, but the man make about three stops on the way. Each time he stop, he eat something, drink something and it take us hours to reach. I'm sorry is so late.'

'Here, Rose,' May said, holding up the lamp. 'Your locket.'

Rose took the locket and tried to put it on until Raphael freed it from her trembling hands and secured it around her neck.

'Let's go home,' May said.

'What about Raphael?' Rose asked, clinging to his arm.

Wilfred stumbled to his feet and clambered into his truck. He hissed at them before shutting the door. 'You all better mind. Anyone in my way will get run down.'

Raphael walked over and bashed the truck door closed. 'Just you drive off if you know what is good for you.'

The headlights flashed on seconds after the engine ignited. Wilfred reversed awkwardly, narrowly missing a tree as he stamped down on the accelerator pedal.

'That man.' May held the lamp higher and shook her head. 'We should get going. Raphael, you'd better walk home with us. You'll have to stay on the couch because you'll never get transport back to Roseau at this hour.'

He looked at Rose and smiled before thanking May for the invitation.

'Don't thank me yet. If you stay, you will have to meet my parents. You think you ready?'

'As long as you can protect me.' He grinned at May.

'I think you can manage to protect yourself.' May shone the lamp in their faces. 'And to get Rose, you will have to meet Mam sometime, so good luck. Come. It's a long walk.'

The sun was not fully risen. Only the soft beginnings of light shone into the bedroom. Rose shuffled as gently out of bed as she could but May groaned and pulled a face.

'Shh, I'm getting up,' Rose whispered.

'Well be quiet, it's Saturday, I want my rest.'

'Especially after all the dancing and rum.' Rose flung the cover back over her her sister's head and tiptoed into the living room. She could hear her father snoring from her parents' room. It wouldn't be long before her mother was up, preparing breakfast before Rose had to get off to market.

Raphael lay on his front on the couch, still asleep, an arm dangling to the woven rug. He had taken off his shirt and hung it neatly over a chair. Both parents were asleep by the time the three got home the night before. May had offered Raphael a sheet to cover himself with, a finger on her lips before she'd retired to bed, pulling Rose with her. Rose had only been able to wave before going to the bedroom. She had so much to say to Raphael, so much she couldn't say on the walk home, as May had started the interrogation she knew her mother would take up the second she saw Raphael.

He inhaled deeply before opening his eyes. Rose smiled at him and put a finger over her lips, her eyes gesturing to her parents' bedroom door. He sat up and took Rose's hand before kissing it and getting up off the couch. He reached for his shirt, getting his arms through but had not buttoned it before Marceline walked out of the bedroom.

'Rose Charles! Who is this man, naked in my house on a Saturday morning? I didn't tell you to pick up strangers at that dance.' Marceline's lips were still moving but there was no sound. Rose realised her mother was praying. For deliverance, for guidance, for forgiveness before she took her daughter to task. Rose rushed to her and gently held her arms.

'Mam, don't worry. May invited him because he couldn't get back to Roseau so late. Mam.' Rose turned to Raphael, who looked awkward in bare feet and an unbuttoned shirt. 'This is Raphael. I told you he was coming.'

'But not at night and not naked.'

'Sorry.' Raphael hurriedly fastened two or three buttons in the wrong place and scrunched his shirt tails into his trousers before stepping forward and holding out a hand. Marceline looked down at it.

'And why you didn't arrange a lift to pick you up and take you home like any decent man would do?'

'Mrs Charles, I'm very pleased to meet you.' Raphael gathered himself. 'I arranged a lift both to and from the dance but the driver let me down.'

'How so?'

'A little too much rum, I think.' Marceline pulled in her lips and looked at Rose. 'I didn't have a single sip,' Raphael continued.

'But I did.' May came out of the bedroom and yawned. 'I was trying to catch up on some sleep but so much noise you all making. Morning everyone. Raphael, you sleep well?'

'You allow this man to sleep in my house?' Marceline turned to her eldest daughter who promptly led her out of the living room.

'We are Christians, we help our neighbours. Let me help you make breakfast. Rose have to get ready for market.' May looked back over her shoulder and winked at Rose.

'Come on,' said Rose to Raphael. 'Help me fetch some water in, we need to wash up and get ready.'

Water was fetched, the stove was lit, the breakfast was laid out. Dunstan rose, yawning and rubbing his tummy before shuffling to the table in his pyjamas. Marceline scowled as he sat down, clearing her throat, loudly, and opening her eyes wide at him.

'Am I saying grace?' he asked her.

'Mr Charles.' Raphael rose to his feet and startled Dunstan. 'Allow me to introduce myself. My name is Raphael Douglas. It's a pleasure to meet you.' He held out his hand. Looking baffled, Dunstan reached across and shook it.'

'Oh,' Dunstan said, drawing the word out. '*The* Mr Raphael.' He looked at Rose and grinned. Marceline cleared her throat again. 'Please, Raphael, sit down and join us for breakfast. Maybe after grace you can tell me why you come here so early.'

The girls burst into fits of laughter, and Marceline kissed her teeth before squeezing her eyes closed, making the sign of the cross and preaching a lengthy grace about offering kindness to strangers and hoping the Lord would grant that these strangers wouldn't take advantage of innocent girls and their God-fearing families.

When they finally began to eat, they did so without a word being spoken beyond the Amen of grace. In the silence, the sound from five bowls of cornmeal porridge slowly emptying and the sips of hot coffee all resonated like great gulps by thirsty travellers who hadn't had a meal in days. Their coffee cups being placed down crashed against the wooden table as if they'd been tossed carelessly onto it.

May and Rose gathered the empty bowls and took them out to the kitchen.

'How you think it's going?' Rose asked.

'Not very good.' May giggled softly. 'Don't worry, Rose, I think Mam would already have thrown him out if she didn't like him.'

They returned with cold ham, warmed bread and a plate of rustically chopped tomatoes that May sprinkled with salt and black pepper. The house was as eerily quiet on their return, their mother scouting Raphael's every move with eyes like searchlights.

'So.' Dunstan looked over to Raphael as the girls laid down the food. 'How you finding Dominica?'

'Oh…' Raphael gasped the word as though he'd been holding his breath, waiting for permission to speak. His words tumbled from his lips as he grinned excessively, looked flustered with heat and adjusted his collar as he spoke.

'Dominica is a beautiful island. I been to a few but none have such colour, so many mountains and friendly people. I don't know why I never think of settling here before. I even have a few relatives here, somewhere.' He continued on about first seeing the island as a boy and how in his eyes, as a man, he could see so much potential. He talked about working in Trinidad and his job in the lime factory on the Bath Estate.

Dunstan nodded amicably. 'So, how about the job at the factory? The money good?' he asked Raphael.

'Daddy!' Rose exclaimed.

'Let him answer,' Marceline said, tearing off some bread and watching Raphael from the side of her eye.

'The money good. That's why I came here to live,' Raphael answered. 'But I never realise there was something more precious than gold waiting for me here.' He looked at Rose. Rose smiled and spooned more tomatoes onto his plate.

'Rose—eat your breakfast,' Marceline said and slammed her coffee cup on the table.

'The food is very good.' Raphael turned to Marceline. 'There's nothing like Dominican cooking.'

'It's just breakfast,' Marceline said. 'You haven't tasted real Dominican cooking.'

'I'm very grateful. It's the best I've eaten since, well, since the war.' He exhaled a nervous laugh.

'You were in the army?' Dunstan set down his fork and grinned broadly at the young man. 'You been abroad to fight?'

'Yes, sir. The British West Indies Regiment, 4th Battalion. I was in France for the most part. We moved around. I was last in Italy before I … I returned.'

'Raphael.' Rose looked anxiously at him. 'You didn't tell me you fight in the war.'

'Well, we really haven't had time to—'

'But you have time now,' Dunstan cut in. 'How you come to find yourself in the army?'

Raphael pulled in his lips, shook his head solemnly before looking at Rose. 'For money, duty, to help me try not to think of you. I mean, I was sure I lost you and I didn't know what to do.'

'The army.' Dunstan pulled his chair closer to the table and leaned in. 'How many Germans you kill?'

'Daddy, please,' said May. 'I'm sure Raphael doesn't want to talk about that right now.' She turned to Raphael. 'I read about what happened out there. I listened on the wireless at my friend's house. All those lives. Daddy knows, we all know about the sacrifices our men made and how they were treated. We are very proud.'

'Thank you,' said Raphael. 'And you're right, the breakfast table is not a place for such things as I've seen.'

'Raphael,' said Rose. 'If I'd only known you were there, I would have said extra prayers for you.'

'It was the thought of you that helped me through it.'

They stared at each other across the table. Marceline shuffled her chair back, the feet scraping the floor.

'Rose, don't you think you should gather your things? Albert will come any second for you. Raphael, can you help my daughter, please?'

'With pleasure.' He got to his feet and began to gather the empty plates.

'The girls will do that,' said Marceline.

'It's my habit,' he said. 'All those years in the army. No one there to wait on you. You learn to do for yourself or you won't do at all.'

Marceline nodded, and for a second, Rose believed she saw a glint of approval in her mother's eyes.

'You'll be able to get transport to Roseau from Portsmouth, Raphael,' said Rose, gathering the cups. 'And Mam, is it all right if I talk to Raphael about meeting him in Roseau soon? I mean, between work and everything.'

'As long your father or I going, too,' Marceline said. 'You must have a chaperone.'

'Mam!' Rose looked at her with wide eyes.

'Don't argue. If Raphael is a gentleman, he will understand that a young lady can't go running around far from home with a young man her family still getting to know.'

'You are right, Mrs Charles,' Raphael said. 'You can be sure that I only have Rose's happiness and safety in mind. No question of that. I lose her once before because I was gullible. It won't happen again.'

Rose and Raphael chatted and giggled all the way to Portsmouth, completely ignoring Albert who sat at the helm, clucking and guiding the horse down the winding mountain road. Albert helped Raphael secure a lift back to the capital very quickly so there hadn't been an opportunity for him to meet Rose's market trader friends. Rose spent the morning telling Benjie and Matilda all about him in between setting up and making sales. She told them what a hero he had been at the dance. She was lost in conversation and busy selling, so didn't realise she was being observed.

Elise La Fleur needed to buy some gifts to take to Guadeloupe. The Carib women came down from their reserve up in the mountainous area around Salybia to sell handmade crafts at the market in Portsmouth. Elise was bound to find something among their handmade jewellery, ornaments and woven crafts. She milled around the stalls, listening to the distinct accent of the Caribs and how their yellow skin and jet black hair made them stand out from the other Dominican traders. She picked up a beautiful necklace, and for a reason unknown to her, she glanced over her shoulder to where she knew Rose usually set up her ground provisions. Rose was at her usual spot, chatting to customers, laughing with her trader friends. Elise turned back to her purchase as the woman in the stall was asking her a question.

'You want me to wrap this one up for you?'

However, Elise was distracted; something about Rose made her turn again. The market was very busy that morning and Elise hadn't intended to disturb her. Rose looked happy. She was yawning, though, rubbing her eyes. Elise remembered the dance on Friday night. Rose must have come home late and she would have been on the road to Portsmouth just after first light; no wonder she was tired. But there was something else. Something sleek and shiny dangling from Rose's neck caught her eye. It was a locket. Rose had mentioned a lost necklace to her before. She had never described it but this silver locket on a silver chain looked very familiar. Elise wanted a better look, but the Carib woman pulled her by the arm.

'What is it?' Elise was confused. The woman pointed to the necklace Elise was still holding. 'Oh I'm so sorry. Could you wrap it for me. I'll take it. I just need one second.'

She walked a few steps across the square; a clear view of Rose was blocked by people stopping for a chat, busy getting in her way. She heard the Carib woman call out the price of the necklace, but her feet had taken her several steps closer to Rose's stall and her elbows had barged aside at least three disgruntled women who were having a very meaningful conversation, if she didn't mind. Elise heard herself say, *I beg your pardon*, but only for the sake of saying it. She didn't care who she moved aside: she needed to see that locket, quite urgently, she realised. Elise had got so close to Rose, she could almost pull the locket from her neck. Rose, of course, was completely unaware of Elise's presence and carried on bartering with a woman in a bright blue headscarf, who insisted Rose was taking advantage of her. Staring intently at the shining piece of jewellery around Rose's neck, Elise backed away into the crowd, hurried to the craft stall, placed a shiny shilling in the Carib woman's palm and left without the necklace she'd purchased.

'Is everything all right, Madame?' Cuthbert looked concerned as he took Elise's trembling hand to help her into the back of the carriage.

'All fine, just take me home, Cuthbert. Quickly.'

Nothing was fine. Hadn't she just seen Rose wearing her precious locket? How did Rose think she could get away with this? Just to be sure she wasn't mistaken, the first thing Elise would do when she got back to the big house would be to go directly upstairs and look through her jewellery box. Rose couldn't have betrayed her trust.

1898

He moved closer and closer to Nanette as he spoke. His breath was hot on her face as she backed into the tall windows opposite the door that Mr Lafferty had taken care to quietly shut behind him. The moon, far off over Morne Anglais, provided the only glint of light in the room. Nanette could hear Charles and Barnabas hushing the dogs who always barked ferociously when they were untied for the night. She knew that they, along with the women servants and her beloved Antoine, would be waiting for her to have supper with them, the duties of the day finished.

'I want some hot cocoa instead of milk tonight, Nanette. Can you serve it in my room? You only have to stay a little while. My wife won't know and your husband won't notice.'

'Won't notice what?'

'Won't notice that another white man had a taste of you.' His hands were on her shoulders now, trying to pull her sleeves from them, but they did not give. To see her naked, he would have to pull harder, rip her dress off, but proof of her secret would be revealed so she sighed with relief when he pulled away.

'Nanette.' His voice had softened and so had his body language but he advanced on her. More slowly this time. 'What if I could help you and your husband find a place? A little home of your own. You want to raise babies, don't you?' Nanette tried to edge her way aside, shrugging her body left and right to escape the trap she was in, between him and the window. He moved to stop her each time; she wanted to tear the skin off his face, but she had to keep control.

'Mr Lafferty, if you want me to bring the drink to your room, you must let me go and fetch it.'

'You'll do that?'

She dared to look at him but saw suspicion in his eyes. His hot breath on her skin like an indelible stain.

'Yes. I will fetch it for you.' Nanette faced away and he brought his forehead close to her temple and whispered.

'You aren't going to run away to the kitchen and not come back?' She shook her head, her breath caught in her throat. 'I know you, Nanette, I've watched you. Don't think I haven't. But only know I can make life here as easy or as difficult for you and your husband as you choose.' His lips brushed her skin as he spoke, but she did not flinch. She blinked into the blackness of the corners of the room.

'Very well, Nanette. I will wait five minutes for you. You hurry, you hear me?'

'Yes, sir.' He stepped aside. Nanette brushed past him, her back erect, her step quick as she walked towards the door.

'Liar!' he hissed as he grabbed Nanette's arm and tossed her violently onto the bed. In less time than it took to inhale, he was on top of her, his weight like lead on her full stomach, thrusting his hips against her. She tried to push him off, but he placed a firm hand over her mouth and pressed her head hard into the mattress.

'Think you can fool me, you little witch? Running off to your husband, weren't you? Well, you are going to give me what you give him or the pair of you will be on the street without a penny. Take your dress off, Nanette, and shut your mouth.' He spoke through clenched teeth. The darkness did not hide his intent, his need, his desire. He eased himself off her and sat, waiting. She lay for a moment then got up slowly.

'I can't.' There was a tremble in her voice, a breathlessness.

'You can and you will.'

As Nanette rose to escape, he pulled at her dress. It tore easily from her back as she lurched towards the floor, exposing the white fabric she used for binding her body. She scrambled to the wall in the darkness, but he reached down and pulled her hair to force her to face him. She called out for him to stop, but he knelt before her and trapped her scream with his hand.

'You stay silent or so help me.' His voice sprayed like venom and the strip of moonlight across his face showed nothing but hate. 'Don't you ever think you can deceive me. Not ever, you hear?'

She nodded, though he still wrenched at her hair, hand over her mouth. Nanette tried to hold the ripped dress over her chest. She was too angry to cry and not strong enough to wrestle him off.

'Now listen,' he said in the same soft voice he'd tried to seduce her with. 'Don't make this difficult. I'll let go of you if you just get up and take off your clothes.' He spelled out the words as if she were learning the language, then he released her. She gasped, wiping his hand print from her face.

'Mr Lafferty—please. Don't hurt me. I'm pregnant. Can't you see?' She lowered the dress to reveal part of the bandages that bound her chest. In a swift motion, her head whipped to one side and stung with a prickly heat seconds after his hand left her cheek.

'You people know the rules. We don't raise black babies here.' He got to his feet and neatened his shirt, tucking in the tails and brushing off the front of it. 'On your feet.'

Nanette rose, unsteadily, still trying to hold the torn fabric of her dress to her body. She couldn't look at him. He stood in front of her, his breath heavy. She knew that she and Antoine would be thrown out, but she wondered if he would try to punish them first. He wasn't going to rape her, but he might do something to Antoine. She thought about the corner of the drawer in the old desk in their room. The money they'd saved. What if he stormed in and took it? Would Antoine have to fight with him? She could feel the wave of anger in Lafferty had not quelled and battled with the notion that pleading and begging forgiveness might either buy them some time or make him more lenient. She turned her eyes to the door.

'Get out,' he whispered.

She started to the door but hesitated. 'Just go? You mean just like that? Leave the house?'

'Leave this damned room right now. I'll deal with you in the morning.'

Nanette ran along the landing, trying not to disturb the mistress or the children as she clung to her dress, holding up the skirt so the wouldn't trip in her rush to get to the kitchen. Downstairs, she could hear murmurs of conversation, Audrey giggling and Charity asking what could have kept Nanette. She didn't stop to think about her appearance and rattled open the door. Silence fell among the garrulous staff when she entered the room. As he always did when his wife entered the room, Antoine stood up. Except this time, he stood slowly, looking at Nanette from head to toe, fury building within him, his body rigid yet seeming to shake at the same time. He threw his arms around her body and hugged her head to his chest.

'Nanette? What happen?' Margaret stood now, but Nanette was unable to speak. She stared into Antoine's eyes, telling her story without the need for words and watching the fire heating his cheeks and hate filling his eyes. He squeezed them shut as he whispered to her in French.

'What did he do?'

She did not speak, and Antoine lunged at the table, grabbing for the carving knife. He flew towards the door, and Nanette, still holding her torn dress against her shoulders, pulled at his arm.

'*Rien.* He didn't do anything, Antoine,' she sobbed, gripping his bicep with all her might. Charles and Barnabas threw themselves at him. Charles grabbed the hand carrying the knife, and the two dragged him backwards, shaking the knife loose so that the steel blade crashed onto the stone tile.

'I have to do this,' Antoine shouted, attempting to take the knife again. Charity kicked it away as the men held tight to Antoine.

'No, son,' Charles warned. 'You can't do that. You know that ole fool have a gun? He won't hesitate. He will shoot you dead right here in this house while his children sleep. He will shoot you, and the police won't care. Think about Nanette.'

'He did not hurt me,' she implored. 'He wanted to but I stopped him.' Nanette was in tears. 'Let us just leave. Go, tonight. I don't want to see his face. I don't want to face him again and neither should you.'

Antoine shrugged the two men away and slapped his hands over his face.

'It's not fair he gets away with this,' he said.

'Listen, Antoine.' Charity shook her head. 'I know you angry. We all are. But there is no justice for people like you and me against people like Mr and Mrs Lafferty. None. Nanette have reason. Is best you two just pick up your things and you go.' She rubbed her palms together, signifying they brush this aside and leave. Nanette placed a hand on Antoine's chest and looked up into his eyes.

'Antoine, please. He said he will deal with us in the morning. That can only mean one thing. He knows about the baby now, so our fate is already sealed. We're not staying for him to try to punish us more than having us dismissed.'

'He will try to shame you in front of us,' Charity said. The others mumbled their agreement. 'Line you up and make a spectacle of you both. That's what he does. It happens every time. Once, he even line up his children to watch when he dismiss a servant. Listen, finish eat and go and pack.'

'Let us gather up all the things we can for you that they won't miss.' Margaret drew closer.

'Like what?' asked Nanette.

'You've seen all those little statues and trinkets around the house. They worth a lot, and the mistress have no idea what she even have in here.'

'We can't…' Nanette began.

'Thank you,' said Antoine. 'Nanette, our savings won't get us very far. Remember what it was like the first time we had to go.'

'Leave when they sleeping, and tomorrow we'll say we don't know where you gone,' said Margaret.

Antoine looked at Nanette, his chest still heaving with anger. 'Nanette,' he said at last, 'you must eat something before we go.'

Audrey placed a shawl around Nanette's shoulders and led her to the table. Trembling, Nanette picked up some bread and started to eat. Margaret dished her up some fish and gravy. Antoine sat beside her and watched Nanette for the full hour it took for her to eat half a plate of food. He ate nothing. Charity and Margaret ran around packing supplies for them to take away into the night. Audrey and Barnabas took care of collecting candlesticks and small items of value that would go unnoticed and would be easy to carry.

Charles went out in the dark without a torch to feed the dogs a few minutes before the young couple were due to leave, so that they wouldn't bark and alert the household. As it was, one of them, the one with the shrillest bark, leapt with excitement at the idea of a late night meal. Nanette could hear the scuffling in the dark and Charles' gruff voice hissing, 'Warn yourself,' to the dogs as she and Antoine packed. Mr Lafferty was bound to reach for his gun if there was a disturbance. He had shot one of his farmhands, a young man called Robert who had taken a liking to the two dogs the Laffertys owned at the time. Warned several times not to make them tame, he'd taught them tricks late at night, but one night, the one he named Alfonse got too carried away with the games and barked so loudly Mr Lafferty aimed a shotgun out of the bedroom window to fire a warning shot and hit Robert in the back of his leg. The bullet blasted out of his knee, shattered the bone and he lost half of his leg after the doctor came to the estate.

Antoine and Nanette listened for the click of the kitchen door and waited five minutes for Charles to still the dogs and get hold of them. Antoine carried a large bag with a leather bottom and a thick leather shoulder strap. Everything they owned—clothes, money, stolen trinkets—was inside, including a small blanket that Audrey said might be useful. Margaret had given them some solid silver plates that were hidden at the bottom of a cupboard in the house and would not be missed, along with a tall candlestick from a stack of at least twelve others. Their mistress seemed to collect brass, silver and crystal ornaments the way dew collects on a field of grass. Trinkets were her passion, but when the shine wore off, she abandoned them the way she did her children. As soon as they misbehaved, looked a wrong way or said a displeasing thing, she would send them off to find the nanny. Her trinkets had been cast into a dark place when they stopped shining for her.

'I don't want any trouble for you,' Nanette had said. 'Maybe we shouldn't steal anything.'

'Consider this a leaving present from your employers.' Charity had winked at her, and somehow, that had assured her.

'Besides,' Margaret had said, 'you will be long gone, and if they ever discover anything missing, they'll think it was you and we won't open our mouths about a thing.' Margaret had cried and hugged them both for several minutes before she left for home with Charity, who had packed a bag of food and supplies that could be spared from the kitchen.

'You have to keep up your strength.' Charity had patted Nanette's tummy, free of all the bandages now and looking fuller and heavy as if she were a different person. 'We will miss you, and if you can ever get word to us, please do.'

'Of course,' they'd said. 'We will never ever forget you.'

The house heaved a silence, and a soft gust of air followed them into the yard outside the kitchen. They would miss the smell of Charity's cooking, especially breakfast. Nanette would even miss the shining surfaces in the house, the large rooms and the long windows. It was the closest thing to her old life that she had. Apart from her locket, she had nothing left from home other than memories. It was almost three years since she'd seen her family. Her younger sister would be grown up, married maybe. Her mother would have stopped crying long ago, and maybe, like her father, she might have decided that Nanette was a disgrace, too. She liked to think that they would come to terms with her decision, that her parents would want their daughter home. Hadn't she proven that her love for Antoine was genuine, that it wasn't just a whim and that he wasn't using her? He had stayed with her, married her, he was prepared to kill for her. Antoine had grown up, too. They were children when they met, spoilt, not at all prepared to look after and fend for themselves, but they were doing that now, remarkably well, she thought. They would go on looking after each other, and when the baby came, she would look after her, too. She had always felt she would have a girl. She had just months to discover who her new child was going to be.

They walked miles. Swapping the strap of the bag from shoulder to shoulder, Antoine held Nanette's hand with his free one. She carried the food supplies and insisted that she do at least that because if Antoine had his way, he would carry her, too. They passed the small village with the church, the village where both Charity and Margaret had their homes. Mr Lafferty would be there the next day, making enquiries as to whether anyone had seen his runaway servants.

It was late when they arrived near the coast; the sun would rise in mere hours. They walked through the scant woodland close to the beach; the air was cool and Nanette's lower back began to ache.

'I need to rest,' she said.

'Of course.' Antoine sat her down on the sandy earth and took out the blanket to make a pillow for her head. She wrapped the shawl tightly around her neck and fell asleep with Antoine rubbing her back. With his head against the foot of the palm tree they sheltered beneath he closed his eyes, too.

They woke to the sound of children laughing. Antoine was curved around Nanette's back like a shell. She opened her eyes and smiled at the children.

'Where you come from?' Just one of the questions Nanette could make out above the many the children threw at them with their giggles and pointing fingers.

'We've come from a long way from here.' Nanette sat up and rubbed her eyes.

'You hungry?' The child who spoke was bony, his skin black as night and his eyes bright like a full moon. Like the other three children, he wore rolled-up shorts and a shirt that looked as though they'd belonged to older siblings. He carried a cutlass about the same size as himself and held out a cut coconut full of milk.

'Is this your breakfast you sharing with us?' Nanette asked.

'No,' he said as if she had no sense at all. 'This look like a breakfast to you?'

Antoine sat up beside her and reached for the coconut. 'Thank you. You are very kind.'

'What you doing here?' The boy looked at the large bag behind Antoine, pressed into the tree, unclasped. The boy peered at it.

'We're on our way home,' Nanette said, sipping from the coconut.

'Where is your home?' the boy asked, kneeling in front of her now.

'That is also a long way from here,' she said. 'So, we better go.' She looked at Antoine who folded the blanket and tucked it into the bag before closing the buckle. He helped Nanette to her feet.

'You have a baby in there?' The boy nodded to Nanette's stomach which she rubbed now.

'Yes, our daughter is in there, sleeping.' She handed the coconut shell back to the boy. 'We'll be on our way. No need to tell anyone you see us.'

'We won't.' The boy looked at his friends for confirmation of this and waved the couple off.

'Where *are* we going?' Nanette said to Antoine a little way on. 'We can't walk forever.'

'Charles said Scott's Head is a good place. He used to live there. But it must be half a day away.'

'Let's eat something first.'

They stopped not far from the children, who they could still see, turning somersaults into the shallow waves on the beach, their brown bodies coated in shimmering sand as they rolled and fought and kicked water at each other. Nanette wondered if she'd ever feel that free again. She had felt liberated, like new when she'd left her house to run away with Antoine. Though she'd had knots in her stomach, it was excitement rather than fear she'd felt that night. She knew she would be safe with Antoine, that she'd be happy. Antoine was her home. She had told the boy—and she looked over at him now, his hair white with sand—that she had a long way to go. Now, as she looked at Antoine chewing with gusto on a chunk of cold meat, the grease on his lips, she knew she was already there. Home.

Close to Scott's Head, Antoine and Nanette came across a deserted shack. It was set on a huge expanse of overgrown land with the ruins of a plantation owner's house in the distance. The land must be owned by someone, but there was no one to be seen and no signs of occupancy. They chose the shack because it looked in better repair than the house and they thought they would arouse less attention if they stayed there. Besides, they didn't need much space, just somewhere to sleep and make plans for their future. Nanette was not able to work but Antoine could. He cleaned himself up and prepared to set off for nearby Scott's Head to sell the silver.

'Here,' said Nanette. 'Maybe you should take this?' She hadn't undone the clasp of her locket but she was attempting to.

'Never,' said Antoine. 'We'll get a good sum for this lot and then I'll find a job. I can work the land now, I'll find something.'

'And what will I do when you're not here?'

'Look after her. Stay safe. We'll be able to rent something in Scott's Head. I'll find out all I can.'

He kissed her forehead and went to the door. 'I hate to leave you but I'll be as quick as I can.'

'It's fine. I'll be fine.'

Nanette in her second-hand dress, her arms under her tummy stood in the doorway of the run down shack as her husband left. She watched his strong back, his old silk shirt heavily creased but clean. She blinked a slow tear and went to sit inside, looking through the window at the idle clouds, hearing the silver clanging in the bag as Antoine walked away, and when she could no longer hear his footsteps, she listened for the distant sea.

Chapter 5

May had set off for Thibaud, Dunstan was getting ready to go to his garden and Marceline was making soup for Ma Jacob, who was poorly. Rose stood in her front yard looking down the road with a craned neck and listening for Elise La Fleur's driver. The wagon was over half an hour later than expected. Cuthbert should have been earlier than usual because she was off to Guadeloupe. They would have to go to the big house, collect Madame La Fleur and load the carriage before driving to Roseau to board the ship. She worried that the horse had overturned on the way up to Moore Park. Had Madame La Fleur revised the plans and they'd be leaving later? There was no way of knowing. Eventually, she saw a man pulling his cart and mule up the road and stopped him.

'Mr Arthur,' she called and left her gate to greet him.

'Miss?'

'I wonder if you pass anyone in a big wagon on your way?'

'No, miss, I don't pass any vehicle at all.'

'Where you come from?'

'D'os D'Âne.'

'Thank you.'

She went back to her yard and figured that if the man had come all that way, then surely he would have seen an upturned wagon, Cuthbert fixing a wheel or something. He just wasn't coming. But why? She waited another half hour, sitting on the front steps with her chin on her hand. Marceline popped her head out of the kitchen.

'You sure is today you say you going?'

'Of course is today.' Rose was becoming more and more worried.

'But, Rose, if a ship going to Guadeloupe today, it would already sail from Roseau, you know?'

'I don't understand what happen. Maybe Elise sick. I should go by her house and see.' With that, Rose picked up her woven travelling bag and headed for the road.

'How you going to get there?' her mother shouted after her.

'I'll find a way,' she called over her shoulder.

It took Rose over an hour to make the journey to Picard, having met a couple on their way to Portsmouth and who gave her a lift in their lorry. From there, she'd walked and run the rest of the way. She arrived at the estate, hot and anxious, even more so when she saw the gates closed. Rose peered in at the tall white building and saw the gardener pruning the bougainvillea by the path leading to the front door. The brown oak doors to the house were shut.

'Henry!' she called. Henry turned and waved to Rose. He walked to the gates and swung them open.

'Where is Madame La Fleur? She all right?' Rose was out of breath.

'Yes, she all right. What about you? You look like you could do with some water.'

'No, no. I'm fine. I been waiting and waiting on Cuthbert, but he never come for me.'

'Today?'

'Yes, today. I always come on Monday.'

'But Cuthbert tell me after he take Madame to Roseau, he not working again this week.'

'Maybe so, but he was supposed to collect me first. Where is Madame La Fleur?' She jerked her head towards the closed doors and was about to run up to them when Henry answered.

'But she already gone.'

'Gone? She gone to Guadeloupe?'

'Since daybreak, she go to Roseau, *oui*. Why? You think is work you was working today?'

'I was suppose to go with her to Guadeloupe. She never send Cuthbert for me.'

'He never say he going by you, Rose.'

'But she asked me to go with her—I can't understand. She never say anything? No one else here?'

'Only Lucinda and the girl, Jane, doing her washing. Lucinda upturning the kitchen to clean it.' He chuckled to himself, but Rose was not amused at all. He stopped smiling and put his hands in his pockets. 'So. All you have any misunderstanding?'

'What misunderstanding we could have? She and I get on so well…' Rose's voice trailed off. She knew full well they hadn't fallen out. They were laughing and joking the last time they were together. Both looking forward to the trip.

'*Ou vlé yon bwé*?' Henry asked.

'No thank you, I'm not thirsty.' She looked at the oak doors. 'Is the door locked?'

'I pulled them to stop the flies, but you can go in.'

Her legs were leaden as she climbed the painted steps and pushed open one of the heavy doors. The doors to the inner rooms were closed, but Rose went into the lounge half expecting to see Elise sitting by the window in the large chair with a book under her nose. She would look up at Rose and say, *Bonjou* Rose. *Jodi sé yon bèl jou*. But there was nothing beautiful about the day. It should have been. Since the day Raphael walked through the rain and back into her life, each day had been beautiful. But this day … this one. It was supposed to have been very special.

Rose found herself halfway up the stairs on her way to Elise's room just to check she wasn't sleeping and that everyone was wrong about her whereabouts.

'What you doin' here?'

Rose turned to see Jane at the foot of the stairs carrying some folded sheets over her arms. She always looked such a mess. Rose couldn't understand why Elise had kept her on. Yes, she had been recommended by Lucinda, but her work was shoddy and she constantly spied on Rose. Walking back down the stairs, Rose ignored Jane and headed for the door.

'You don't hear me? I say what you doing here?'

Rose stopped. 'I came to make sure Elise was well.'

'Elise? Is that you calling her now? Well, you of all people should know that right in Guadeloupe Madame go.' She began to giggle. 'And she leave her poor little Rose behind.' Rose left then, practically stumbling down the stairs from the porch, Jane calling after her, 'They tell me you going, too. What happen?'

Henry looked up from his work. 'See you soon, Rose.'

She didn't answer but exited the gate, stopping to look up and down the private road as if she'd forgotten the way. Her stomach felt knotted and uncomfortable, her legs weak, so she sat on the curb. She had so much built up excitement and nowhere to channel it except through tears that rolled down her cheeks. She heard Henry call her, but she didn't look over, didn't answer him, she just swiped at the tears with her thumb. She smoothed her new skirt over her knees, hoping she hadn't made it grubby by sitting like a lost soul on the roadside. She remembered her handkerchief, one Elise had given to her, and searched for it in her bag. She dried her face and sat for a while longer, puzzling over what had gone wrong. Why the confusion, and why on earth would Elise leave without her and not send a message?

Her confusion, disappointment and sadness followed Rose back to Moore Park. Her feelings had turned to frustration and anger by the time she walked into the house. Her mother said nothing but went to the kitchen to fetch her daughter a glass of sorrel.

'Sometimes these things happen for a reason,' her mother said and left her to sit on the couch. The glass of sorrel, red and still on the table beside her, went untouched for a good hour.

By dinnertime, Rose was talking again. May had done everything she could to cheer up her younger sister, reminding Rose that on Saturday, she would be seeing Raphael after market and she better not have that face when she saw him. It made Rose smile, and May squeezed her hand. When they retired to bed, May whispered to her that everything would be fine, she would see. But it would take Rose hours before she fell asleep, and the week of waiting to see Raphael would seem interminably long.

Come Saturday, Rose finished her market duties early. To her market stall friends' amazement, she was not full of fancy tales about her trip; in fact, she avoided the topic completely and talked about Raphael instead.

'Is that why you dress like you going to church?' asked Benjie.

'Yes,' said Rose and nodded to her father who was chatting with Wilfred's uncle across the way. 'And that's why I have my chaperone. Mam doesn't trust me to be alone with him.'

'Well, if he's as handsome as you say,' said Martha, 'then I'm not surprised. You mind you don't spoil your dress before you meet him.'

'You sound like my mother now.' Rose laughed. For the first time all week.

She and Dunstan hitched a ride into town in the early afternoon and met Raphael by the port at the very spot they'd said a goodbye in the hope they would meet again soon. Dunstan shook Raphael's hand then nodded and took his leave, leaving Rose surprised but happy that she could be alone with Raphael.

'Am I late?' she asked.

'Only by four years.' He grinned at her and took her hand. They walked along the harbour road. As they did, a small merchant ship sailed away from the pier and out across the ocean. Four years ago, Raphael would have been sailing with them. Rose wondered what would have happened if they had been able to keep their rendezvous. She thought about the lost years, feeling Raphael's palm, warm against hers. They had only ever kissed once, but she'd missed that kiss. She'd tried to relive it, but in the end she couldn't bring it to memory. She'd begun to forget his touch, his smile, even the sound of his voice. She would be ashamed to admit it. She'd imagined being with him and then fought to forget the conjured-up picture of him as it was too painful to wake up and realise he wasn't really there. She couldn't remember when she had stopped dreaming of them meeting again, but at some stage, she had. Had he forgotten her at all? Had he loved another girl when she wasn't there?

They walked along the seafront. The cobalt sky hung still as a canvas, framing the boat as it grew smaller. They stopped at a low wall where waves rolled close to their feet and sat down.

'Something is wrong.' Raphael's voice penetrated the depths of her thoughts.

'How you mean?'

'You're not so chatty as the last time I saw you.' He put his hand on her lap and she looked at the long fingers, the strong hand that had held her waist as they walked in the dark after the dance.

'I'm sorry. But don't think I'm not happy to see you. We have so many things to talk about, I don't even know where to start.'

'Tell me about the day you tried to come to Roseau to meet me.'

'Oh.' She sighed a laugh as she remembered the impetuous teenager, hell-bent on meeting her love. He would have laughed at her tenacity or been angry at her for taking such a risk. She tried to relay the story, Raphael looking intently at her, not letting go of her hand for a moment. When she'd finished, he kissed her fingers.

'If only I had known. I would have got the first ship or found a boat and sailed out the next day. I would have found you sooner. I trusted that my messages would get to you, that I could see you.'

She thought of the nasty lies that Wilfred led Raphael to believe. Raphael could have found her just weeks later; instead, they'd had to wait all this time.

'And then you joined the army.' Rose shook her head. 'I can't believe you were away so long, in another part of the world. All the time, I thought you had met another girl. Got married.'

'And I thought you must have a family of your own in Guadeloupe. So much time wasted.'

'I don't want to talk about it anymore. I want to know about the war, about everything that happened since the day of the hurricane. But we have time now. Don't we?'

'All there is.' He kissed her lips.

'I brought food. Would you like some lunch?'

'Yes, please.'

They sat and ate the roast breadfruit and fried plantain that she had brought, chatting endlessly.

'And what of Guadeloupe?' said Raphael as he wiped his hands and mouth with a cloth. 'You haven't said a single thing about your trip. It kept us apart for a whole week.'

Rose put her head down as she packed the lunch things away.

'Not as good as you hoped?'

'I don't know because I never get to go. Madame La Fleur leave without me.'

'True? But why?'

'I still don't know. She gone. She never send word. I don't know if she even turn back yet.'

Raphael screwed his brow. 'It doesn't sound right. Something maybe happen and she couldn't tell you in time?'

'But she go and she never leave a message with anyone. Everyone know I was going, and yet she just gone. I think is something I do wrong.'

'You? Impossible, Rose. You yourself tell me how well you get on. She seem to me like she really like you. You two could be mother and daughter. And sometimes mothers and daughters fall out.'

'That's the thing. There was nothing like that. She just change her mind.'

'I think is best not to think about it for now. And don't worry, whatever is the matter is nothing you do wrong.' Raphael put his arms around her shoulder. 'You'll see. Come Monday morning, she will have her driver come for you and everything will be fine.'

Someone behind them cleared their throat, and the couple turned around. Dunstan stood holding three sodas.

'Marceline would kill me if I leave you too long on your own.'

Raphael relieved him of two of the American soda bottles sweating in the heat. A cold fizzy drink was what they needed in the lazy afternoon sun.

The ship to Grenada was no longer visible on the horizon. The three sat on the wall as if posing for a painter, watching the sky turn hazy and the lazy waves drifting in and out on the sand but not quite touching their shoes.

Dunstan disappeared for another hour, having gone back to a bar where he'd met with some old friends from Roseau. Raphael and Rose spent the time on the beach talking each other through the journey of their lives, only plotting the main points because they had the rest of their lives to fill in the details and to carve out a life together with stories that they'd share. By the time Dunstan returned saying he'd secured transport to take him and Rose home, the couple had cried, laughed, hugged and planned a future that did not involve more time apart than was necessary. They grinned to each other as they parted company, their plans secret to themselves.

Rose was up and ready for Elise's driver who did arrive, as Raphael had predicted, early on Monday morning. They rode down to Picard in silence as Rose went over in her head what she should say to Elise. She couldn't be accusing. Raphael had thought there may have been an emergency and it could be a sensitive one, so she shouldn't rush in declaring her disappointment. She must be patient and listen to what Elise had to say.

The house stood as it always did, imposing yet ageing. The gates were open this time and so were the oak doors. Henry walked by and touched the peak of his straw hat.

'Good morning, Rose. She back.'

'Good morning, Henry. Thank you.' She smiled to mask the worry on her mind and slowly climbed the stairs, clutching the handle of her bag, packed for the week as normal though nothing felt normal to her. The air inside the house was chilling. The drawing room door was slightly ajar, and Elise called for Rose to enter.

'Elise!' Rose, suddenly more happy than worried at finally seeing her employer, practically ran into the room. She wanted to throw herself at her employer's feet and start apologising for whatever she'd done, but the atmosphere was not a happy one and Rose stopped dead in the middle of the room, halted by the icy glare in Elise's eyes. Rose's skin prickled. The curtains were only partly drawn to block the morning sunlight that usually poured into the rooms at that side of the house.

'Something wrong, Elise?' Rose stood and waited. Elise didn't speak at first. Her eyes sank to the floor. She looked as though she was in pain or about to cry. She coughed slightly then raised her head. The look of steel was there again.

'The first day I met you, Rose, I told you about how those girls I had working here were a burden to me.'

'Yes.'

'And can you tell me why that is?'

'I don't understand.' Rose struggled to call her Elise when, under the circumstances, Madame La Fleur seemed more appropriate.

'If there is one thing I can't abide is dishonesty, Rose.'

Rose shifted uncomfortably from one foot to the other. She didn't want to interrupt but thought if Elise would only say how she had been dishonest, she could prove her wrong. Rose would never lie to her.

'I don't want a big fuss or commotion here today, Rose. I just want you to know that I don't need you to come and work here anymore. I have to think about who I can trust. I might just pack up and go back to Guadeloupe. My cousins would welcome me with open arms. This house is far too big for one person, and I wouldn't need to employ anyone, anyone who could let me down.' Rose could see the disappointment in Elise's face.

'But Madame La Fleur. *Please.*'

'Rose, your money for the week is on the table by the front door. Please take it and go.'

'Just like that? What happen for you to make me go? Don't you find I work hard enough? Did I do something wrong?'

'I don't need anyone here, Rose. And that's the end of it. I can cope for myself. I just want you to go, and I don't want *any* fuss. You hear me? Now go. Cuthbert have instructions to take you back to the Indian River. There have plenty transport from there.'

Rose stood in silence. She shook her head. She turned to leave but swung back to face Elise, arms outstretched, shoulders high. Elise La Fleur did not even look in her direction. Finally, Rose started out of the room.

'Rose.'

'Yes.' Rose turned quickly.

'Is there anything you need to leave behind on the table before you go?'

'No, ma'am. I don't...' Rose was confused.

'Very well, Rose. Goodbye.'

Rose walked out into the hot Picard morning, the envelope with her weekly wage in her hand. She reached into the front of her blouse and felt for her locket. Ever since Rose had discovered that the locket had been a present from her birth mother, she fingered it in moments of worry, sadness or contemplation. Calling for guidance from the resting spirit of the Creole mother she never knew and seeking wisdom from the educated father she would never meet.

The money in her hand meant nothing, had no value. All that mattered was the way Elise had regarded her in those few minutes that changed her world. Elise had come to be more than an employer to her. She was the only friend that Rose really had, apart from May. At the gate, Cuthbert sat on the wagon. She stared vaguely through him and continued past as if the sight of a horse and wagon and a waiting driver didn't exist.

'Miss?' She heard his voice from a distance and walked on. She was at the coast road before noticing she'd arrived and stood for a while wondering where to go, what to do with the rest of the morning, wishing she had Raphael to turn to. He was sensible; he'd help her puzzle out what she'd done wrong. There was nothing she was aware of, that was the maddening thing. She felt like she needed to run back and plead with Madame La Fleur to tell her what she'd done.

She owed her that. Hadn't she been a faithful servant, attended to her every whim, kept her privacy? Then why?

Now she walked without direction towards the sea rather than towards the mountain road to find transport back to Moore Park. What would she tell them at home? They would think she was bad at her job; they would think ill of Madame La Fleur. Maybe they should: she was being unfair, she judged and condemned her without a fair trial. She held her hand against a swaying palm tree, the sea as restless as her mind. She put down her bag and sat at the edge of the grove of palm trees, feeling for her locket, rubbing the smooth silver and running a finger along the tiny clasp. Once she'd discovered where the locket came from, she had wished that there had been pictures of her lost parents; she would have loved to have talked to them now about what was happening. She allowed the anger she felt about the situation to bubble up, redden her face until she couldn't bear the feeling any longer and seethed the frustration like vapour from a boiling pot. All she was left with now was despair. Above all else, she'd lost Elise and she didn't know how.

Elise shook her head when she heard Rose's footsteps in the hallway as she stopped to pick up her wages. The main door creaked, and she could sense Rose standing there for a moment before closing it. She got up and walked to the oak doors and stood watching Rose leave the front gates. She noticed Rose hadn't accepted the ride from Cuthbert and puzzled over that. Had the girl repented and felt she could no longer accept any more of her kindness now that she had been found out? A bitter taste came to her mouth, and she turned to see Lucinda hovering in the hall.

'Madame? Would you like me to serve your breakfast now?'

Elise shook her head. 'I don't have the stomach for it.'

'So, we not going to see Rose again?'

'No Lucinda. Not again.'

'And would you like me to find you a new girl? Maybe Jane…'

'No, not her and not anyone. Thank you, Lucinda. I going and lie down for a while.'

'Very good, Madame. I'll send Jane before she leave to ask if you need anything.'

'No, no, don't fuss. I will come to you if I need something.' She turned and started to mount the stairs.

'Madame?'

Elise stopped, gripped the bannister but didn't turn around. 'What is it Lucinda?'

'I mean, I don't know what the problem is with Rose. Is it very bad, what she do?'

'It's between us, and I don't want a lot of gossip building up. You hear me?'

'Yes, Ma'am.' Lucinda took her leave, and Elise continued up to her bedroom.

She sat on the edge of her bed, tears welling in her eyes. She wished she hadn't had to talk about Rose: it was only making her sad after she'd steeled herself all morning to be able to handle the situation. So upset by Rose being capable of stealing from her so blatantly, she knew she would have to be harsh, leave no room for pleading or begging. Elise would not have been able to stomach it. She should not give Rose an opportunity to ask for forgiveness because she might be tempted to accept and it wouldn't be long before Rose took advantage of her again. Since she'd discovered that Rose had stolen her locket, she'd told no one. Her cousin in Guadeloupe had mentioned that she wasn't herself, and Elise had shrugged it off, tried to act normal. All the while her heart was breaking. She had come to love Rose; she didn't know how. Maybe because she saw in her a daughter she never had. She was certainly the best companion she'd had.

She looked over to the grand dressing table with its wide, ornately framed mirror and the perfumes and trinkets that lay there, waiting to bring her comfort. But her jewellery box and fine *eaux de parfums* could not rouse her from the ennui that would consume her for days to come. No, Rose had broken her heart and left her convinced that this would be the last time she would ever trust anyone to come this close to her.

Rose stood outside the lime factory of the Bath Estate in Roseau. She saw the ensemble of workers leaving and stood sideways on beside one of the acacias that lined the small road leading to the factory gates. She didn't want to be recognised by anyone, she had no business being there and she didn't want to have to explain herself. Three girls walked past the tree, linking arms, giggling about something or someone. They looked so content that they practically skipped. Perhaps she could get a job there herself; she could work alongside Raphael, find a home with him in Roseau.

She heaved a sigh, holding back thoughts of what her parents would say if they knew she'd been fired, what May would say. She saw Raphael leave the gates, adjusting his cap, and ran to him.

'Rose! How you come to be here?' Raphael held her arms and looked down the road and around. 'Your father not here?'

'No, is just me.' She looked down. Raphael took her bag from her and put his arm around her waist.

'Come.' He led Rose down the road and stopped when he came to the parade of shops and offices outside which they'd had their grand reunion in the rain. 'Is it something to do with Madame La Fleur?' he asked.

Rose began to cry now. She hadn't all day, stopping herself by blinking away tears, wringing her hands and chewing her lip. Anything but cry because she knew once she started, she'd never stop. Besides, crying might make this whole ugly affair true. Not a terrifying dream she was waiting to wake from.

'You go to her house?' Raphael asked, guiding Rose to a wooden bench outside a grocery store.

'Yes.' Rose sniffed and tried to dry her face with the cuff of her blouse. Raphael handed her his handkerchief.

'Rose, you can't cry like this. People will stare.'

'Let them. Let them know I never do anything and she just tell me to go.'

'She is angry about something. You should go back and clear it up. I'll go with you.'

'Is too late. Whatever it is, is too late.'

'Maybe not, Rose. She has you wrong. Maybe someone told her something about you.'

Rose stopped sniffing and looked up. 'That Jane girl, she don't like me and I don't like her.' She turned her damp face to Raphael. 'But why would Madame believe a lie about me? Because anything that girl could say must be a lie. I don't do nothing.'

'I know that, Rose.'

'She never even tell me why, and I didn't even try to change her mind.'

'All I know is that you are a good person and maybe she isn't as good as you thought.'

'I don't believe it. Not her. Something make her change her mind about me.'

'And you can't torture yourself if she don't give you a chance. So, if you not going back to plead your case, then you have to move on, best you can.' He stroked her hair and then took the handkerchief to dry her eyes and dab at her nose. Just then, her stomach groaned. Rose hadn't eaten all day, she'd just sat at the beach near Picard, staring out at the unchanging horizon, her emotions leaping from anger to pain and all the colours in between. Her mind jumping from thought to memory, trying to make sense of it all.

'I'll get you something to eat, Rose.'

They bought grilled fish from a vendor near the sea; they drank ginger soda, the gas bubbling in Rose's tummy until the anguish healed and her hunger abated.

'I'm sorry,' she said as they walked aimlessly towards the deserted market square. 'I shouldn't have brought this to you.'

'Then who else? Rose.' He stopped in front of her, put down her bag and held her hands. 'I want to always be the one you come to, if you have a problem, for everything.'

'I know. But still…'

They stood silently; the sun would set soon, streaks of magenta glowed in the sky and the light was dimming. The rare sound of a motor vehicle hummed from somewhere unseen, and the salt of the ocean was present in the air.

'It's late, Rose. You want me to take you home?'

'Not to Moore Park. I want to stay with you.'

'But, Rose…'

'They don't know, do they? They don't know I'm here. As far as Mam knows, I'm by Madame La Fleur. I could stay with you until Thursday and then go home and tell them Madame don't need me anymore.'

'You shouldn't lie to your parents.'

She looked down. 'I know, but I really want to stay.'

'One night.'

They walked back to Ma Lawson's house, not far from where Rose's family home used to be. By distracting his landlady, Raphael was able to sneak Rose into his room. It was an extension to her house that had a door leading straight into it from Ma Lawson's yard and another connecting it to the rest of the house. As usual, she had left food for him on the stove and he took it and shared it with Rose. They waited until it was completely dark and they could hear the thin walls of the house rattle with the cacophony of both Ben and Ma Lawson's snoring before they stripped off their clothes and lay in Raphael's bed. They shared everything that night: secrets, dreams, promises. Their skin perspired in the warmth and tangle of their limbs and blankets until they fell asleep, Rose's head against Raphael's chest, heartbeats lulling them into slumber.

Raphael was late rising in the morning. He and Rose had spoken in whispers, their fingers interlaced for hours until they'd fallen asleep. He'd told her a little more about his time in France; he didn't mention that his best meal had been with the French woman he'd slept with. He would have to keep a lot from her now that he had Rose back in his life, especially the whole truth about the war years, many of his memories of those days, the day when he longed for her and cried silently into the night for there never to have been a hurricane. No Wilfred, no distance and no time passed. The sun from the window warming his arm told him it was late.

Although her husband, Ben, left the house early, Raphael knew that Ma Lawson wouldn't be going to her mother's house until later and he had to wait so that he could leave with Rose. They spoke with hand signals and mouthed conversations while Ma Lawson gathered herself to go. She usually said a goodbye to Raphael and offered him morning coffee and something light to eat, but this morning she knocked on the door.

'Son, you late today,' she called from the other side. She never went into his room save for when she collected his clothes for washing on a Saturday morning, but only when he was awake and had left the door open for her.

'Yes, I know,' Raphael said. 'I going just now.'

'Me, too,' she said. 'I leave you breakfast and there is enough for your visitor, if she don't eat too much.'

She left then and the couple began to laugh. They had a hurried breakfast. Raphael made sure that Rose had a lift back to Moore Park before he ran all the way to the factory, praying that he wouldn't be dismissed on the spot.

A small bundle arrived for Elise at her estate in Picard. A brown paper parcel wrapped with string containing a red polka dot dress, a silk blouse and a skirt. Elise looked at the contents then shook them out, expecting her locket to tumble to the floor. Nothing. Elise—who had been in despair since she turned Rose away—let the parcel fall onto the Moroccan rug as she got out of her chair.

She walked aimlessly around the house and then around the grounds. As usual, she hadn't had any breakfast. Lucinda had said her mistress was fading away, becoming so thin the wind could take her. Elise had told her to stop fussing. Later, she would call Cuthbert to ready the wagon and take her to Roseau.

'Madame La Fleur.' Mr Bartholomew, the estate agent, was a Grenadian. He'd come to Dominica as a boy, had made good progress at school and had been shipped over to America to complete a brilliant college education. He returned to Dominica with a plan to buy and sell land having seen what potential a place like Dominica had when the decline of the government and laws concerning land ownership had come into question since the abolition of slavery. Over several years, the landscape had changed; money and property changed hands at an alarming rate, though none of it fell into the hands of the former slaves, who, for years after, worked as if they were still enslaved for a paltry sum. Of the previous slave owners who had stayed on the island, they held onto their land with the benefit of having cheap labour and still charged the ex-slaves rent for living in the small shacks on their property. Europeans coming and going meant deeds and property became big business, and even when there were fewer landowners left in Dominica, the potential to make money remained. Years later, this was still the case. Though the black and brown people became landowners themselves, it would be foreign developers who made the most money.

'To what do I owe the pleasure?' There was too much American in Mr Bartholomew's accent for Elise's liking, but she'd have to tolerate him if she wanted him to help her sell the house. She'd been thinking about it for weeks, months, if she was honest. Her financial situation had been changing for a while, and Mr Bartholomew's constant talk of her floating around on her own filled her thoughts. He may not have been aware of the extent of her situation, the staff certainly were not, but the money she had been left was dwindling. With so much time to think about her situation, she had made trips to her bank, had spoken to her lawyer and it was time for her to make a decision about her future. So far, she had made no mention of selling the house to Henry and Lucinda, her most long-standing servants. They would see Mr Bartholomew arrive to do an estimation on the value of the estate and they would know her intentions. She would eventually have to take them into her confidence.

'You know why I come,' she said. 'I'm considering the idea of selling up.'

Mr Bartholomew, who had been lounging back in his office chair, his hands patting the orb of his stomach, stood up, his eyes sparkling.

'Come in, come in. I haven't seen you in a long time. I was beginning to think you'd stopped considering selling.' He pulled up a chair for her on the opposite side of his desk. 'Cora!' He called across to the girl in the corner by the window of his office. 'Please set out some coffee. Or would you prefer tea, Madame La Fleur?'

'I would prefer a glass of water. Thank you.'

'I have to say, you are looking very lovely today.'

Elise cleared her throat and crossed her legs. She had bought the dress in Guadeloupe where the fashions were for a shorter length than they wore in Dominica. Her cousins said the new style was very American and they wore them that length in Europe, too. She would have bought a dress for Rose, had she been there. Put a feather in the new style of headbands and laughed until they were helpless. They'd listen to jazz and ragtime on the gramophone and learn the new dances from New York. Elise had not been in a dancing mood for some time. Her eyes were dull now, remembering her sadness during her trip. Cora arrived with a tall glass of water and propped it on the desk for her.

'Thank you,' said Elise. 'Listen, Mr Bartholomew. I'm very clear on this. I want you to price up the house and the land. I will even sell the furniture. I feel it's time I make a new life for myself. There is nothing here for me in Dominica again.'

'You don't have family, maybe, but you do have friends.'

'Yes, this is true and I will be saying goodbye to those as well. Even they considering leaving. Dominica is not the place it was.'

'It is changing, that's for sure. It is still a beautiful island. It will probably develop in time, but I suppose, that is irrelevant to you. You will have moved on to pastures new.'

'So you think you could find a buyer quickly?'

'How soon were you thinking of leaving us?'

'As soon as possible. I've already written to my cousins, and they know to look for a small house for me.'

'This is quite some turnaround, I have to say. But you just leave it with me and I'll start looking for a buyer. I'll come to you on Thursday for a proper valuation, but in the meantime, I'll have to see who's buying.' He began to chuckle, his eyebrows raising up and down as if he were taking her into some amusing confidence. She rose to leave. Mr Bartholomew stood, too.

'Let me walk you out.' He shook hands with Elise at the door. She breathed a sigh of relief on leaving the estate manager's office. She thought she would be sad, but the weight of finalising the decision to leave was in place and she would not be going back on it.

After Mr Bartholomew's evaluation, she gathered the servants in the lounge and told them about her decision to leave. She informed them that Mr Bartholomew was optimistic about there being a buyer very soon and that they could start to look for new positions straight away if they wanted to but she would appreciate their staying until she was ready to pack up. Lucinda looked solemnly at Henry, who in turn looked at Cuthbert, who lowered his eyes.

'Well,' said Jane. 'I think I will go now and start to look for work. Dominica don't have many jobs you know?' She looked accusingly at Elise.

'I'm sorry you feel that way, Jane. Thank you for your time here. I'll have your pay ready at the end of the week.'

Jane bobbed a curtsy, something she never did, and stomped out of the room.

'I apologise for her,' said Lucinda. 'I'll be here until you don't need me, Madame.' The other two were both in agreement and slowly began to take their leave.

'Before you go.' Elise stood up. 'I thought I would have a dinner with my friends very soon. I haven't seen them in ages, and I think is about time this house had a bit of life in it.'

'That's a good idea,' said Lucinda. 'At least if you have a dinner, you might eat something yourself.' Lucinda raised her eyebrow. Elise grinned.

'I know I haven't had much of an appetite lately, but I want things to change. I tired of wallowing like some miserable old lady.'

'Praise the Lord,' said Lucinda and quickly covered her lips with her fingers. 'I'm sorry, Madame, but you have us all worried.'

'And I shouldn't be like this. I'm sorry, too. It's just that I lost something that means a lot to me.'

'You mean, Rose?'

'It's nothing to do with Rose,' Elise said abruptly. 'I think that was all I had to say. You can go back to your duties.'

Cuthbert and Henry left the lounge, but Lucinda held back.

'What is it, Lucinda?'

'Madame, I'm sorry but I have to ask about Rose. Why you ask her to leave so sudden and why she never even come to tell us goodbye? You see, that's not like her.'

'People aren't always what they seem. You know that.'

'All I know is one day she was here, the next she gone and it doesn't seem right.'

'Lucinda, please. We've known each other a long time and I know you look out for me. You were the person I turned to when I lost Sebastian. I remember how you comforted me, and I've always respected you and appreciated your kindness. We are friends. So as a friend, I'm saying to you, I can't trust that girl and I can't have her in the house.'

'But, still…'

Elise sat again, raising a weak hand to make a barrier between herself and Lucinda. 'Enough. I don't want to—'

'The truth always have a way of coming out, Elise. For you to sell your house over something she do must mean is something big and, as a friend, I wish you would trust me with the truth.'

Elise turned sharply to her. 'Not this truth. No one needs to know.'

'Then, fine.' Lucinda started towards the door. 'Anyway, I'm here for you, Madame. As ever.'

'Thank you.'

Lucinda left the room and closed the door behind her. Elise went to the open window and folded her arms around her waist as she looked out at Henry cutting some roses across the lawn, getting up to swipe at his brow and stretch his back.

Elise hadn't walked in her garden for days, she realised, but Henry knew to cut fresh flowers and refresh the vases in the hallways, the main rooms and her bedroom. In months, maybe weeks, she would be saying goodbye to all of this. This life. The life she had made with Sebastian and the wonderful times they'd had. Apart from him being taken away from her far too young and long before they'd even fulfilled half of their dreams, it had been a wonderful house to live in. She'd dreamed of raising at least three children here. They had not had a single one. Rose had been the closest she had come to having a daughter. She'd ached for children and imagined a life with them so deeply, she'd felt they were there. With names, faces and characteristic gestures that she imagined they would have. She missed them as if they had been real, just as she missed Sebastian. She missed Rose, too.

Rose walked among the tall bushes by the river. In her bare feet, the ground felt cool, twigs and brambles pricked her toes but she continued into where the denser part of the forest grew, where the sun couldn't reach. She had been doing the laundry at the river with May when, once again, she was thinking about Elise La Fleur. There were moments when she tried so hard to forget what happened between them that she forgot where she was. Moments later, she would be shaken—sometimes physically—from a reverie, to find an angry Marceline, a frustrated May or a worried Raphael staring at her, wanting to know why she hadn't been listening. She had grown weary of quizzing everyone about what they believed she could have done wrong and became aware, rather quickly, that everyone was becoming weary of her questions. So she'd tried to bury her feelings, forget the whole sorry affair and learn to live with the not knowing. In time, she'd find out. She told herself this over and over, and still the sorrow hung over her, and she knew that, if anything, it was only becoming darker.

From somewhere outside her inner turmoil, she heard her name. May was calling her. She'd told her sister she needed to stretch her legs and she'd be back. But Rose had kept on walking. She looked around now seeing how far she'd walked and turned to run back to the spot she and May had been washing clothes. As she ran, she landed on a tiny sharp stone that embedded itself into her bare foot.

'Damn, it.' Rose dropped down to try to dislodge it.

'It's your own stupid fault for going around here without shoes.' May knelt in front of her. 'Here, let me look.' She lifted Rose's foot up and inspected it. She rubbed at it and produced the tiny piece of rubble causing all the pain then tossed it behind her.

'Rose, you're crying.'

Rose stood up and dusted off the back of her dress.

'Is it that painful?'

Rose shook her head. 'No, of course not. Let's go. We need to wring out the sheets.'

'I've already done them.'

'By yourself?'

'What choice did I have?'

'I'm sorry.'

'You are sorry about a lot of things these days, Rose. Anything you want to talk about?'

At the riverbank, the wrung-out sheets were rolled up and soggy. They sat in two large metal pails filled with other wet clothes.

'Nothing,' said Rose, picking up a pail, about to heave it onto her head.

'Wait,' said May. 'You'll need this.' She handed her sister a folded cloth and Rose placed it on her head before sitting the pail on top, one hand up to hold its side. May did the same with the other pail before they started off home.

'If you really have nothing to talk about, could you at least tell me if you heard anything I was saying before?' May was behind Rose who stopped, suddenly, and turned to her.

'I forgot my shoes,' she exclaimed.

May held them up. 'I have them. Keep walking, this is heavy.'

'I don't remember what you said.' Rose spoke over her shoulder.

'I know,' May called. 'I suppose you weren't interested in your sister getting married.'

'What?' Rose stopped again, unexpectedly, and made May stumble and lose the pail to the ground, the wet clothes rolling and unravelling on the grass.

'Rose! What the hell?'

'Mam wouldn't like it if I told her you swore.' Rose giggled as she put down her pail.

'We're going to have to take these back and rinse them through again.' May stooped to gather the sodden laundry, but Rose threw her arms around her sister so that they both fell backwards, laughing as they lay looking up through the spaces between the leaves above them. Rays of sun splashed their faces; grass and earth cradled them as they held hands.

'My big sister is getting married,' sighed Rose. 'I'm so happy. Have you told Daddy and Mam?'

'I've only told you. You're the only one who knows I've been seeing him.'

'Why the big secret?'

'It's not. I just know Mam is going to cry because I'll be leaving home. She thinks we're still little girls.'

'I know.'

'And she knows you and Raphael must be on your way to the altar soon. She's worried about you because he's poor and she doesn't know his family.'

'I can't help who I love.'

'I know you love him.' May squeezed Rose's fingers. 'But that doesn't seem to be enough for you.'

Rose turned to her. 'How you mean?'

'Rose.' May propped herself on her elbow. 'You walk around in a trance all day. You're hardly eating and Raphael is the only one you really talk to. You have to let go of what happened up at Madame La Fleur's. It was a nice job while it last, but you will find another one.'

'I'm still sad about it.'

'But you can't dwell on it forever. You did right to return her presents. Now you have to take back your friendship and your loyalty and give it to the people who love you. Who care about you.'

Rose sat up now, pulling up a wild flower and aimlessly pulling at the petals.

'I know. I will, May. I promise. Now we better sort out the washing.'

They got to their feet.

'Correction,' May said fixing her pail back onto her head. 'You have to sort it out. I already washed them once. It's your turn.'

Rose protested all the way back to the riverbank and all the time that May sat resting while Rose rinsed soil and leaves from the wet clothes and wrung them out as she stood knee-deep in the river.

Raphael waited at the foot of the hill until the service at Rose's church ended. It wasn't easy to get transport on a Sunday from Roseau to Moore Park, and he'd had to walk a lot of the way. It was very early when he set off. The sun on the mountain road was sultry, the air close, rain threatening to spill. He hoped it wouldn't because he was at the back of the wagon he'd flagged down in a new shirt: crisp cotton and pale yellow that reflected off his cinnamon skin.

'I not going very far,' the man had said to him. 'But you welcome to take a ride.'

Raphael had been so grateful because by the time he'd got to Glanvillia, he was perspiring and he'd wanted his new shirt to be spotless.

'No church for you this morning?' the old man in the wagon called over his shoulder. Raphael noticed for the first time that the man had no front teeth. He smiled so hard, it forced a grin from Raphael who had been concentrating on what he was going to say to Rose when he saw her.

'No, not for me. Neither you it would seem.'

The man turned his eyes back to the road. 'Not for some time.'

It had been quite some time since Raphael had entered a church. He'd walked into a nearly empty sermon in the little

French village his battalion had been stationed at, days before moving to the front line. By then, he'd been at war for a year. He'd felt several years older than his twenty-one years, his body sore, his bones aching. He'd seen too much, seen so many men die or have limbs hacked off because it was the easiest solution on the battlefield. He used to worship back home out of duty, but in the cool, echoey church in the French village, Raphael had sat in a back pew and prayed with all his might and hoped his prayers would be answered. He prayed not to have to stay another day in Europe, that it would all be over soon, that he would not have to kill another man, that he would not have to see another man die, that he wouldn't lose his friends, that he would see his parents again. His eyes were squeezed so tightly that they turned dry, and he nearly jumped out of his skin when the priest came and put his hand on Raphael's shoulder, looked down at him and smiled. The priest had walked from the altar to the back of the church with the communion cup and offered him the sacramental bread. The few other worshippers were all looking back at Raphael when the priest said something to him in French and held out a thin wafer. 'Amen,' Raphael had said and slipped the wafer into his mouth. The priest returned to his flock and continued the communion rite while Raphael stared up at a stone statue of Jesus. He let the wafer dissolve on his tongue.

He had no room in his life for God after that. He hadn't answered his prayers after all. Except for one, he thought, as the church at the top of the hill opened its doors and the congregation began to spill out. He caught sight of the demure beauty of the woman he had loved for four years and whose hand he had not been able to hold for most of that time. He realised now that Rose had always been his prayer, maybe even before he'd met her. His prayer and his answer.

Raphael bowed politely to Rose's family as Rose led them towards him, holding her straw bonnet for fear of the wind blowing it off as she sped down the hill.

'And you didn't think to at least come in and say a prayer, Raphael Douglas?' Marceline was still fanning herself with the large fan she always brought to church, breathless by the time she caught up with her daughter. 'And what of your family? They don't go to church either?'

Dunstan linked one of her arms and May the other, but she shrugged them off.

'They do,' said Raphael. 'Both of them. And I am not shy of church.'

'Well, my daughter do go and pray and I think you should at the very least consider the benefits.' She looked him up and down as if her head was on a well-oiled pivot.

'Thank you,' he said to her. 'I will take your advice. And consider them.'

Dunstan and May led Marceline away, May inviting Raphael to breakfast.

Rose grinned as she watched them go, her mother still bickering to herself.

'Mam won't eat a thing until I get back home.'

'Well, one thing I can say about your mother, she don't look like she starving.'

Rose playfully slapped his arm. He caught hold of her elbow and led Rose away from the departing congregation. Her mother called after her, but Rose shook her head as if she couldn't hear her as Dunstan and May dragged her home.

Raphael still had hold of Rose's elbow. He bowed down to whisper into her ear. 'Rose I want to marry you.'

Rose looked up at him, smiled and walked hastily towards the nearby wood.

He followed behind, confused. She walked towards a shallow river that forked into two distinct streams, one trickling gently away, the other a little deeper and flowing quickly past an old autograph tree. Raphael caught up with her, reaching for her hand so that she couldn't go any further.

'Rose? You didn't hear me?'

'Yes, Raphael, but I needed to hear you ask me, ask me properly, somewhere more private.'

'And will this do?' He pulled her to face him. 'It's just you, me and the river. So, I'm asking, the best way I know how, if you will marry me, Rose?'

'My answer is yes. Always yes to you Raphael.' She threw her arms around his neck and hugged him closely. He held her chin between his thumb and forefinger and looked into her eyes. He could read in those eyes exactly what she was thinking and feeling; she couldn't hide anything from him. But as happy as he felt, he knew there was a heaviness in Rose's heart. He kissed her lips.

'You have to forget about her, Rose.'

'What? Who you mean?'

'Elise La Fleur. You know who I mean. You haven't spoken about her in weeks, but I know she's there, somewhere in that mind of yours.' He smoothed her bonnet off and held it. She looked down.

'It's hard, Raphael. But I won't talk about her, about any of it, because this is so much more important. I think I can forget her, I just don't know why it is taking so long.'

'Look, all right, let's not talk about her. Instead, let's go to your father and I will ask for your hand properly. Like a gentleman. What you say?'

'I say yes.'

Her guests had brought some fine full-bodied bottles of port for after dinner, and Elise had ordered some wine from Guadeloupe, the French wine she'd enjoyed on her last visit. Every now and again, she made plans, plans about how she was going to live her life in Guadeloupe. Her cousin had told her about a small house on a windswept hill that was available for sale. Elise knew the area well; it wasn't far from the town where her cousin lived. The hills were velvety emerald in the sun. They'd taken a drive to visit friends, and Elise had seen a young boy driving his sheep across the hill and towards a farm. Even then, she'd pictured herself in a place like that, letting go of the big house one day, probably asking if Rose would ever consider being her companion in Guadeloupe some time in the future. Rose might have considered it at one point. She had said, once, that she was not likely to marry, that there was no one there for her. But then, someone did show up for her. Raphael. And things changed. Rose changed. Perhaps it was her young man who'd thought Rose could secret away some of her valuables so that they could run away together. But the young man had seemed honourable and Rose wasn't like that. Perhaps she'd fancied wearing the locket to look nice for Raphael and would have put it back or confessed to borrowing it. Elise would never know because she hadn't given the girl the opportunity to speak. It was all too late. It was all ruined, and she wished Mr Bartholomew would quickly find a buyer for the house, as he'd promised he would.

She looked at herself in the mirror, absently lacing her finger over the carvings of one of her jewellery boxes. What should she wear to cheer herself up, to brighten her demeanour before her guests arrived? Lucinda was downstairs setting the table. She'd asked her to put out the tall candlestick holders, and Henry had already cut some deep red roses for the centrepiece.

Elise stood and looked at her dark blue dress in the mirror. She looked fashionable with a dress that fitted like a tube with a velvet sash at the hips. She touched her throat and decided not to wear a necklace tonight.

They drank a lot, talked a lot and, with her guests, Elise was able to laugh for the first time in weeks. She allowed herself to drink more than she usually would. In fact, there had been several occasions when she'd sat in the high-backed chair in the drawing room and drank whisky late into the night. It helped her to sleep these days. She told herself she'd stop needing that late night shot. One of these days.

'Elise, I cannot get over how young you look in your new fashions. I think if you leave here, you should really go to New York, or London or even Paris. You'll make your West Indian neighbours so jealous in Guadeloupe.' Antoinette Leonce was very drunk, she held the stem of her wine glass as if it were a flower and drops of red tippled out as she gestured to her host. Her husband took the glass from her.

'What you mean,' said Marguerite Lamont, 'is that you are jealous of her clothes. We love your new style, Elise. It suits you so much. Speaking of which...' Marguerite tapped a palm to her cheek. 'I've become so forgetful in my old age.' She got up and left the dining room, walking in a way that told everyone that Antoinette was not the only one who'd had a good amount of wine. When Marguerite returned, she leaned over Elise's shoulder and placed a closed hand on the table beside her.

'When you came to us for dinner the last time, you left something in your room. Here.' She spread open her hand and revealed Elise's locket.

Elise gasped, her eyes glistening as if an old friend had returned from the past. Several layers of sadness—ones that she'd hoped had been well masked—stripped away and she took up the locket, holding it in both palms.

'You want for me to put it on?'asked Marguerite. Elise nodded slowly. Marguerite fumbled and squinted but couldn't get the clasp to behave.

'It's fine, let me,' said Elise. She shook her head, blinking, a smile spreading wide across her face.

'You obviously missed it,' said Marguerite. 'And please forgive me for not letting you know sooner. I was going to send it to you, but I can't always trust that boy I have doing my messages. So I put it in a safe place and forget all about it. Can you forgive me?'

'Of course I do.'

Her problem would be that she would never forgive herself. At least not for a long time.

Days after the dinner party, Elise had not decided what to do about her returned locket. She had not told anyone why she had terminated Rose's employment or what had made her finally decide to leave Dominica. She was glad she hadn't openly accused Rose of theft. It was easier to hide the shame she felt. She would have ruined Rose's reputation and prevented her from finding similar work. If anyone knew now how quick she'd been to point a finger at someone who was as honest as Rose, she would die of shame. She spent a lot of time wondering if she should go and apologise to her. She'd imagined Rose would have moved on with her life, seen Elise as some eccentric woman with too much time on her hands. It was easy to tell herself that Rose would be too angry, would turn her away and not give her the opportunity to ask forgiveness. And who would blame her? No, she would say nothing and she would leave the island along with her secret and regrets.

Elise walked out into the back garden where she saw Henry busy tending to the flower beds along the path leading to the river. It was the third time that morning she'd done that, walked aimlessly outdoors and commented on the weather before going back inside.

'Madame La Fleur.' Henry nodded to her again. He waited in case she had something to say, an instruction, a comment about his work, but when she just stared out towards the tall hedges, he continued working. Elise walked around for a while but came to hover close to where Henry was finishing up, about to collect his gardening tools.

'It look lovely,' she said.

'Thank you.' His knees creaked as he got to his feet. 'You know, my wife tell me that Rose getting married soon. She marrying that man from Grenada.'

Elise stared at him, lips parted.

'They going and live in Roseau, she tell me.'

Elise wandered back into the house. She'd expected this news but had hoped it would be Rose rushing to her one morning, breathless and breaking it to her when she brought her early morning drink. Listless, she went up to her room to rest.

She lay on her bed, legs folded at the ankles. She hadn't taken off her shoes. Just then, Lucinda knocked on the door.

'Yes,' she called lightly.

'Madame La Fleur, where would you like me to serve lunch?' Lucinda opened the door.

'I won't be having lunch today.'

'You should eat something, Madame. You've been like this for days. I thought you were better. I thought whatever has been troubling you had passed.'

Elise did not answer. She could hear Lucinda hovering by the door, imagined her shaking her head as she always did in that motherly way, though she was not old enough to be her mother. Softly, Lucinda closed the door behind her, leaving Elise to her thoughts.

1899

Antoine had managed to find odd jobs here and there as a field labourer and cleaning fish by the pier. The money was usually only enough to buy dinner for him and Nanette. The sailors said they would take him out on the boat with them and teach him how to fish for himself but so far hadn't followed through on their promises. The money he'd made on the silverware from the Hudson Estate didn't get them very far. They could eat but they'd had to stay in the dilapidated shack, and a whole month later, they were no closer to finding a place they could afford to rent. They had tried to make the old place as comfortable as possible. The shutters on the only two windows had rotted. Antoine had done his best to patch pieces of wood onto what was left of them, only because Nanette didn't like the idea of lizards or creeping insects coming in at night. The insects had found other ways inside the shack, either via the cracks in the old wooden walls or marching boldly through the door which didn't shut firmly, often blowing in when the wind picked up.

They had ventured into the big house on the estate. No one had shown up to claim it. They'd kept an eye out for anyone arriving in a wagon or carriage along the road up on the hill. No one came. The bracken and hedges were so overgrown, anyone would have to cut them away to even spot a road beneath all the foliage. It must have been a grand place, one of the biggest estates, most likely abandoned since the declaration of emancipation, the owners unable to sell it. Still, they made use of the old building, Antoine always insisting that they move in. At least the roof wouldn't leak and the termites had not ravaged the wooden floors, once highly polished, they imagined. Balls and parties like the ones their respective parents had thrown would have taken place in that house.

'I would like, once, to at least see my sister again,' Nanette said as she stared at her tightly fitting dress in the long mirror in one of the bedrooms of the big house. The only dress she could fit into was the one Margaret had given her, but now it squeezed against her chest and the fabric pulled across her stomach. She had searched the wardrobes in each of the once grand rooms, but there was not a stitch of clothing still hanging in any of them.

'Don't be sad, Nanette. I'm sure you'll see your sister again.'

'I am sad. My father didn't even come looking for me.'

'How do you know that?'

'It's not so big an island they couldn't have found me if they'd looked. They just didn't look.' She sat on the high four-post bed, covered only by a yellowing cotton sheet. Dust motes flew up from it and the smell of damp rose out of it.

'If you want, if you'd really like to, we could go and visit your parents.'

She looked up, her face brightening. 'Really?'

'Of course, my love. I don't want you to be sad.' He sat beside her. 'When the baby is born, we can go.'

'And don't you want to see your *maman*?'

'If I tried to see my mother, I have a feeling my father would shoo me away. He told me he'd throw me straight out of their house if I was with you. He wouldn't want to see our child. He most definitely wouldn't want to see me.'

'But your *maman* would. She would plead your case.'

'She has no real say,' said Antoine, swallowing hard. 'She agreed with everything he said about me and you. I wouldn't give them the satisfaction. You and I, we will be fine. We'll find a house. I'll find work. Maybe become a sailor.' He laughed at how ridiculous it sounded. 'And your parents could come to visit, even if mine wouldn't.'

'I think if I showed up at the house, my mother would take one look at me and feel so much shame, she'd probably lock me away forever. They would try to break us apart, ship the child abroad.'

'Well, then maybe we shouldn't go back.'

'I'd like my sister to know what became of me.' Nanette sounded close to tears.

'Then we'd find a way to tell her.'

'Oh Antoine, we are people with no history. At least not one we can talk about to our child. I want our child to feel as if she belongs to someone, to her family. I would never dream of casting her aside.' She lay back on the old mattress. Antoine rested on his elbow and gently rubbed her tummy.

'This baby will always be wanted, always be loved. We might not tell her our history, but we can build a future for her. A good one. We'll make sure of that.'

She held his hand on her tummy, closed her eyes and felt the baby moving around, as if she could hear their promises, as if she was happy about them.

They'd gathered lots of things from the house over the month—a mattress, a table, a couple of chairs—and put them in the old shack. Antoine had learned from one of the fishermen that the shack had once been owned by a slave family. When they were freed, the family grew food and kept chickens but were forced to leave when the Land Tax rose too high for them. The estate owners wrapped up the sugar plantation as they could not afford to run it. The few shacks on their land, except for the one the couple now occupied, had since collapsed. They had been set far away from the main house and obscured by a cluster of trees and shrubs. So the owners took off, completely ignoring what they couldn't see. No one knew who the land had been sold to until a relative from England turned up and started throwing grand parties, and most of his money away. They say he'd lost the house and the land to a rich American whom no one had laid eyes on and who allowed the fields to fall fallow and nature to diminish the house's once beautiful exterior.

In the dark shack that was now nothing more than rough planks of wood held loosely together by nails, with a corrugated iron roof over its one room, the couple sat and considered the dwindling amount of money they had left. They'd already thought to search the grand house for any hidden treasures, but of course, there were none. Probably already sold, shipped away or stolen. Nanette insisted, yet again, that Antoine try to sell her silver locket, and again, he refused.

Now, with only weeks to go before the baby was due to be born, Nanette became desperate and scared.

'I can't have my baby here, Antoine. Is there a doctor or a midwife nearby? And if there is, will we have to pay them?'

'I don't know.'

'What? You don't know if there is a doctor or if we have to pay someone to deliver the baby.' She was furious with him.

'I don't know, I don't know. I'll ask. I'll find out. Just don't you worry.'

'Don't worry?' she screeched. 'You think we can do this alone, Antoine? We can't. I need someone. I want my mother.'

'You really want me to get her here? Here to this place so that they can say, "I told you so"? I can't have that. I will find a way. You'll see.'

He left her for several hours. It was getting late. Antoine had left for work before sunrise that day and had come home with his shoulders blistering and his cheeks flushed beneath the constant tan he now wore. His milky white complexion had faded years ago. Neither of them looked themselves anymore. Nanette's hair was long, wild and bushy. She tied it back in a piece of silk fabric she'd found lying in the house. A ripped petticoat, perhaps. She had managed to leave her comb and hair brooches behind when they'd run away from the estate. The finest of her clothes that had no longer fitted her had been bundled away in a forgotten corner of the room, and she'd told herself they had no room for it and made the decision to leave her good things behind. She craved them now. Those and a warm, comfortable bed. The baby turned constantly, it seemed, and she hadn't had a peaceful night's sleep in weeks. She knew she'd treated Antoine awfully. It wasn't his fault they were this destitute. He'd been trying hard to keep her fed, happy, and she felt guilty for hurting him. She looked through the gaps in the shutters and saw the light dimming. She went outside to look for Antoine, wishing him home again so that she could say sorry. A dull pain in the lower part of her back troubled her and she began to rub it. The muscles of her tummy tightened involuntarily and she thought that something was wrong. A dark feeling fell over her as she looked across the landscape, up to the big house and back towards the road leading to the sea, from which Antoine usually appeared after a day of work. It was almost dark and there was no sign of him at all. She touched the silver locket and thought of her sister wearing hers, a memory returning of Elise laughing to her through the reflection of the mirror while Nanette combed her hair. How she wished she was back there.

She lay on their mattress, sleepy but staying awake until, finally, Antoine returned.

'You were so long.' She sat up, one of the lamps they'd scavenged from the main house alight on the floor beside the mattress.

'I said I would ask around and I did.' He sat and took off his boots. The fine leather, streaked and creased with wear and tarnished from work, came off easily. Nanette saw how worn the heels were, too.

'Antoine, I'm sorry. I was upset before, and I shouldn't have shouted.'

'I understand.' He came to sit next to her. 'I had a long time to think. No matter how you look at it, we can't stay in this hovel, Nanette. Even if we could get a doctor out here, this is no place to raise a baby.'

She touched his hand. 'What are you saying? We should move on? Now?'

'Before the baby comes, we need to travel back to Roseau. Dr Le Maitre was our family doctor. He will help us. You'll have the baby, and then we will find somewhere to live.'

'But Antoine, where will that be? We have no money and you'll be without a job in Roseau. You do not eat—you give me most of the food we buy.'

'I will do whatever it takes, Nanette. I will make a home for us. Even if I have to work for the people my parents dine with. You'll be close to your family. You can see your sister.'

'I would love to, but all I want, all I want in this world is to have you and this baby. Nothing else matters.'

'But you know we have to do this. You know we must go.'

'I know,' she whispered. 'I trust you. We'll go.'

They dowsed the light and lay in the dark.

'We have travelled so many miles only to find ourselves going back to where we started,' Nanette said.

'True, but sometimes you have to travel a long way to find home and maybe that home is in Roseau.'

'My home is you.'

On the Saturday, they packed the things they could carry. Antoine had arranged for a ride back to the capital on the back of a wagon. Nanette had been experiencing mild pains in her stomach for several hours. They had started, unexpectedly, before light. Antoine had fumbled with the lamp, trying to organise what they could take. He continuously asked Nanette if the baby might be coming.

'I hope not,' Nanette had said. 'It's too early.'

'But only by days. She wants to come now and we're not ready.'

'Perhaps she's not coming yet. Surely I would know.'

'Well, no matter, we have to go.'

They both checked the tiny space for anything important they may have left behind. As if sharing a thought, they looked at each other and acknowledged that if anything had been forgotten, it was probably too decrepit to bother with. And off they went, a fresh wind from the coast helping them on. Nanette walked slowly behind Antoine who was laden with two heavy bags.

A few of the townsfolk that Antoine had befriended were there to wish them a safe journey. Nanette didn't know any of these men. She had not had any involvement in Antoine's life outside the grounds of their temporary house and wondered for a brief moment if she could have fitted in with these people. If only Antoine could have been better paid and able to rent them a house in town. If. But there was no time to wonder. A new chapter was about to start, and with a flick of the reins, the wagon began its trundling descent of the hill towards the mountain road. Antoine sat in the back with Nanette against one side of the wagon. On the other side was some furniture that the driver, a skilful carpenter, had made and was taking to Roseau. There was a small table and a couple of round stools. Expertly smoothed and polished and covered by a piece of coloured fabric was a baby's cradle, one that rocked. Antoine and Nanette looked at each other. How naive they'd been to think they could carry on as they were with nothing to call their own and not a thing for the baby that was about to be born. He squeezed her knee. They smiled at each other, both reading the fear in the eyes of the other.

The driver, Mr Carl, had to make a few stops *en route*. As was the way: if someone was travelling any distance with a vehicle, they would always be asked to carry messages, drop things off, pick things up. And so Mr Carl stopped three times in the first leg of the journey. He had to pick up a package from one woman in Laudat, and she offered them something to eat. It was late morning and the couple hadn't eaten since the evening before. They'd had grilled fish at the edge of the beach while there was still light in the sky and they had some bread left over to go with it. They had run down their food reserves in preparation for leaving but hadn't thought to pack something to eat on the way. It was about a two-hour journey by wagon to Roseau, but with stops for messages, it would take them closer to three. They were grateful for a break, to eat, to stretch their legs and for Nanette to rub her back because of the pains she was having.

The woman who'd offered to feed them had a house that appeared to be set in a bouquet of flowers. Roses adorned the gate, yellow and red rose bushes surrounded the yard. Bougainvillea in pink, white and lilac surrounded the front of the house like air, and countless other colourful plants and shrubs crowded every possible inch of soil.

'Sit a while,' the woman said, looking especially at Nanette. 'How long to go?'

'Less than a week,' Nanette said, breathless.

'I don't think you have as long as that.'

They ate a good breakfast and took to the road again. The woman wrapped a bunch of red roses in some brown paper and handed it to Nanette.

'I saw you admiring them. I hope you find somewhere nice to put them where you're going.'

'Thank you so much.'

Back on the coast road, the sea air was cooling but the sun was relentless with its streams of heat so Mr Carl and his passengers had no shelter. Nanette began to feel faint, and the pains in her abdomen became more intense. She was moaning with the pain.

'Nanette?' Antoine's brow creased as he pulled her to him.

'She's coming, Antoine, I know she is.'

Mr Carl stopped the wagon. 'What for me to do?'

'Keep going,' said Antoine. 'How long until we get to Roseau?'

'Over an hour to go. I have one more stop, you know?'

'Please, just hurry.'

At the next village, Mr Carl jumped off the wagon and disappeared from sight. He'd stopped the horse by an avenue of trees and told them he would be quick. He had to deliver some money to someone at the first house in the village. He pointed to where he meant and rushed away. Nanette and Antoine got out of the wagon because Nanette needed to pace. She was in so much pain, she told Antoine, she couldn't take any more and that maybe they could find someone who could help her in the village.

'It's not too far to Roseau, Nan. I think it would be safer if we had a doctor we can trust. We don't know anyone here.'

'It's true, but I'm getting scared.' She squeezed her eyes closed, cradling her lower abdomen.

'Look, I can ask around for a midwife,' said Antoine.

Nanette looked desperately for signs of life but could not detect any beyond the avenue of trees. There was no house in view, let alone the one Mr Carl said he was going to.

'No, I think we should go.' She straightened up. 'I would prefer your doctor. Where is Mr Carl?'

'I don't know.' Antoine hugged her to him. 'Ah, I see him.'

Mr Carl came running towards them carrying a baby goat, tripping on the way. In doing so, he lost his hold on the kid and it trotted away. He chased it up and down before being able to take hold of it again.

'What are you doing with that?' said Antoine, his cheeks reddening as he perspired.

'One more stop. I have to deliver him.' He tied the kid, who bleated in fury, in the front of the wagon beside him.

Antoine helped Nanette back onto the wagon, shaking his head. 'I'm sorry,' he whispered. 'I had no idea this would take so long.'

Nanette gave a weak smile as she tried to make herself comfortable. She felt the cramp in her limbs, and she wanted to bathe away the sun and dust from her hair and skin. She wanted a soft comfortable place to have the baby. She feared the baby would arrive in the rattling wagon with a noisy goat complaining of being dragged away from its mother and Mr Carl continuing to make stops and relay messages on the way.

She turned her head away from Antoine and dabbed away the tears.

Far into the distance, the church spire in the centre of Roseau could be seen. Nanette's groans and cries of pain had unsettled both Antoine and the driver.

'We're nearly there,' Antoine kept saying. Nanette puffed heavily as she held his hand.

'Please, Antoine, the baby is coming. Tell him to stop. I can't make it to Roseau.'

'Yes, of course. And don't worry.' He stroked her drenched brow. '*Monsieur*, stop at that convent up there, *s'il vous plait.*'

The convent was not far from the road. Mr Carl cracked the whip as the tired horse tried desperately to pick up a pace that it couldn't find in its legs. It grunted in protest, steam rising from its shiny black body.

They stopped at the front gate of the low-built convent, and Antoine helped Nanette down from the wagon. She was hot and disoriented and clung to his sleeve as he guided her to the door and banged on the wooden panel. Mr Carl turned his wagon and rode it away, wishing them luck. A little further on, he pulled the wagon to a stop, jumped out and ran back to them carrying their bags and the bunch of roses.

'You will need your things.' He grinned at them and rushed away again to continue his relay to and from Roseau.

Antoine called their thanks and banged on the convent door again. Shortly afterwards, a nun with very black skin pulled open one of the doors. She smiled, looked at Nanette and ushered her in without words. She led the couple into a cool corridor and opened the door into a small room with a single bed, a chair, a stool and a low table. The window was narrow and let in very little light. The nun and Antoine helped Nanette onto the bed and removed her shoes.

'This is a fortunate day for you to arrive.' The nun had an African accent. 'There is a nurse visiting today. Sister Mary Celeste was taken ill and she is being attended to. I will go and see if the nurse can help you, too.'

'Thank you so much,' said Antoine.

'It is my pleasure, and I'll collect your things at the door.'

'I'll help,' said Antoine, about to follow her.

'You stay with your wife. I'll return soon.'

Very shortly, three other nuns appeared in the room. Their headdresses were crisp and white and fanned like wings at each side of their head, their garments long, dark and heavy.

The older of the nuns introduced herself as Mother Jeanne Marie. She asked Antoine if he was French and proceeded to speak with him in French, asking how he and Nanette came to find themselves at the convent. He explained everything as hurriedly as he could, and when Nanette let out a cry of distress, he went to her side and looked pleadingly at Mother Jeanne Marie.

'But my wife…' he said.

The nuns stepped aside and a woman with the same headdress but a simple black dress stepped up to the bed, held Nanette's hand and told her not to worry, she was a nurse. In French, the black nurse asked how often she was getting contractions.

'*Très souvent*,' said Nanette and rolled onto her side in pain.

'Then we must make you comfortable and I will examine you. My name is Cecile.'

Mother Jeanne Marie beckoned the nuns out of the door.

'Come, *Monsieur*,' she said to Antoine.

'No. I'll not leave her.'

'Cecile is both a nurse and a nun,' said the Mother. 'Your wife is in good hands.'

'He stays,' breathed Nanette and held out her hand to Antoine who knelt beside the bed and took it.

'I'm not going anywhere.' He looked from Cecile to Mother Jeanne Marie who exchanged glances.

'Sister Mary Agnes,' said Cecile to the dark-skinned nun who had first welcomed the couple. 'Boil some water, find some clean sheets and towels and be quick about it.'

Mary Agnes curtsied and hurried off, closing the door behind her.

It was dark when the baby showed herself to the world. A tiny bundle with a slippery body and a cry so loud it must have woken the other nuns. Cecile lay the naked baby onto Nanette's bare chest and the baby stopped crying in search of comfort from her mother's breast. Antoine grinned at Nanette. Her eyes looked hazy and her lids fell heavily, a slight twitch in her lips as if she wanted to smile but couldn't.

'Something…' she whispered to Antoine. 'I don't feel right.'

Antoine swivelled his eyes to the nurse at the foot of the bed.

'We have a lot of bleeding,' said Cecile. 'But I think it is easing.'

'Is it all right? Will Nanette be all right?'

'I believe so.' She continued to attend to Nanette, not once looking at the couple.

'I think she will be settled now,' said the nurse after a short while. 'The bleeding has stopped.'

Nanette looked at Antoine and sought his attention with her eyes, beckoning him closer so that she could whisper. 'Tell Elise that someone else will be wearing the other locket.'

'What do you mean?'

'And I want our baby to be called Rose.'

'Yes, my love, but why are you speaking like this?'

'Take her.'

'You hold her. Feed her. She's hungry.'

Nanette's head lulled from side to side and she tried to lift the baby from her breast.

'Please. I love you.' Her voice faded and her eyes blinked shut, and he knew as he looked from the tears leaving her closed eyes to the baby wriggling in the palms of his hands that he had lost her forever and the weight that landed in his chest would never lift.

Cecile sat cuddling the baby girl she'd wrapped in a blanket. The baby did not cry. She was good, Cecile thought. In a pouch was the silver locket and some money that Antoine had begged from an old friend in Roseau, where he'd ridden to on horseback shortly after bidding his child farewell. The nurse also went back to the capital, but by canoe. The oarsman followed the tall reeds by the river to the house of Marceline and Dunstan Charles.

It was only just light when Dunstan came to the door, rubbing his eyes and letting out a loud yawn.

'Is that you? Cecile? Marceline is expecting you?'

'And good morning to you, Mr Charles.' Cecile's smile was full and bright considering she had been up all night after the birth, trying to appease a hungry, crying child whose parents were no longer there to look after her. The baby was asleep now and weighing so little in her arms, she could forget she was there.

'Come in,' said Dunstan. 'I'll call her.'

'No need to call no one. I'm up.' Marceline wrapped a towelling dressing gown around her wide middle and stared with open eyes at the bundle in Cecile's arms.

'I know I am taking a big liberty here,' Cecile said. 'But I know you have been waiting for another child for nearly three years. We've all been praying for you, and finally, He has answered your prayers.'

Marceline smiled, confusion on her face as she looked from her goddaughter to Dunstan and then at the sleeping baby.

'But how?'

'A young girl came to the convent when I was there tending to one of the sisters. Sadly, the girl died and this little one is alone in the world. I thought…'

'Yes,' said Marceline, reaching to take the tiny bundle from Cecile's arms.

'A boy?' asked Dunstan.

'A little girl. Her name is Rose. All she has is her name and this.' Cecile held out the pouch. 'There's money and a locket from her mother that she must always wear. When she is old enough, I suppose.'

Dunstan opened the pouch and revealed the silver locket.

'Beautiful,' Marceline said.

'She is,' said Cecile. 'So you think you can take her?'

'You came to answer my prayers, Cecile, and I thank God for you. I'm sorry for her parents, but I promise you and Him that we will love her and we will look after her and she will be our daughter. She has made our family complete.'

A small girl came running out of the bedroom.

'What is it?' she said.

Marceline crouched down to show her first daughter the new addition to the family. 'A little sister. All for you, May.'

May screwed her tiny pink lips.

'Hope she do more than sleep.'

'We'll see what she do,' whispered Marceline. 'We'll see.'

Chapter 6

Applause, peals of laughter and voices raised in joy rang out into the early afternoon air surrounding the small wooden church on the hill. Marceline had fussed all morning and cried through most of the ceremony. May had helped Rose dress: Marceline, being too emotional, was all fingers and thumbs and only able to help by telling May what to do.

When Dunstan saw his youngest daughter standing in the doorway of her bedroom in her wedding gown, he'd cried.

'Dunstan, don't be foolish. It's just a dress,' Marceline had said, but her eyes were so watery with tears, she could barely see her daughter.

'Both of you, please. You going and make Rose nervous.' May had been straightening Rose's veil.

The dress was of pure white cotton overlain with a delicate layer of white lace. The sleeves were long and close-fitting, of plain white cotton with a long row of pearl buttons to fasten the cuff. The neckline lay at the base of Rose's neck. Around her waist was a pink cotton sash tied in a bow behind. The dress fastened at the back from the neck with white pearl buttons mirroring those on the cuffs. On her head, she wore a mobcap headdress with stiff white netting forming a veil all the way to her hips. White slippers adorned her feet over white stockings. Her bouquet was a small posy of pink, red and white orchids with allamanda. Around her neck, she wore her silver locket.

Raphael had bought a brand new suit. He had borrowed a tie, although it was very worn; the smile he wore when he saw Rose walking down the aisle on her father's arm more than made up for it and the uneven heels of his shoes, polished as highly as his nervous hands could make them. Once Raphael had placed the two-shilling wedding ring on Rose's finger and the priest had pronounced them man and wife, the applause was overwhelming.

The church doors were thrown open; the warmth and happiness that flowed down the hill touched the woman standing beside a tall tamarind as she placed a delicate hand on her heart.

Elise La Fleur could not take the distance any longer. It was Lucinda, after she'd confided in her, that had told Elise that she needed to swallow her pride.

'Madame, your heart is breaking and you don't look well at all. If nothing else, the girl is owed an explanation.'

'She will be so angry with me.'

'And so she should. You were wrong, and now you know you wrong, is time to put things right.'

'I don't know how I will even begin to make amends. She will never accept an apology from me.'

'You don't know that.'

'She will have changed her opinion of me, and she probably won't want to see me.'

'Well, she will have to decide. Just as you must decide to do right by her.'

Elise turned away, wringing her hands. 'I don't know what I will do when all of this has gone.' She looked up at the ceiling and around the walls of the living room. The framed painting of her and Sebastian on their wedding day was always supposed to hang there, but soon, she would have to move all her grand things and sell most of them. The new home she intended to buy was not big enough to house it all, and she needed to make as much money as she could from the property and its contents.

'You will be just fine, Madame.'

About a week later, she took a trip to Moore Park. Cuthbert had already left her employ, having taken a new job when he knew there was a buyer for the house. She had to rely on a friend of Henry's, her groundsman, to arrange a ride for her. She had never been to that part of the island. In fact, she'd only ever driven into the countryside a few times with Sebastian, but even then, she'd never come this far into the mountain villages. The land was lush with rolling hills of wild and abundant forests. So different to the manicured hedges and neat lawns of her grounds. The driver put her down at a clearing where a couple of houses built on either side of the road had their doors flung open. A woman came out of one house with a screaming child over her shoulder.

'You lose your way?' she asked Elise.

'I trying to find the home of Rose Charles.'

'*Rose*?'

'Yes, you know her?'

'What she want?' The woman in the house opposite came out in a white petticoat and a red headscarf, the knot on top of her head. Her hands were wet, and she was carrying a bucket of soapy water which she splashed across the flowers in her front yard.

'She say she looking for Rose,' the woman carrying the crying baby called. She shifted the child to her other shoulder, and it seemed to quieten him.

'And what you want with Rose?' The woman in the headscarf put down her bucket and crossed her arms.

'She know you?' The baby was settled, and at last, the women stopped shouting across the road at Elise who stood looking from one to the other as they fired questions at her.

'She used to work for me,' Elise said.

'Oh! You the one that let her go?' Both women shook their heads from side to side.

'Please,' Elise pleaded, 'if you could just point me in the direction of her house.'

'Just up so the house is. But Madame, you know is Sunday and they at the church?'

Elise looked at her wristwatch. 'Still?'

'Is a long service today.' Both women looked in the direction of Rose's house and presumably the church. It seemed that everything she needed, she'd find if she continued up the narrow road. Elise waved to her driver to signify she was going by foot.

It was past eleven and most Christian services should have been finished by now, but Elise noticed that most of the houses were empty. She imagined something important was happening. A little way on, she spotted the church. In fact, it was the voices coming from the church that drew her attention. The voices were loud and melodic; a huge choir must be gathered inside. Elise hurried along, thinking she could take a look inside the church. She hadn't been to mass in a long time, the frequency of her church visits diminishing after Sebastian's funeral until her faith in God left her altogether. She felt glad that Rose still had Him in her life, and perhaps, her religion might allow Rose to forgive her.

At the bottom of the hill, she stopped. The singing ended and so might the sermon, so she decided to stand by a tall tamarind and take some shelter from the sun. The air was quite different from the coastal air, and she had to catch her breath. Suddenly, the people inside the church began to laugh and clap. The clapping grew louder as someone threw open the doors. Elise looked up the hill and saw a young couple emerge, closely followed by the congregation who were still applauding, chattering and waving. Elise saw the bride in a dress that reflected the sun and glowed as bright as her smile. It was her Rose. She placed a hand on her chest to still the rapid beat of it. She wouldn't have been able to stop the tears if she tried.

The guests showered the couple with their congratulations and kisses, shaking Raphael's hand until Rose feared it might fall off. As a woman with a damp face kissed Rose on her cheek, she thought she caught a glimpse of someone who looked like Elise, standing by a tree down the hill. The woman stepped away from the tree, held up a hand and gently waved.

'Raphael, just a moment,' whispered Rose. 'There is someone I need to see.'

'Where you going?' Marceline looked puzzled as Rose left the crowd and began to walk towards Elise. The people whispered and pointed. They wanted to know what this high-class Creole woman was doing in Moore Park. Marceline made it her duty to loudly reiterate the injustice this woman had done to her daughter.

Rose held her bouquet as she stood in front of Elise, not knowing what to do with it. 'Madame La Fleur?'

'Rose, congratulations. You are the most beautiful bride. I'm sorry to disturb your wedding day. I had no idea. I came hoping I could talk to you. But, of course, I can come back.

I...' Elise paused mid-sentence and stared at the locket around Rose's neck.

'I can talk for a few minutes.' Rose put her fingers to her locket as Elise continued to look at it.

'It's incredible,' Elise gasped.

'What is?'

'It's, it's, your locket.' Elise pulled a silver chain from beneath her blouse but kept her hand around the pendant that hung from it. 'I need to find a way to explain something to you, but this isn't the day. I should come back. You have all these people here.'

As she said this, Marceline appeared at Rose's side and stood with hands on hips, screwing her eyes at Elise La Fleur.

'Mam, this is the lady I worked for.'

'I know who she is. What I want to know is what she doing here?'

'I was about to leave,' stuttered Elise. 'I came to talk to Rose, they didn't tell me it was her wedding day when they directed me here. Again, congratulations, Rose. I see you marry your sailor at last.' Teary eyed, she cracked a wide smile. 'I'm happy for you. Had I known it was today, I would at least have brought a present.'

'Why?' demanded Marceline. 'We wouldn't want your present.'

'Mam, please. Let us have a few words.'

'It's fine, Rose. I can come back.' Elise went to leave.

'Madame La Fleur,' Rose said. 'You know how long I waited for you to come and explain what I do? Too long. You come all this way, so is best you just tell me.'

'You're right, Rose. God knows this has gone on too long. I did something awful. I made the biggest mistake when I let you go like that. You see, just before the trip to Guadeloupe, I come to the market and I saw you. You were wearing the locket you have on, and, you see, I took it for mine.'

'So!' Rose exclaimed. 'That is why you leave me behind. You think I steal your locket?'

Raphael walked down the hill. Rose's family and a few members of the congregation followed but gave the women a little distance to talk.

'Rose, I'm so sorry. I know you will never forgive me.'

'Forgive you? I cried big, big tears from the day you go to Guadeloupe and don't take me. Why didn't you just walk on me so you could see is not your locket I have.'

'But Rose, it is. I mean, it's the same locket. I couldn't mistake it. See?' She opened her palm to reveal her own locket. 'Can you see? Mine was an original design. Especially made. I would know it from miles away. I never believed there could be a third.'

Rose and her mother inspected both lockets.

'And how you come to have this locket?' Marceline asked Elise.

'My father had them made. One for me and one for my sister, who died.'

'What was your sister name?' Marceline drew nearer and folded her arms.

'My sister's name was Nanette.'

'Papa God, bless us.' Marceline threw her arms up in the air.

'What is it, Mam?' asked Rose.

'Tell me,' Marceline said to Elise. 'How your sister die?'

'She die in childbirth.'

'Just over twenty years ago in a convent just outside Roseau?' asked Marceline.

'Yes, but how you know?'

'I know because the nurse who deliver her baby was my Goddaughter. Is she who bring the child for me to raise. Her father, a white man, send some money and her mother locket with the child.' She slapped both hands to her puffy cheeks and called on the Holy Virgin in a long, drawn-out voice. '*La Sent Vyèj.*' By now, the whole wedding party had gathered closer.

With shaking hands, Elise held Rose by her wrists, the bouquet between them. They smiled, one face reflecting the other; unnoticed until now, the similarity of their smiles.

'Elise, you are my *aunty*?' Rose was light-headed.

'Rose, please. I'm so, so sorry I let my stupidity get in the way. I have allowed bitterness to rule my judgement. I wish I had behaved differently, better—'

Rose threw her arms around her aunt before she could finish her sentence.

'Please, come and join us for a drink and some wedding cake,' Rose said.

'I feel I should come back another day. You make this day all about you and your husband, Rose, and if you permit me, I will return.'

'Of course I permit you. I want you back in my life again … aunty.'

They both grinned. Elise dabbed Rose's damp face with a silk handkerchief and used it to dry her own tears.

'Enjoy your day, Rose, and I'll send a message to ask when is a good time.'

Rose took her hand. 'Any time is a good time. But I will be moving to Roseau with Raphael very soon, so I'll send word when I settle down.'

'Of course. And I will have time buy you a wedding gift.'

'The only gift you can give me is to tell me about my mother.'

'It would be my pleasure.'

Raphael put his arms around Rose and the two watched as Elise walked away along the grassy track to the road. Dunstan announced that it was time for a drink and some food and led the group to the village centre where a lavish lunch had been laid out and three elderly women stood fanning flies away from the feast.

After they'd eaten, Raphael's parents called him and Rose to the side with some news.

'We're not going to America,' his mother said, squeezing his hand. 'We decided we will stay here.'

'By "here", your mother mean we selling up and finding a place in Dominica,' said his father, all three of them hugging in celebration. Rose laced her fingers together at her chest. The day was complete. The celebrations continued long after the last drop of rum was poured into Dunstan's glass.

***

The dry season drifted idly by until the island became enlivened by the fiery, stormy months. Rose and Raphael found a house in Roseau close to his job at the lime factory. He would prefer to have the sun on his back all day and work the land, but until they could save enough for a country dwelling, they would make do in the two-room house close to the sea and only minutes from the place they first met.

It was a time for change with May's wedding coming close behind Rose's. During the ceremony, Marceline cried so hard for losing both of her daughters to men who'd move them so far from home that all attention was on her and not on the bride. Rose had looked at her mother—who

245

suppressed a wailing sound—trying to shush her, though her efforts were in vain. Dunstan had threatened to have her removed from the church. May's wedding was a memorable affair. Up in Thibaud, where the sea crashed relentlessly into the rocks by the coast. The big white church swelled with the voices of the choir as May married her beloved Timothy, also a teacher and nine years her senior. The couple settled in Thibaud, despite Marceline's protests.

One of the hardest changes for Rose to accept was that Elise La Fleur was leaving.

'I'm putting the sale on hold for a while,' said Elise. 'I'd like to be here for at least a while so I can get to make up for what I did and to rekindle our friendship.'

Elise and Rose sat in the garden of the big house as they had done in the days when Rose was working for Elise. Now she was visiting her aunt.

'I'm so happy you're staying a while. I cried when you said you were selling up.'

'Well, there was a time when I thought there was nothing here for me and I had no choice.'

Rose reached across the table set up on the lawn and took her aunt's hand.

'But now,' Elise continued. 'I can leave with a clear conscience, knowing that you forgave me for my stupidity. You are so understanding, Rose. I wish my father could have been when he allowed your mother to walk out of our lives, never to return.'

'So you never knew about me?'

'Antoine came back. He told me there was a baby, but he never told me that Nanette had passed the locket on to their child. I was still a young girl when he told me about you. I asked mother if we could try to find you, but my father stopped us and my hands were tied. I could only put you in my prayers and hope that you were well. Antoine said you were with a family in Roseau who would love you, and I had to satisfy myself with that.'

'And what about him? My father is he…?'

'As far as I know, your father is still alive. He went back to France. His family wanted nothing to do with him, and he said he would leave and try to find work. He was so heartbroken. He told me that everything about Dominica reminded him of Nanette and that he was a broken man.'

'That is so sad. I wish I could find him. Tell him I'm happy, tell him about me.'

'It is the hardest thing in the world to go on living without the people we love, Rose. But in the end, I think he found happiness.'

'You saw him again?'

'No, he used to write to me. My family knew I had spoken to him, and father said I was forbidden to talk to him or his family, but I used to send messages and he sent some back to me. That's how I know he went to France. A year after he left, he sent me an address. Now, don't get excited, Rose. I don't know where he is now. Not long after I got married, his letters stopped coming. I wrote and wrote, and he never returned a letter. So I have no idea where he is.'

Rose lowered her head. 'It's a shame, but I don't suppose I will ever go to France. Or that he will return.'

'Rose, don't fill your heart with sad thoughts. Years after Nanette died, your father wrote to say he was getting married, that's how I know he found happiness again. He married a French woman, a seamstress. They had twin boys, Benoit and Giles, if I remember rightly.'

'I always wanted brothers.' Rose smiled.

'Be happy for your father, Rose. If he found love again, it's the best outcome.'

'It's true. I am happy for him. Even though I never knew them, I love him and my mother. And I miss them, too.'

'Don't worry, Rose. I suspect that one day you will have a houseful of children and no time to miss anyone.'

'I will miss you.'

Marceline continued to bemoan her sadness and loss to anyone who cared to listen to her, wringing her hands, distraught now that both her daughters had abandoned her. Worn down by his wife's malaise as she went about her day-to-day life, Dunstan had threatened to leave, too, if she continued in that way.

'You forget why I marry you, Marceline?' he asked one day.

'What you mean?' She stopped what she was doing and looked into his eyes for the first time in a long while.

'I marry you because I wanted to spend the rest of my days with you,' he replied. 'If that's no longer enough, if I'm not enough, then I will leave here, too.'

'Dunstan, what you talking about? You can't leave me.'

'Why not?'

'Because I want to spend the rest of my days with you.' Her demeanour spoke of frustration with her husband, but her eyes told a different story. She folded her arms.

'So you love me then?' Dunstan's forehead creased in expectation.

'Yes, I love you, ole fool.'

'Well, stop complaining your daughters leave and give me a kiss.'

Marceline kissed her teeth and then kissed Dunstan where they stood in the front yard, much to the amusement of a couple passing by.

'Now, Dunstan, shut up, go inside and sit down while I bring you your dinner.'

Elise La Fleur had spent nearly two years in financial difficulty. The cost of keeping such a big house once the money from her late husband's coffee plantation neared its end, meant her days of clinging onto the house were running out. Just she and Lucinda alone remained. The gardens were overgrown, and most of the rooms were kept closed, the furniture covered in dust sheets. Mr Bartholomew called her constantly to remind her that with every month, she was losing another buyer. Her cousins in Guadeloupe sent endless letters saying that although she had missed the opportunity to buy the house she originally liked, another opportunity had come up but she must act quickly. She just didn't have the heart to leave Rose and her family.

A year after Rose and Raphael got married, Rose gave birth to a baby boy. He was the most darling child that Elise had ever seen and she spent hours at Rose's small house in Roseau, feeling at last that she was part of a family. She had coped with the heartbreak of, firstly, losing her sister, not being able to have children of her own and then losing her husband. Rose's baby brought new meaning to her life.

One day Rose made another of her frequent visits to her aunt with her new baby.

'I know what is happening,' Rose said to Elise who held the baby boy. He spluttered and gurgled, and Elise could not take her eyes off him.

'What do you mean?' Elise said, distracted.

'Aunty, I know things are not going well for you and that money is, well, it's a problem now.'

Elise handed the baby back to Rose. 'Lucinda had no right coming to you.'

'Of course she had. We worry about you, aunty. Look at this place. Before I get married, you were determined to go to Guadeloupe. You had your heart set on it.'

'Only because I didn't think I had a life here. But now there's you, Rose. And this little one.' She stroked the baby's cheek.

'I want to give you back the money you gave us for our wedding present.'

'Don't be silly, Rose. I can't believe you still have it.'

'I kept it for a rainy day. And this is a rainy day.'

Elise got up. 'This is my rainy day, Rose. Besides, I know what's happening with Raphael's job at the lime factory. I know they might close it.'

'You knew about that?'

'I read about it. The newspaper said the production of citric acid crystals has lessened and the production of lime is declining all over the island. We're all going to be as poor as each other, so we need to help ourselves.'

'And you must help yourself. You can live a simpler life in Guadeloupe if you sell this place.'

'How can I leave? It would break my heart.' She returned to the sofa where Rose sat, the baby being lulled to sleep in her arms.

'Me too, aunty, but we don't have a choice.'

It was a hot and sunny morning in February when Rose and Raphael stood with their son at the port to say farewell to Elise.

'Rose, we will write all the time and I will come back to see you whenever I can.' Elise was tearful, and she trembled as she hugged Rose for as long as time would allow. Raphael stood a little way behind holding their son.

'I will write to you, aunty. I'll tell you how we are all doing. If I ever can, I will come and see you in Guadeloupe.' Rose was also in tears and had been distraught when she'd found out that Elise had finally booked her passage even though she knew the day would come. She would miss her aunt but would always be grateful for finding a piece of herself in Elise.

Rose and Raphael waited at the port until the ship was out of sight. The sea was calm, and Rose was sure that Elise would have been watching the island disappear before finding a seat on the ship.

The baby struggled. His father, Raphael, held him closely before placing him gently into his mother's waiting arms. Raphael wrapped a warm arm around Rose's shoulders and led her away from the port. It was time to go home.

Thank you for choosing

The Long Way Home

I really hope you enjoyed it. Your thoughts mean the world to me, and I'd love to hear what you think. If you have a moment, please consider leaving a review—it makes such a difference in helping new readers discover the book.

You can share your review at your preferred retailer.

I also love connecting with readers on social media, so please do follow my journey and say hello on Instagram and TikTok. @franclarkauthor

Thanks so much for your support!

Fran x

Now read the next book in the Island Secrets Series: *When Skies Are Grey*

Connect:* Hop onto my *website* for links & info!
franclarkauthor.co.uk

And: Join my ***mailing list*** for a Free Read! And be ahead of
all my offers, news and updates!

Also by Fran Clark

Lovers

Other books in The Island Secrets series:

Holding Paradise

A Prayer For Junie

When Skies Are Grey

The Hope series:

Wherever You Will Go

However Far We Fall

About the author

Fran Clark is an author of emotive women's fiction, whose stories are deeply rooted in the connection between London and the Caribbean. Born to Dominican parents and raised in West London, her work explores themes of identity, resilience, and the strength of women—often inspired by the vibrant storytelling of her mother.

Her first novel, *Holding Paradise*, was published in 2014 and later reimagined as the first in the *Island Secrets Series*. Fran holds an MA in Creative Writing from Brunel University and lives in the English countryside, where she teaches vocals and leads a local choir.

She also writes contemporary fiction under the pen name Rosa Temple.